"I think your wife was crazy to leave you," Paula said

"There'll be a dozen women waiting to fill her shoes," she added.

Dane looked at her, amused. "A dozen? I'll have to line up help."

"Now, now." She grinned. "Don't be modest. A man who makes his living in combat survival should be well equipped to handle twelve women."

He frowned. "My record isn't great so far. One's divorced me, and one's giving me fits."

It took her a moment to grasp what he meant. "We're coming to like each other," she said finally. "That's all it is. The...other...is just enforced proximity, close quarters, cabin fever."

"The other," Dane said, sliding down on the sofa. "You're deluding yourself, you know. You're falling in love with me."

"No, I'm not," she replied mildly. "I don't want that anymore."

"Afraid?" he asked quietly.

She looked him in the eye and answered honestly, "Yes. I am afraid."

ABOUT THE AUTHOR

The beautiful Siskiyou mountain region in Muriel Jensen's home state of Oregon is the backdrop for her third Superromance novel. Like her latest heroine, she loves cats and cross-stitch, because, she says, the only skill it requires is the ability to count. "I once took a manual dexterity test when applying for a civil service job," she reports. "A woman with her right arm in a cast from fingertip to elbow beat me by two minutes." Muriel Jensen is married and has three children.

Books by Muriel Jensen

HARLEQUIN SUPERROMANCE
422–TRUST A HERO
468–BRIDGE TO YESTERDAY

HARLEQUIN AMERICAN ROMANCE
283–SIDE BY SIDE
321–A CAROL CHRISTMAS
339–EVERYTHING
358–A WILD IRIS
392–THE MIRACLE
414–RACING WITH THE MOON
425–VALENTINE HEARTS AND FLOWERS

In Good Time

MURIEL JENSEN

Harlequin Books

TORONTO • NEW YORK • LONDON
AMSTERDAM • PARIS • SYDNEY • HAMBURG
STOCKHOLM • ATHENS • TOKYO • MILAN
MADRID • WARSAW • BUDAPEST • AUCKLAND

Published August 1992

ISBN 0-373-70512-3

IN GOOD TIME

CHAPTER ONE

DANE CHANDLER stepped aside as a small housemaid ran past him, clutching a tweed sports jacket and a cashmere sweater in her arms.

A tall, elegant older woman peered around the bedroom door next to which he stood. "Is my daughter here yet?" she asked breathlessly.

He shook his head. "Not yet, Mrs. Emmett."

The woman's frightened dark eyes settled on him, curiously unnerving him. "*You* should have gone for her," she said. "Your brother insists that you're the best. Why didn't he send you to pick her up?"

"Buck was closer," he replied gently. "They'll be here soon, I promise."

"Maybe Hailey got here faster than Kurt expected. What if he's intercepted them? What if..."

"He hasn't, Mrs. Emmett," Dane said quietly. "Hailey escaped only two hours ago. He couldn't have made it from Arizona to Los Angeles in that time."

"Gangsters have long reaches."

"He's not a gangster," he said, guiding her back into her room. "He's just a crazy."

That wasn't entirely a lie. According to Kurt's psychological profile on Hailey, he was a crazy with a frighteningly twisted flash of genius, but she didn't have to know that. "Have you finished packing?" he asked, trying to distract her.

She indicated the suitcase on the foot of her bed and gave him a grim smile. "If we come out of this unscathed, please don't let the tabloids know that Paul Emmett's wife went *anywhere* with only one suitcase. I'm sure Paul will have three. Louise is still packing for him."

Dane smiled back. He hadn't expected to like Kurt's clients, but he did. Paul Emmett, white-haired star of the nighttime soaps, was a barrel-chested, big-voiced man who liked things his way but would listen to reason. Barbara Emmett, his wife, was simply a nice lady. Dane had had little enough experience with that species to appreciate one when he met her.

As he picked up her suitcase, she put an overnight-sized bag in his other hand. "This has some of the things Paula leaves here to wear when she helps her father. She won't be pleased with the choice, but since there isn't time to go to her place..." She shrugged helplessly.

"I'll carry these out," Dane said. "Why don't you have a last look around. Make sure you haven't forgotten something you can't live without."

She caught his arm as he moved toward the door. Her eyes were wide and urgent. "The only thing neither Paul nor I could live without is our daughter, Mr. Chandler. Don't let anything happen to her."

"He won't." Kurt Chandler appeared in the doorway. "He's the best man I have, Mrs. Emmett. Paula will be safe. Dane, I need to talk to you for a few minutes. Leave Mrs. Emmett's bag. I'll get it later."

Dane kept his grip on the suitcase and replied stiffly, "I'll take them both out. I'll be back in a minute."

It was apparent Kurt didn't like his mild defiance, but he said nothing, simply walked away. Pleased with himself, Dane took Barbara Emmett's bag to Kurt's car, and her daughter's to his own.

He found Kurt in the Emmetts' enormous kitchen. At a utility island covered with hand-painted tiles, Kurt glared at him. "First, I'd appreciate it if you stopped looking at me like I'm Charles Manson."

Dane remained calm. His brother's gift for strategy and detail always made his directness seem out of character. "You remind me more of Benedict Arnold," Dane replied.

Kurt shifted and jammed his hands into his pockets. "Look," he said, "Joyce walked out on you, I didn't send her away. I wish you'd get over it and stop blaming me."

The hot anger that had lived in his gut for a year flamed to life. But if twelve years as a Marine had taught him anything, it was to remain calm under pressure. "You didn't send her away," Dane replied, "but you didn't tell me she'd left, either. I didn't find out until it was too late for me to do anything about it."

"You were in Saudi Arabia," Kurt reminded him. "Did you want me to call the Pentagon and have them send you back?"

Dane looked him in the eye. They were both tall, both big, both tough. All their lives they'd been competitive, but with a love and loyalty under their rivalry fed by the dark years of their childhood and the need to stick together. They'd grown to manhood with a bond between them Dane had thought nothing could sever— until Joyce left, and Kurt let her.

"I'm sure you were pleased," Dane said, "to have such a good excuse to let me lose her."

"Why in the hell would I be pleased?" Kurt roared. "Besides the fact that she was a five-star bitch?"

In an instant, Dane had Kurt's shirtfront crumpled in his fist, the other fist pulled back to strike. Kurt made no effort to free himself. He simply looked back at him with an all-knowing, big-brother superiority that had been making Dane crazy for as long as he could remember.

"Do it," Kurt said. "You've been itching to hit somebody since you came home and found her gone. Go ahead. See if it changes anything."

Dane tightened his grip. "You never wanted me to have her," he said harshly, "because you'd had her first and she preferred me."

"I never wanted you to have her," Kurt replied, "because I knew she was poison. You wanted her because I'd had her. And now you're paying because you wouldn't listen."

The fire in Dane's gut became a conflagration. Raw anger had drawn his fist back, but long years of training made him stop and think. That was something to be settled another time.

He pushed Kurt away from him and drew a deep breath, trying to remember why he was here. He leaned a hip on a stool and willed himself to calm down.

Kurt straightened his jacket. "We'll get to that when this is over. Right now I have a client with a lunatic after him." He paced across the room to a small round table, beckoning Dane to follow. He sighed, obviously having difficulty with what he was about to say. "I want to thank you . . . for coming to help on a moment's notice—particularly considering the way you feel about what happened."

That was another quality Dane had always resented and respected about Kurt: his ability to direct his anger only at its source.

Dane gave him a brief nod. "Sure. You promised money. Had you asked me to do it for old times' sake, I'd still be packing."

Kurt raised an eyebrow. "But you'd have come?"

Dane picked up the folder on the table. "Yes. So what's this Hailey's problem? I read the trial transcript. The guy's weird. But why direct his hatred at Paul Emmett?"

"The crazed fan is becoming more and more of a phenomenon. This one hates Emmett because of what his character in the soap did to Candy Malloy, the actress Hailey fantasizes is his soulmate."

"You're sure the family's in danger, too?"

Kurt nodded. "The daughter, particularly. Hailey wrote threatening letters while he was in jail. When he made his attack on Emmett at the airport in Phoenix, Paula was traveling with her father. She hit Hailey in the face with a purse she was carrying, and the clasp put his eye out."

Dane frowned and studied the black-and-white photo of a lean-faced man wearing an eye patch. The good eye was the eye of a maniac. He closed the folder and handed it to Kurt. "Why me? You have a staff of security elite."

Kurt shrugged. "She's very precious to the Emmetts. When I explained that I wanted to separate them from her in order to make Hailey's job more difficult, Emmett said he'd only allow that if I swore to him that the best man I knew would be guarding his daughter. You're the best."

Dane leaned back in his chair. "I love these low-pressure assignments. But isn't this overkill for just one man?"

Kurt shook his head. "Hailey's connected with a weird group of survivalists in Idaho. I'll spare you the details, but his letter to Emmett's daughter said he and his friends were all coming after her."

Dane frowned. "That doesn't fit the profile for this kind of nut, does it? I mean, don't they usually plot and brood and carry out their plans alone?"

"Usually, but not in Hailey's case. He has dangerous tendencies and dangerous friends, and he's diabolically clever. That's why I wanted you."

Dane's mouth quirked wryly. "Takes one to know one, you mean? So what do we know about the daughter?"

"She's divorced," Kurt replied with a sigh, as though, for the moment at least, he was glad to put the subject of Hailey aside. "Founded Pretty Lady Cosmetics and is now its CEO. Yearly sales in the millions." He grinned. "Guaranteed she'll look pretty for however long you're stuck with her. If all goes well, we'll get him the instant he tries anything, and you'll collect your pay for nothing more than a few days relaxing in the wilderness with a beautiful woman."

Dane couldn't help looking skeptical. Murphy's Law had always applied to everything he'd ever done—personally or militarily. That hadn't changed in the year he'd been a civilian.

Paul Emmett walked into the room, silk paisley scarf tucked into the neck of a one-hundred-dollar casual shirt. Despite his privileged circumstances and his flamboyance, he had good nerves, Dane thought. Except for the attentiveness with which he treated all Kurt's suggestions for his own and his family's safety, it was impossible to tell that he was concerned about

Hailey. Emmett was either a man of iron control, Dane judged, or simply a good actor.

"I guess we're ready," Emmett said to Kurt. "Your man arrived with my daughter?"

"Not yet," Kurt replied, getting to his feet.

A frown line appeared between Emmett's eyes, the first sign of worry Dane had seen. "Shouldn't they...?"

The kitchen door opened and one of Kurt's men leaned his head in. "Buck's coming," he reported.

Dane and Kurt followed Emmett into the living room where his wife was already waiting.

Dane watched in surprise and considerable interest as a woman ran through the front door, which the housemaid held open, and into her parents' embrace.

"Are you all right?" she demanded, hugging her father, then her mother.

The way Barbara Emmett talked about her daughter, Dane had expected a quiet, fragile young woman with a gentle manner like her mother's. Even his knowledge of her executive status hadn't altered that impression. Her business was makeup, after all.

But this was a mature woman who did not appear to be quiet or fragile. Of average height and above-average physical attributes in a slim gray wool suit, she looked as though she were every insecure man's worst nightmare. Dark red hair was caught at the back of her head in a severe knot. A small, well-shaped nose attracted attention from a tight, though nicely angled jaw. She turned to size up Kurt and him with a presence that came only from deep-seated self-assurance or an experienced bluff. Dark brown eyes flashed. He'd known tough, leathery sergeants who'd been less daunting.

Dane, standing several paces behind Kurt, asked quietly, "This is the woman with whom I'm going to spend a quiet week in the wilderness?"

Kurt gave him a quick, wry backward glance. "Good thing you have the Gulf War behind you." He covered the distance between him and Paula Cornell and offered his hand. "Mrs. Cornell," he said, "I'm Kurt Chandler."

HE WAS PROBABLY YOUNGER than she was, Paula thought. Early thirties, maybe. But, then, she'd reached the age where everyone seemed to be younger than she was. He was big, fit and good-looking.

She shook his hand. "I trust you know your work, Mr. Chandler."

"I do, Mrs. Cornell," he replied. He drew the man standing behind him to his side. "This is my brother, Dane. You'll be going with him."

This man was even younger. His good looks were rougher, less refined, but a family resemblance was apparent. His smoky-green eyes seemed to be weighing her. She sharpened her stare, waiting for the uncomfortable shuffle that usually resulted. It didn't come.

He finally offered his hand, saying politely, "Mrs. Cornell."

His hand was warm and strong, enclosing hers firmly without the restraint a man usually showed when shaking hands with a female. She held back a wince. Upstart, she thought.

"Mr. Chandler," she replied coolly. Suddenly his brother's words registered with her. She withdrew her hand and frowned at Kurt. "Going with him?"

Kurt nodded. "Into hiding. He's your bodyguard."

"No," she said firmly. "I am not going into hiding."

Kurt turned to Paul Emmett. "I thought you explained to her on the phone...."

"He did," Paula said, folding her arms. "And I told him I wasn't going. I'm negotiating the sale of my company, Mr. Chandler. I can't go into hiding."

Dane put his hands into his pockets while Kurt continued to reason with her. Were it up to him, he'd simply put her into the car, but he knew from experience that the Marines moved in when diplomacy failed. He waited.

Paul Emmett shepherded them into the living room. With everyone settled on a sectional near the fireplace, Paul put an arm around his daughter. "We're not going to pretend that Hailey isn't going to make his way to Los Angeles, look us up, and try again."

Paula nodded. "Very wise. You should hide out for a while. But I . . ."

"Your mother and I are going with Kurt," Paul interrupted. "You're going with Dane."

Dane admired the man's style. Paula Cornell was the kind of woman to whom a man spoke plainly and with conviction or he wouldn't stand a chance against her. He silently applauded the man's ability to do it in the face of what was bound to be strong and stubborn opposition.

It came immediately. "No," she replied simply.

Paul countered without flinching, "Yes. Paula, you're the one who put out his eye. You're the one he threatened in the letter."

Paula studied her father a moment, obviously planning strategy.

"Dad," she said finally. "I appreciate your concern, but I'm hardly your little girl any longer. I'm almost forty. I'm a career woman on the brink of a deal that will set me up for the rest of my life. I am not going into hiding. If Hailey—"

"Mrs. Cornell," Kurt said reasonably, "there's little point in staying to negotiate a deal you might not live to benefit from."

She gave him a dark look. "This deal means more to me than money, Mr. Chandler."

Dane leaned forward and caught her eye. As it had always been in his relationship with his brother, Kurt was the brains and Dane was the muscle. It was looking as if the pattern would continue into his temporary sojourn into the security business. And sometimes muscle could be applied emotionally as well as physically.

"The longer we delay by arguing," he said into her watchful dark eyes, "the more you endanger your parents."

She raised a haughty eyebrow and got to her feet. "Don't try to manipulate me, *sonny*," she said. "There is no argument. I am not going into hiding and that's final."

"Paula!" Emmett scolded.

That small slur brought Dane's usually latent temper to boiling. Accustomed to respect from the men in his command, this woman's derogatory reference to what was probably a five- or six-year difference in their ages made him wish he were back in uniform again. He could think of several ways he'd make her pay for that superior attitude, each more delicious to contemplate than the next.

"I apologize for her, Mr. Chandler," Paul said.

Paula ignored him and turned away—only to come face-to-face with her mother. "Sit down," Barbara Emmett said quietly, enunciating each word.

Paula rolled her eyes. "Mother, I . . ."

Barbara put a hand on her daughter's shoulder and pushed. Paula landed on the sofa with a bounce, her eyes now surprised as well as angry. Barbara sat beside her and said with quiet deadliness of purpose, "You listen to me, Paula. You can play out your death wish some other time—not when your father's life is at stake. For all our sakes, you will do as you are told, I don't care how old you are or if you're negotiating with Queen Elizabeth, herself."

The room pulsed with tension. Dane had no idea what Barbara Emmett's curious choice of words meant, but it had the desired effect. He watched in amazement as Paula lowered her eyes and leaned back against the sofa cushions, her face pale.

"Now," Barbara went on, her gentle self once again. "Simply ask your vice president to explain that a family emergency has you unavoidably detained. Italians place a strong emphasis on family. I'm sure Ms. Ferrante will understand."

Dane watched Paula glance up at her mother. Her eyes said that it was far more complicated than that, but the words never left her lips.

Paul Emmett put an arm around his daughter and held her close. Over the top of her head he gave his wife a scolding look. Barbara accepted it and turned away. Dane found something very familiar in the small exchange. Brains and muscle again at work. It was probably harder to be the one with the muscle, he guessed, when one was a woman.

"Dane's the best," Paul said bracingly. "You'll be safe."

Paula looked at her father a moment, then kissed his cheek. She still looked shaken from that small exchange with Barbara. "Then he should be the one watching you and Mom," she said.

He shook his head. "You're most important to us. So he's watching you."

Paula looked at Dane, her expression openly skeptical of his legendary reputation.

He grinned. "Want to go two out of three falls and see for yourself?" he asked.

Paula sighed and turned to her father. "Where are you going?"

He shook his head and took her hand. "I don't know. And we don't know where you're going. Mr. Chandler thought it safer that way."

She rolled her eyes. "So we can't be tortured into telling?"

"Don't be smart. You know how dangerous Hailey is. You were there."

She put a hand to her eyes for a moment as though to block out the image of a memory. Then she dropped her hand and looked at Dane, asking with a straight face, "I hope someone told *you* our destination."

He gave her a small smile. "I always know where I'm going."

"I'll need clothes," she said.

Kurt nodded. "Your suitcase is in the back of Dane's car."

PAULA FOUGHT against the annoyance she felt when things were done for her. She liked to control things herself, to know in advance her next move. She didn't like being forced at a moment's notice to abandon her daily routine. She didn't want to be taken to some unknown destination for God knew how long while a crazy man stalked her and her parents.

She particularly didn't like the idea of going into hiding with the man sitting opposite her. He seemed like such a boy. She took a closer look and amended the conclusion. The boyishness was just a trick of his smile. As he looked back at her, she noted the curious paradox of smoky-green eyes that reflected a knowledge of things, good and bad, and taut tanned skin without so much as a suggestion of a character line.

His hair was dark and closely cut, his angular face, clean-shaven, his mouth relaxed, but his jaw stubborn. One got a surface impression of youth, but under it was a look of jaded worldliness. She wondered what accounted for that. Either he was older than he looked, or he'd lived a lot in a short time.

At the moment, however, there was little she could do but cooperate. She hated to admit it, but the kid was right. She'd die before she'd willingly endanger her parents further.

"When do we leave?" she asked.

Kurt Chandler stood. "Now," he said. "You have ten minutes to call your office and talk to your parents alone. Then we're out of here."

Her father turned to her as the two men left the room to wait outside. He smiled gently, his eyes filled with love and the unqualified adoration she remembered seeing there from the time she was a little girl.

"Everything's going to be fine," he said, "if you do what he tells you. I hired them because they know what they're doing. I trust them. Please, Paula."

"What he's trying to say," Barbara said, sitting on the other side of her daughter and putting an arm around her, "is don't be your usual difficult self. Your life is in his hands. If we're all going to survive this, you're going to have to cooperate."

Paula looked into her mother's eyes and saw a desperation that had grown familiar over the past few years. They'd lost the closeness they'd known during Paula's growing-up years and early adulthood. She looked as bereft as Paula sometimes felt. With maternal mercilessness, she said, "You can be tough without being a pill, darling. And Dane Chandler doesn't look like he'd stand for a lot of resistance. Make it easy on yourself. Let's have the old Paula back until this is over."

Paula shook her head at her mother. "She no longer exists, Mom," she said quietly.

Barbara caught her chin and pinched it as though she were eight years old. "Yes, she does. She isn't dead, she's just sedated." She put her arms around Paula, held her firmly for one moment, then stood.

Paul embraced her, too. "Take care of yourself, baby. We'll see you in a few days." He kissed her cheek and drew away to smile at her. "Old Paula or new," he said, "I love you. Go make your call."

Paula went out the door and didn't look back as she allowed Dane to help her into the Scout. Dane waited, watching his rearview mirror until his brother had loaded his passengers and backed out of the driveway. Kurt gave one tap of his horn which Dane returned. Buck Mitchell followed Kurt in the red pickup.

The driveway now clear, Dane turned the key in the ignition and the Scout purred to life. He gave his passenger a quick glance. Beautiful, but brittle, he thought.

He guessed he could put up with it for a week, though he'd sure as hell had enough of that sort of woman to last a lifetime.

He wished he was home, mowing his lawn. Better yet, he could picture himself behind the counter in the hardware store on which he'd just made an offer in Heron River, Oregon.

Paula's voice snapped him back to the irrevocable here and now. "Anytime today would be nice, Mr. Chandler," she said.

With a sigh, Dane pocketed his dream, swallowed his temper and smiled at her. "Buckle up and we'll be on our way."

Paula drew her seat belt around her, then looked at him consideringly before snapping it into place. "What if I paid you twice what my father's paying you to take me back to my office? Your brother and my parents are gone. What they don't know won't hurt them."

For a moment, he just looked at her and she turned to him expectantly, thinking there might be a chance. Then he covered her hand with his and pushed the end of her seat belt into its slot.

"The deal's already made, Paula," he said, turning the Scout in a tight circle. "You and me together until the Hailey business is settled. Don't fight it."

With a small groan Paula leaned back against the headrest and closed her eyes. That was the problem, she thought grimly. Lately it seemed imperative that she fight everything.

CHAPTER TWO

IT WAS EARLY EVENING when Paula opened her eyes. She hadn't slept, but keeping them closed had helped maintain a distance between herself and the man entrusted with the preservation of her life—such as it was.

She had no idea what to say to him. It had been two years since she'd made polite conversation with a man. She'd talked business with them, negotiated deals, had lunch in the interest of landing a new account. She was a master at diverting the topic from anything personal back to business, and at dousing interest that did not relate to Pretty Lady Cosmetics. She'd lost proficiency at small talk. She felt uncomfortable. She hated that.

They were somewhere in the central valley where lush, fragrant fields of herbs and vegetables stretched out on both sides of the highway to the mountains, turning purple in the gathering dusk. Paula sat up, stretching her cramped arms out in front of her.

Dane glanced her way. "Getting hungry?" he asked.

She wasn't, but eating meant less time to talk. "Yes," she replied.

At least she wouldn't talk his ear off, Dane thought. A lot of men hated that. Personally he appreciated a little sparkle in a woman, but it was a different world, he knew. Somehow, in the twelve years he'd spent in the military, things had changed and women now wore suits much of the time and behaved like female men. Except for Joyce, who'd looked all woman outside, but had none of the warm and wonderful qualities that defined the word. He'd given up trying to understand it. He just did his best to live around it.

A tiny, fast-food spot the size of a telephone booth, and a restaurant and lounge on the side of the road with neon flames promising Cinders—Good Food appeared to be the choices. Dane pulled into the parking lot of the restaurant.

Paula unbuckled her seat belt and pulled the visor down to check her hair and makeup. No vanity mirror.

Dane noted her frown. "Sorry," he said. "Not a luxury car. You look fine."

She gave him a withering glance because she was sure she didn't. She knew her mascara wasn't smudged—it was a guarantee Pretty Lady stood behind. But her blusher and lipstick were undoubtedly gone and her chignon was probably starting to self-destruct.

She reached for the door handle, but he stopped her with a hand on her arm. She turned to him, further annoyed. "What?" she demanded.

He took a moment to study her snapping eyes before he answered. When he did reply, his voice remained quiet, but she suspected he was no less annoyed than she was. "Let me come around and help you down."

She rolled her eyes. "I have two good legs. I'm not helpless."

"You have two *great* legs," he corrected her, "but until this is over, I want you within arm's reach."

She opened her mouth to protest but he countered quietly with, "It's not open for discussion. Wait there."

In the face of such blatant autocracy, Paula could think of nothing to say. On top of his comment about her legs, his tyranny kept her silent until he came around the Scout, opened the door, and offered her a hand down.

She thanked him coolly and walked stiffly beside him into the restaurant. It was dimly lit with dark, low-quality, low-style paneling, and bright red carpeting. Beyond the lineup of booths, bat-wing doors opened into a corridor that led to rest rooms, a public telephone and rusty hooks on the wall, presumably for coats. From beyond the corridor came the sound of jukebox music, loud male laughter and the smell of alcohol. The lounge.

A smiling young waitress led them to a booth and dropped two menus on the table. She was back in a moment with water and coffee.

Paula saw the waitress glance at Dane, catch his eye and blush. He returned her shy smile with a grin and watched her as she walked away to pour coffee at another table. Kids, Paula thought with mild impatience.

"Should you let yourself be distracted like that?" she asked airily, scanning the menu.

She felt him look up. "I wasn't distracted," he said.

She looked at him over the top of her menu. "How can you watch her hips and guard me?"

He hooked a finger in the fold of her menu and pulled it down until he had her full attention. "It was her smile that appealed to me," he said, his tone ripe with implication. "I haven't seen one since we left your mother."

"I didn't know that was required of a client," she said, her tone underscored with sarcasm. "Perhaps you should be providing security at a dental convention."

A ten-mile hike with full field pack might dilute some of that nastiness, Dane thought. Then he wondered why he was even considering solutions. Their enforced relationship wouldn't last that long and it wasn't his business, anyway. He was happy to let her be some upwardly mobile business genius's problem. He pushed her menu back up in front of her face and busied himself watching the traffic pass on the highway.

After they'd placed their order, Paula picked up her purse. "I'm going to wash my hands," she said. She scooted out of the booth, then stopped halfway up the aisle when she sensed Dane following her.

"Tell me you're not coming with me," she said.

He grinned, enjoying her look of distress. "I have to make a phone call," he said. "This would be a good time."

In the ladies' room, Paula washed her hands, dampened a paper towel and patted her face and neck. She'd been right, she noted with a small sigh. Her makeup was gone, and her hair was slipping out of her chignon. She looked closer—closer than she'd wanted to in some time—and saw that the complete lack of appeal in her reflection was the result of much more than shoddy grooming.

Everything she used to be was gone. Vacant, her eyes said. Nobody home. She made herself smile but it didn't help because it meant nothing, reflected nothing. It would never catch someone's eye the way the waitress's smile had caught Dane Chandler's attention. For the first time in two years she knew a sense of grief for what she'd lost personally, as well as for what had happened.

The Paula Cornell of two years ago had been so full of life, so full of plans. Now all she wanted to do was sell Pretty Lady and put herself out to pasture. Retired. Vacant. Nobody home.

Impatiently she combed the straggling sides of her hair back into place and fixed them there with the tiny hairspray can in her purse. Too bad. No point bemoaning her fate. What happened, happened. That part of her life was over.

A little shaken by what she'd seen in the mirror, but determined to put it out of her mind, Paula walked out of the ladies' room—right into the arms of a wall wearing a green-and-gray plaid shirt and topped with a baseball cap that said Blitz—Breakfast of Champions.

"Well, hello, sweets." Out of a red beard came a gravelly chuckle and a case of halitosis from hell. A hand closed on her chin and another around her waist. "Aren't you a pretty, prissy little..."

Another male hand closed over the fat wrist at her chin and pulled it away. Before Dane could do anything more, Paula reacted. Fueled by a temper that had had to be controlled one time too many in a day filled with unspeakable aggravations, Paula brought her heel down hard on the wall's instep. As he cried out in pain and surprise, she rammed her fist into a large stomach the texture of sourdough starter. Then she turned on Dane.

"I can take care of myself!" she shouted at him. "You may have to follow me around, but I don't want you butting into my life. If I want your help, I'll ask for it!"

The wall caught his breath, towering a good six inches over Dane's six feet plus. Dane grabbed his shirtfront and pulled his face down. "And if you don't behave yourself," he threatened, "I'll let her have you." He walked back into the dining room, wishing he was carrying the M-1 he'd left in the car, rather than the Smith & Wesson 10 mm under his jacket. He was sure before this was over, the lady would have more than one enemy stalking her.

Still, he had to admire her style. She had a little to learn about diplomacy, but she was long on courage and resourcefulness.

She was picking at a chef's salad when he returned to their booth. She glanced up at him, her eyes still stormy but her manner quiet. "I'm sorry I screamed at you," she said. He suspected the apology was sincere though she appeared to have trouble offering it.

He leaned across his steak sandwich for the A.1. sauce. "I'd nobly tell you to forget it," he said. "But I really hate being shouted at. You might do it one time too many, then we'd probably both end up being sorry. So watch it, all right?"

She dropped her fork with a gasp of indignation. "Don't threaten me, young man," she said fiercely.

He put the bottle of sauce down with great care and drew a steadying breath. "How old are you?" he asked evenly.

"Thirty-nine," she replied without flinching. "How old are you?"

That surprised him, but it didn't alter his case. "Thirty." He looked at her steadily. "So you have a few years on me, and probably a lot more sophistication, but what's needed here are survival skills and the ability to kill, if necessary. How good are you at that, Paula? If it comes down to you and Hailey and nothing but a butcher knife between you, can you do it?"

Paula had never let even her father know how that episode with Hailey had terrified her. She'd been close enough to see the madness in his eyes, to feel the superhuman strength hate gave him when he grabbed her arm, trying to ward her off. Even now, her insides shook as she thought about it.

She tried to imagine herself in the circumstance Dane described and had to close her eyes against the picture. She'd always been a strong woman, and she'd grown a tough shell over the last few years, but she had to admit she wasn't sure she could kill. She didn't answer, but one look into those watchful eyes told her she didn't have to.

"That's what I thought," he replied quietly. "I can do it without thinking twice. So I think a little respect is in order. You don't have to think of me as a superior. You don't even have to consider me an equal if that's too difficult for you. But try to appreciate my ability to do something you can't—particularly since it involves the preservation of your life."

As Paula lowered her eyes, Dane suddenly remembered the curious words her mother had used to bring her into line. "You can fulfill your death wish another time," she'd said. Death wish. If she truly had one, he thought, that was something he had to know. "Unless staying alive isn't a priority of yours," he added, his tone questioning.

She glanced up at him with something so sad in her eyes that he felt it as if it were his own pain. He recognized it as something he'd lived with for a while. Loss. But there seemed to be no anger entangled in hers. It was simply hurt—pulsing, screaming hurt. It so surprised him that for a moment he didn't know what to say. Instinctively he reached out to put a hand over hers.

Paula looked into his eyes, momentarily touched by the compassion she saw there. His hand was warm and strong over hers. She wanted to turn hers into it, lace her fingers with his and draw courage. But she couldn't.

Compassionate understanding always made her shield slip, and behind it were things she couldn't deal with.

She pulled her hand away and picked up her fork. "Of course being alive is a priority," she said. It hadn't been for a while, but it was now. Of course, some people wouldn't call it life. Her mother called it retirement from life—coasting. She was disappointed in her, Paula knew, because she couldn't get it all together again. That was part of the rift between them. Paula regretted it, but she was powerless to change it. "I'm about to put together the deal of a lifetime. That is, if the other side of the deal understands my sudden disappearance."

Dane understood her withdrawal. Hands off. She hadn't misunderstood his instinctive touch, she'd simply rejected it. He was becoming uncomfortably familiar with rejection. At least he was being paid to deal with this one.

He picked up his sandwich. "You mentioned selling your business," he said.

She smiled with satisfaction. "For seven figures to Faces by Ferrante." She grimaced and speared a bite of ham. "Provided my mother was right and Giulia's little Italian soul does understand the obligations of family when my vice president calls her in the morning."

"What will you do after that? Try something new?"

She shook her head. "I'm going to cruise around the world. Take my time. See everything."

Dane raised an eyebrow. "Seriously?" he asked.

She straightened defensively. "Yes. Why?"

He chewed a bite of sandwich then sipped at his coffee. "That strikes me as an adventure for a senior citizen."

She shrugged. "I told you I was almost forty."

A short bark of laughter escaped him before he could stop himself. When she glared at him, he explained, still amused, "Hardly time to send for your AARP card. What is this age fixation you have, anyway?"

"I don't..." she began to deny.

"Yes, you do," he persisted. "You're very pretty, you deal in beauty, yet you dress like the stereotypical maiden aunt with a low libido, you tie back that gorgeous hair and you act like a dragon with PMS—an eighty-year-old dragon."

No one ever talked to Paula that way. Well, her mother did, but no one else. Anger swelled in her, but somehow her mind held on to the cloaked compliments in his diatribe—"pretty, gorgeous hair," and earlier he'd told her she had "great legs." Those words made it difficult for her anger to build up a full head of steam.

"Maybe if you weren't such a kid," she said, annoyed with herself for reacting to his badgering, "you'd see it differently. I've worked hard. I..."

"This *kid,*" he said, "has spent twelve years in the Marine Corps and seen more of life than you can probably even imagine—particularly if your idea of living is a cruise around the world. You're putting this age thing between us because it makes you feel safer around me."

She made a scoffing noise and reached for her coffee. "That wasn't a suggestion that you consider me a sexual threat," he said calmly, making her feel foolish for implying it. "I don't understand it, but it has something to do with this power front you present. It's to keep people away, isn't it? Men, particularly?"

She took a long sip from her cup then put it down with deliberate care. "A bodyguard who reads Freud. Daddy sure knows how to pick them."

He covered her hand with his again, but this time it wasn't to comfort, but to capture. "Look," he said. "I need to keep you within reach for safety's sake. That doesn't mean you're in any danger of physical or emotional intimacies from me, so relax. Lighten up. This could be a very long couple of days."

It certainly looked that way to Paula.

They finished their meals in silence. Paula made another trip to the rest room and perversely slipped out the door while Dane was taking care of the check. She wasn't planning to escape, she just didn't want him to think he'd alarmed her into being amenable.

Darkness had fallen and the night air had the bite of autumn. It also had a fragrance one seldom enjoyed in downtown Los Angeles, and Paula took a deep gulp of it. She choked on it when a hand closed over her mouth and another grabbed her around the waist, forcing the air out of her.

"You didn't let me finish, pretty priss," the bearded man from the bar hissed in her ear. The sour stench of alcohol and tobacco wound around her face, contributing to the choking sensation. "Now, instead of telling you what I'd like to do," he went on, carrying her toward a truck where two laughing companions waited, "I'm gonna just do it."

Cold, real fear ran down her spine. His hand muffled any sound she might make. Her arms were pinned to her sides, and though she kicked frantically, she struck nothing but air. Her captor tried to hand her to one of the men who'd leapt into the truck. At least that finally gave her feet a target. She landed a high heel to his jaw before he finally caught her ankles with an oath and a rough yank.

Suddenly she was on the ground beside the man who'd accosted her. He didn't appear to be moving. There were blows and grunts in the darkness, and in the dim light from the neon sign, Paula saw the body of the man she'd kicked make an elegant arc into a bank of oleander bushes that separated the parking lot from the highway. The third man had fled.

A hand yanked her to her feet. Curiously, after what she'd just been through, she recognized the touch as Dane's. It was hard, even angry, but it didn't hurt. "Move it!" he ordered, leading her at a run across the lot to the Scout. "We don't need police or angry truckers out for retribution."

They were several miles away before he took a long look in the rearview mirror, then glanced at her, his eyes angry. "You're deaf, right?" he asked. "That's why I'm having so much trouble with you. It can't be that you don't understand the danger. It must be that you can't hear."

She had no defense to offer; it had been a thoughtless, foolish gesture. It hadn't resulted in the danger he'd warned her against, but her predicament had been grave all the same.

"I'm sorry," she said quietly.

He glanced at her again. "Now *I* must have lost my hearing. I thought I heard you say you were sorry."

"I did," she replied. "There's no need to be sarcastic. And thank you."

"Thank you?" he repeated. "Now my mind must be going."

"I suspected that the moment I met you," she said. She gave him a swift, reluctant grin, then closed her eyes and leaned her head back. Issue closed, her action said.

She'd apologized and thanked him. She wouldn't listen to any more scolding.

He rapped his hand against the side of her knee before she could convince herself she'd handled him. Her head came up immediately, her eyes snapping open.

"You do that again," he warned, "and I'll have to show you who's in charge here."

She glared at him a moment, then closed her eyes again and leaned back. "I think you've already done that. Are we stopping for the night or driving through to wherever it is we're going?"

All right, Dane thought. Let her think the issue's closed. Until it comes up again.

"I'll put another few miles between us and your admirers," he said, "then we'll put up for the night. We have a full day's drive tomorrow."

"All right," she replied.

Dane glanced at her again, noting her pallor in the darkness. She looked tired, and was probably frightened, though he was sure she'd die before admitting it. He suspected something even deeper and more painful than fear and exhaustion haunted her. He wondered what it was.

She stirred, and he turned back to the road, trying to turn his mind back to his job. What was in her head, even in her heart, had nothing to do with him. He was to protect her body—that was all. Solving the mystery of a pretty woman with great legs and a death wish was not his responsibility.

Trouble was, he'd never been one to let someone else dictate the scope of his duty.

PAULA GUESSED that the Mountain Meadow Cabins just south of Stockton didn't rate one point on one star in anyone's travel guide. The coming winter's first storm would probably knock them down. They had no such amenities as ice and soft drink machines, telephones or televisions.

She was relieved to discover that the room did have a bed and a bathtub. She didn't even question Dane's renting only one room; she knew the drill. He needed her within arm's reach, and he was the boss here. Very male. Very predictable. At the moment, she was too tired to care.

She was sure she was safe with him; she'd just had concrete proof he could protect her from outside threats. And she was in no danger from him personally. He'd told her so in no uncertain terms. And she was, after all, nearly ten years older than he was.

"You can have first go at the tub, and the use of the bed," he said. "I'll sleep on the floor."

"That's silly," she said with what she thought was extravagant aplomb. "I don't mind you using the other side. I don't budge when I sleep, so I won't bother you."

He looked at her a long moment, long enough to cause a strange little stir in the pit of her stomach. Then he pulled his jacket off and sank into the room's only chair. "I've spent a lot of nights on the ground," he said. "It's not a problem. But I am anxious for a bath, so if you'd hurry it up a little..."

Paula opened her suitcase and found it packed with clothes she kept at her parents' to wear when she helped with the gardening and her father with the various redecorating projects he loved to tackle without hiring professionals. She groaned at the collection of old jeans and sweatshirts. She dug down, looking for a nightgown. She reached the bottom without finding one.

Unaccountably her cheeks grew hot. "Who packed for me?" she asked.

Dane looked at her suitcase, then up into her blush. "Your mother gave orders to a nervous little lady in a maid's uniform," he replied. "Problem?" He wanted desperately to smile. He didn't know exactly what had upset her, but seeing her royal demeanor so ruffled was worth having to find a solution to whatever it was.

She cleared her throat. "No nightgown," she said. The blush deepened despite her attempts to resume her usual aplomb. "No long sweatshirts, either. Just old, shrunken ones. She remembered my cross-stitch, but no nightgown."

He really struggled with the smile now. Not that he found her embarrassment funny, but because he'd never expected to see her so discomfited. He guessed he was right about her often waspish disposition. She was hiding behind it. And only vulnerable women hid.

Dane opened his backpack and pulled out a T-shirt. "This do?" he asked, offering it.

Paula studied it a moment as though it might attack. Then common sense reestablished itself. He was a good eight or nine inches taller than she. The shirt would fall at least to midthigh on her. She forced a smile, accepted the shirt with a thank-you and disappeared into the bathroom.

When she inched the door open to see if it was safe to come out again, he was arranging a blanket on the floor and didn't look up. Deliberately to satisfy her modesty, she was sure. Thoughtful, she thought grudgingly, walking quickly to the bed. Not usually a male trait.

"Tub's all yours," she said, curling into the lumpy pillow. "See you in the morning."

Dane took his time in the tub, leaving the door slightly ajar so that he could hear Paula. She was already asleep, body curled, shoulders hunched, her nerves still taut. Whatever haunted her, did so even in her sleep. He let himself wonder about that for a moment, then leaned his head against the back of the tub and closed his eyes. The question intrigued him, even unsettled him a little, but he had other things to worry about: such as where Hailey was now.

PAULA OPENED HER EYES to blackness. Her first waking thought was of Natalie. It was always of Natalie. She lay still and let the taloned pain walk over her, shuddering with it, knowing it would pass in a moment. It wouldn't be gone, but the intensity of it she experienced every time she awoke would subside. Then it would just ache. She'd learned to live with that.

She drew a deep breath as her body relaxed a little. Water. A tall, cold glass of water would taste wonderful. She sat up, swung her legs over the side of the bed and headed for her bathroom.

Just as it was beginning to register in her drowsy brain that the sheets under her bare legs hadn't been silk and there was no carpet under her feet, she tripped over something long and solid and went down with a cry. She gritted her teeth against impact and suddenly found herself suspended inches from Dane's body stretched out on the floor, his strong hand splayed across her ribs, supporting her, the other catching her shoulder. Both her hands were braced against his warm, bare chest.

For one interminable moment they stared at each other in the darkness. As her eyes adjusted, she saw the amused light in his, the whiteness of his smile. She became aware of the muscle and body heat under her hands—and a sturdy heartbeat. Silence and shadow seemed to thrum around her with the rhythm of his pulse. There was no air in her lungs.

"I'm...sorry," she whispered breathlessly. "I...forgot where I was."

Dane looked into the pale face hovering over him, felt the silky ends of hair dangling against his face and the fragile warmth of woman under his hands. Need raced with his blood. Not desire, but need. His life had been devoid of a woman's love, a woman's compassion, a woman's comfort and laughter. On the surface, this woman was stiff and cool. But once in a while he'd glimpse softness in her, vulnerability, likability. He found himself longing to explore those possibilities. But she was a client—Kurt's client. And that facet of his life was already too complicated.

He sat up, pushing her gently back onto her knees. "Are you all right?" he asked briskly.

She had to clear her throat. "I wanted a glass of water and forgot you were sleeping on the floor." She pushed herself to her feet, tugging on the shirt. "I'm sorry. You're sure I didn't hurt you?"

"Positive," he replied. Then he grinned. "Stop apologizing. It's the nicest thing that's happened to me in some time. Get your water and go back to bed. Tomorrow's going to be a long day."

Eager, relieved to comply, Paula quickly put the bed between them then closed the bathroom door behind her. She was shaking again, but this wasn't pain. It was...no. Couldn't be. She closed her short-circuiting mind on the thought, downed a glass of water and went back to bed.

"Good night," she said into the dark.

"Good night," Dane replied.

She closed her eyes, comforted by the sound of his reply. It seemed as if it were forever since she'd shared the darkness with a man.

CHAPTER THREE

THEY HAD JUST CROSSED the border into Oregon. Dane had been driving since dawn with a concentration that left little opportunity for conversation. Paula didn't mind. She wouldn't have known what to say to him, anyway. After last night's curious episode they seemed to be back to their mutually antagonistic relationship.

Paula's stomach began to grumble.

"You should have eaten something when we stopped for lunch," he said without looking away from the road. It was narrow, with a sheer drop to a stream on one side, and fir- and cedar-covered hills on the other. They'd left the main highway some time back.

"Grease burgers aren't my thing," she replied. "The cholesterol in what you ate would probably kill me faster than Hailey."

He gave her a quick glance that was critical and a little pitying. "No dim sum or escarole salad in this neck of the woods, I'm afraid."

"No nothing, it appears," she said, looking out at the beautiful landscape. It had been an hour since they'd seen another car.

"That's the idea," he replied. "Ever climb with a pack?" he asked.

She turned to frown at him. "Stairs? Ladder? Rope?"

"Mountain."

She'd been afraid that was the point of his question. She'd never been very athletic, and she simply wasn't a very physical individual. When her friends played tennis and went hiking, she'd been reading and taking extra business theory classes. Mercifully her slenderness was an inheritance from her mother.

"No," she replied with a bravado she didn't feel. "I've never climbed a mountain with or without a pack. But I've run for planes at LAX in high heels with a purse filled with samples over my shoulder. Can't be that different."

It was.

Dane nosed the Scout into a thicket at the base of a steep trail that led up into yet more Douglas fir. From behind the back seat he pulled two packs and a leather rifle case. One of the packs she remembered from the night before when he'd given her his T-shirt. He handed her the other.

"Take whatever you need out of your suitcase and put it into the pack," he said.

While she worked, he pulled his jacket off and she caught a glimpse of a shoulder holster that contained something shiny and probably lethal. He shrugged the pack on over a dark blue sweater, then shouldered the long scabbard. He tied the jacket around his waist by the sleeves and instructed her to do the same with hers.

Only part of what Louise and her mother had included would fit in the pack, but considering it consisted mostly of her grubbies, Paula didn't think she'd miss what she'd have to leave behind. Making sure she had the T-shirt Dane had loaned her, and her cross-stitch, she stuffed her purse in on top then fastened the flap. She noted in alarm that it was heavy.

Dane took it from her with one hand and turned her around with the other. He put the pack on her shoulders and secured the straps. "Comfortable?" he asked, turning her to him.

She was pleasantly surprised that it was. She nodded, relieved. "Yes."

"Good." He indicated the trail. "You go first. The cabin's about two miles in. Stop when you need a break."

Paula's relief lasted about ten minutes. A full pack might be comfortable when one was standing still, but it quickly became a miserably lumpy ton of bricks on a steep, uphill climb.

"Keep your shoulders straight," Dane ordered as she began to stoop under the weight.

She complied without turning, already gasping. She trudged on, her breath now coming in burning gulps.

"Stop!" Dane called.

"That's the death rattle, isn't it?" she asked, puffing heavily as he pulled her pack off and shouldered it by one strap.

His grin was half scolding, half amused. "That's the sound of a woman who doesn't exercise," he said. "You're worse than a boot."

"A boot?"

"A green recruit."

"I didn't enlist," she said, swallowing and gasping, "for an endurance test. Anyway, I'm ten years older than you are."

"Nine years," he corrected her, "and that has nothing to do with it. I know grannies who could leave you in their dust. You've got to care, Cornell. You've got to put some effort into life. And I'm not talking about Keogh plans."

Breathing more evenly now, she blew her bangs out of her eyes and looked bored. "Are you the guru everyone climbs the mountain to ask questions of? To talk to about life and truth and the importance of a fit cardiovascular system?"

She thought for a moment she'd annoyed him enough to earn an uncontrolled reaction, but he simply turned her around and gave her a light push upward.

By the second mile, she was leaning heavily on him and she judged it best to save all hostile observations for another time. He certainly did have endurance—and the strength to keep them both climbing.

The hill finally flattened out into a meadow. Several hundred feet away she could see a cabin at the edge of a woods.

"Is that it?" she asked, not sure if she was chagrined or relieved. It didn't look as if it were much from where they stood, but then, a milking stool under a lean-to would have been a welcome sight at that point. Anything to sit on.

"That's it," he replied. There was something in his voice when he said it. A little pride, a trace of wistfulness, and probably the same relief she felt.

"Your place?" she asked.

"Kurt's and mine," he replied. "You going to make it?"

"You go ahead," she said. "I'll crawl from here."

"You're such a pansy." He tightened his grip on her waist. "Come on. I'll get you there."

"And probably remind me every chance you get," she prophesied, doing her best to hobble along with him.

"Damn right," he said.

The cabin was built of rough logs in classic Northwest style. Three steps led up to a plain, railed porch.

"Oh, God. Steps," Paula groaned. "I can't do it, Dane. I'll just sit right here at the bottom and you can throw my food and a blanket down. If I see Hailey coming, I'll shout for you."

Dane leaned the rifle on the stairs, tossed her pack onto the porch, shrugged out of his and did the same with it. Then he anchored her to his side, lifted her until her feet cleared the ground, and walked up the steps. "Super pansy," he said, putting her on her feet in front of the door and reaching into his pocket for a key.

"I thought people in the wilderness left their cabins open for other travelers," she observed, leaning heavily against the wall.

"That was a hundred years ago," he answered, pushing the door open. "And they weren't expecting Hailey. Sit down. I'll bring the packs in."

The cabin was small, spartan and surprisingly tidy. The main room held an eclectic collection of odds and ends of furniture, a fringed wine-colored carpet under a very plain old steamer trunk that served as a coffee table and a scattering of candles and oil lamps. Of course, Paula thought. No electricity. No television. No telephone. She and Dane were completely cut off from civilization. And, hopefully, from Hailey.

"How do we call someone if we need help?" she asked as Dane put one of the packs down in front of a small stone fireplace.

He carried the other into the kitchen separated from the main room by a low counter. "We have a radio," he replied. "Kurt's men hiked it in with our food." Dane removed a bag of gourmet coffee from the pack, then he began to build a fire in an old wood stove. "They're out there somewhere." He made a vague gesture with his chin toward the window over the sink. "Otherwise, you and I are the only help each other has."

She hobbled toward him on feet that felt worn to her knees. "Seriously?" she asked gravely.

He looked into her eyes as though surprised by her concern. "Seriously. Can you handle it?"

He expected a blustery reply, or a flip one. She surprised him again when she replied candidly, "I hope so, but I don't know. I'm not an ex-soldier like you are. In a boardroom I could give Donald Trump a few bad moments, but in hand-to-hand combat..." She shrugged eloquently.

"Basically," he said with a smile, "the same principles apply. You get your mind right, know your opponent as well as possible and go in with no thought of giving up. The other guy'll know that the minute he touches you—or you touch him. Courage and determination scare the hell out of an enemy. And I'm not an ex-soldier, I'm an ex-marine." He grinned. "We're sensitive. How about a cup of coffee?"

"Sorry," she replied. "I meant the word in its most generic sense. And I'd love a cup of coffee."

As she shifted from one sore foot to the other, he suddenly put the bag of coffee aside and lifted her onto the counter.

Paula sat there, completely shaken. She had to stop reacting this way when he touched her, she thought. It meant nothing. Judging by the way he went back to his task without missing a motion certainly indicated it meant nothing to him. How could it? She was old enough to be his mother. Well, his older sister, anyway.

"You packed a five-pound bag of gourmet coffee all the way up here?" she asked, just to show him and herself that she could handle being swept around as though she were a girl.

He reached into an overhead cupboard for a battered old coffeepot. "I can handle bad luck," he said, "bad times, bad women..." He slanted her a grin. "But not bad coffee."

She watched his economical movements, fascinated by his quick, long-fingered hands. "You're quite the philosopher," she said. "Isn't that unusual in a sol...a marine?"

He put the coffeepot on the wood stove. "Not at all. Few people think harder than those in a life or death struggle. Can you cook?"

It took Paula a moment to answer. He had a confusing habit of stating a profound truth, then tacking on a mundane question. She needed time to shift from rhetoric to practicality.

"Ah...yes," she replied, "but I don't like to."

He nodded. "Neither do I. We'll rotate KP. You start with dinner."

She grimaced. "As soon as my feet stop throbbing, I wanted to look around a little. I almost never get out of the city, I..."

"No," he said without turning away from a visual inventory of the cupboards.

The mellow mood Paula had been carefully cultivating dissolved and she felt the hair on her neck bristle. "Excuse me?" she said haughtily. She wasn't accustomed to being denied. And she particularly wasn't accustomed to being ignored while she was being denied.

Dane turned at her tone and came to stand beside her, leaning a hand on the counter near her thigh. "I said no," he repeated mildly. "You never leave the cabin without me."

"Where could I possibly go?" she asked reasonably.

"That's not the question," he replied patiently. "If Hailey or anyone else does get near us, I don't want you out alone."

"We're miles from nowhere."

"*We* got here. Do you think Hailey couldn't?"

"I doubt even Hailey's as bullheaded as you are."

"Let's hope not."

As he started to walk away, she grabbed his shirt-sleeve and leapt off the counter. She didn't even feel her sore feet as she squared off with Dane.

"This may seem like a small thing to you," she said hotly, "but I don't like your attitude. I know you're used to ordering tough guys around, but I respond much better to please and thank-you. I have a few years on you, you know. I've earned a little respect."

Paula was surprised—and deeply annoyed—when he grinned. "Why do you do that?" he asked, studying her with all apparent fascination. "You're at an age when a woman's just getting interesting, and you act like you should be buying a cemetery plot."

Paula lifted her chin, stammering a retort. But he wasn't listening.

"You have my respect for what you've accomplished in business," he said, returning her glare with cool equanimity, "and because you're a woman, you automatically have my respect. That's what my grandmother taught me. But you'll have to earn my respect as a person, just as I'll have to earn yours. And you won't do it by hiding behind the years between us. There aren't that many."

Speechless, Paula stormed off toward a door at the far end of the main room, praying as she approached it that it was a bedroom and not a closet. She saw gratefully that it was. She walked into it, then came back to the doorway.

"Who gets the bedroom?" she demanded.

He turned away from the fireplace, a chunk of wood in his hands. He grinned again. "We'll share it."

She folded her arms. "What?"

"Take a moment to look," he said patiently. "You'll notice two beds. And, anyway, you'd have *shared* a bed with me last night."

"I wasn't this annoyed with you last night," she said and slammed the door.

Dane, still smiling, started a fire in the fireplace. He was beginning to enjoy her reactions because he was seeing more and more of the flustered woman behind the controlled goddess image she tried to present. This sure as hell wasn't going to be the quiet week in the wilderness Kurt had predicted.

DINNER WAS EASIER to prepare than Paula had anticipated. Because the cabin had no electricity and, therefore, no refrigeration, the small kitchen was stocked with an extensive variety of canned goods. As Paula opened a can of stew, turned it into a pot and put it on the stove, she glanced uneasily at the full shelves. Apparently finding Hailey was expected to take time.

From outside, Paula could hear the rhythmic crack of an ax against wood. Peering out the kitchen window, she saw Dane at work in the encroaching darkness, a lantern on a stump lighting his task. She experienced a startling sensation of having been thrown back in time. It crystallized her situation for her, made it even more dreamlike than it had been.

She was setting two places at the small table when Dane shouldered his way into the cabin, the wood in his arms stacked up to his chin. He dropped it noisily into the wood box near the fireplace and added a log to the quieting flames. He brought two handfuls of smaller kindling into the kitchen and put them into the stove. Then he placed the bright lantern he'd used outside on the counter beside her to light that dark corner of the kitchen.

She looked up at him, discomfited by his brawny competence and the interest in his eyes.

"Doing all right?" he asked.

She stirred the stew to have something to do. "So far. Do we have bread or rolls to go with this?"

"Yes." He put a hand on her shoulder and reached to the bread box on the shelf above her head. "Wheatberry or French?" he asked, his body curved over hers. His shoulder rubbed the back of her head while he waited for her answer. Air whooshed out of her lungs like smoke up a chimney. She felt closed in, cut off, cornered.

"Wheat," she said thinly.

He pulled the bag of rolls down and stepped back. She let her breath out slowly, forcing herself to relax. She refused to let the "What is happening to me?" question form. If she pretended this strange tension surrounding her wasn't there, perhaps it would go away.

"Bowls?" she asked.

He reached into a cupboard under the counter and handed her two chipped pieces of blue pottery. She filled them and carried them to the table while he put the rolls on a plate, pulled forks and spoons from a drawer and brought them to the table. He lit a white utility candle in a simple brass holder and set it in the middle.

"Ah," she said, her tone exaggeratedly cheerful. "Elegance in the wilderness."

"Atmosphere," he replied, holding out a chair for her, "can make even stew out of a can taste like chateaubriand for two."

The quietly spoken, suggestively intimate remark made her cast him a quick, discomfited glance before she sat down. "Let's hope so," she replied lightly. "Or the menu could get pretty dull around here if we stay longer than two days. Thank you."

"Trust me to be resourceful," he said, taking his place opposite her. "There's a stream in the woods, and I'm not a bad fisherman. Why don't you let your hair down?"

Again, it took her a moment to catch up with him. She put a hand to the tight knot of hair at the back of her neck and gave him a mirthless laugh. "Is this where you pull out my hairpins and I shake out a breathtakingly sexy head of hair, decimating the antagonism you feel for me and turning it to attraction?"

He grinned at her while reaching for a roll. "I don't know. Want to try it?"

Annoyed that he seemed unaffected by her sarcasm, she picked up her spoon and dipped it into the stew. "I wear my hair this way because it keeps it out of my face. I'm a busy woman."

"And it contributes to the matronly impression you're trying to make?"

Hurt, she glared up at him. "And what impression are you trying to make? Sexy adventurer who wants to add an older woman to his list of conquests?"

He'd asked for that, Dane thought. He shouldn't push her. It was just that she looked as if she needed a good shaking to jar her out of what appeared to be a downward rush to middle age.

"I work in a hardware store and I've just made an offer for one of my own," he said, tearing his roll in two. "How sexy and adventurous is that?"

She frowned at him, surprised. "I thought you worked for your brother."

He shook his head. "Just this time. My boss gave me two weeks off."

She grimaced. "You mean I'm being protected by a hardware clerk?"

He laughed. "A hardware clerk with twelve years' military experience, five of them in Force Recon, the Corps' equivalent of Special Forces. You're safe, Paula."

She knew that. He would do all in his power to protect her from physical harm. But suddenly that wasn't the most serious threat. "Isn't hardware a little mundane after life in Force Recon?"

He nodded, smiling. "Precisely what I was after when I got out. I've had the dream for a long time. The military was supposed to be a stop-gap measure—a way to get an education when I couldn't afford one. I turned out to be good at it, so I stayed longer than I intended."

She nodded. "That's how I feel about my business. Though you seem to think travel is frivolous, I thought I might write a book afterward."

He inclined his head in a conciliatory gesture. "I didn't mean to scoff. Your future is your own business, it's just that sometimes..." He hesitated, knowing he was overstepping again. But two people confined together for an indefinite period were bound to learn each other's foibles and secrets without the gradual intimacy most relationships allowed.

She looked at him wryly, suspecting she wasn't going to like what he had to say. "Go ahead," she prodded.

"Sometimes," he went on quietly, "you behave as though you don't have a future."

He thought she might deny his observation. Instead she simply held his gaze for a moment, then went back to her dinner. "I feel that way often," she admitted, without looking at him. "I mean, I know I have years ahead of me, but...that's not the same."

He frowned over that, quelling the urge to ask her to explain. If she wanted to, she would. If she didn't, that was fine. There were a lot of things about himself he wouldn't want to share.

After dinner, he pumped water into a small copper basin and carried it into the bedroom for her. Then he pumped water for the dishes and did them while she got ready for bed. It was still early evening, but it had been a long day.

Her cat-wash finished, her hair brushed, the long T-shirt on, Paula opened the bedroom door a crack and called, "Good night."

Dane's response was immediate. "Good night, Paula." The rich, quiet sound of his voice filled her with the same contentment it had the night before.

She crawled into bed, truly concerned about herself. All right. He was nice looking. He was competent. His job was to protect her life. That was a triple-powered whammy bound to make any woman feel things inappropriate to the situation.

In her case, she hadn't felt those things in several years—had turned them off. So she was more susceptible than most to broad shoulders and quiet confi-

dence. But he was young, and she'd had her chance.
That part of her life was over. *Get it together, Paula,* she
told herself severely. *Get a grip!*

On the sofa, Dane listened to Paula toss and turn. It
was almost 2:00 a.m. and he'd been staring at the ceiling since nine. Judging by the sounds of the springs in
the bedroom, Paula had stared at the ceiling, the floor,
the wall and the window.

A shadowy image ran across his mind of her in his
T-shirt, shapely legs white in the darkness. It was a
memory he'd stored from the night before. He'd refused to concentrate on it. He'd pushed it to the back of
his mind several times today, but it refused to dissolve.
That was why it seemed wiser to spend the night on the
sofa.

She was a client, he reminded himself. A client who
considered him a kid. He smiled as he thought about
that. He hadn't been a kid since the first time his mother
was picked up when he was seven. With an impatient
sigh, he turned over and buried his nose in the pillow.
Why was he giving the matter a second thought? She'd
grown up in Beverly Hills, and he'd spent part of his
youth with Kurt and his drunken mother in a one-
bedroom apartment in East Los Angeles, and the other
part as a ward of the court. It wasn't as though they
could find something to talk about that didn't involve
Hailey or the way they annoyed each other.

The sound of the bedroom door opening quietly
made him turn over again. "Glass of water?" he asked.

Her voice sounded wry and resigned. "I want a cup
of coffee, even if it's cold. I can't sleep. Why don't you
sleep in the bedroom?"

Dane reached to the coffee table to turn on the Coleman lantern. Paula bloomed out of the shadows like a

light in the fog. She'd put on jeans and a sweater, but she'd untied her hair. It captured his attention, and he stared at it for a moment. It lay around her face and shoulders in dark red disarray, a cloud of smoky fire more beautiful than he'd suspected. The lamplight picked out its copper tips. She pushed a wave off her forehead, unaware of the picture she made, and light rippled through it as it settled back against her cheek.

He forced himself to look away from her hair and noticed the floral fabric bag in her hands. "What's that?" he asked.

"My cross-stitch," she replied, looking away from Dane's broad chest, disappointed that her severe talk with herself had such little result. She dropped her bag onto the coffee table and turned toward the kitchen.

Dane's hand closed over hers, stopping her. He knows, she thought desperately. He thinks I'm coming on to him. He thinks I'm an over-the-hill broad looking for a rejuvenating fling. While part of her mind absorbed her own scolding, the other part was thinking how warm and strong his hand was, how easily it braceleted her wrist, how immobilizing it was.

He stood, barefoot in his jeans. He looked down at her, and she knew his eyes read every thought that had crossed her mind in the past few seconds. She swallowed, waiting.

He reached down to hook a finger in the handle of the lantern. "Take the lamp with you," he said, raising the hand he held and transferring the lamp to her fingers. He gave her a strangely melancholy smile. "Don't want you falling over anything. I put the pot over the coals in the fireplace. You sure you don't want to take your coffee back to bed?"

Relief and disappointment warred in her breast. "No," she replied, taking the lamp across the small room to the fireplace, hoping a little distance from him might help her relax. "I don't sleep well under the best of conditions. Between wondering where Hailey is, and worrying about my business, it's almost impossible." She touched a hand lightly against the pot and found it still hot. She went into the kitchen for a mug as Dane left the blankets on the sofa and went to the bedroom door. She came back, poured her coffee, then saw him still standing there. "You take the bedroom," she encouraged him with a smile. "I'll be fine. If I hear anything weird, I'll call you."

"I'll leave the door open," he said, a frown wrinkling his brows. "If you hear anything, I'll hear it, too. Good night."

"The lamp will keep you awake."

"No. Good night."

Bone weary but as taut as piano wire, Dane crawled into the larger bed, the one Paula had been sleeping in. The lamp wouldn't keep him awake, but her scent might. He buried his nose in a pillow that smelled of gardenias and knew it was going to be a long night.

Paula put the lamp on the coffee table, methodically separating her embroidery floss and carefully unfolding her project. It was a wedding sampler for her secretary, who was getting married at Christmas time.

Folding a knee in a corner of the sofa, Paula sat back on it and was immediately enveloped by Dane's body heat in the blanket he'd left behind. She closed her eyes and let herself absorb it, enjoy it—and accept for the first time in the thirty-six hours she'd known him that her life had taken a frightening, dangerous twist that had nothing to do with Hailey.

CHAPTER FOUR

PAULA ROLLED onto her back, emerging from a deep, dark sleep. Even before she opened her eyes, she was aware of being vaguely headachy. Other processes borne of long habit also began to work. She had to get Bill's and Natalie's breakfasts. Call the office. See that... Then she remembered. A groan came from deep within her, and the day felt dead before it even began.

The aromas of coffee and something spicy as yet unidentified wafted past her nostrils. Her eyes still closed, she frowned. Was someone already cooking?

In a lazy movement intended to hold on to the half-wakeful state as long as possible, she stretched an arm and a leg—and came fully awake instantly as pain ran the length of her. Everything cramped in protest from her ankles to her shoulders. She focused on the ceiling, wondering what on earth was wrong with her.

Her frown deepened. There was no art nouveau, leaded-glass lampshade suspended from an oak-paneled ceiling. She saw rough half timbers steepled overhead. Hanging from one crosspiece by a leather thong was a thick candle in a wrought-iron base.

She heard the crackle of a fire, and the gentle clang of iron pans against an iron stove. A melodic whistle completed the collection of domestic sounds. Paula groaned again and let an arm drop across her eyes as memory brought her to full awareness. That's right.

She'd walked for miles yesterday with a backpack. She was on the lam with a man who probably didn't even remember the miniskirt.

"You getting up sometime today?"

Paula lowered her arm to her waist and looked up into quiet, smoky-green eyes. Dane braced his hands on the back of the sofa, his broad torso covered in a thick dark blue sweater. He smelled faintly of wood smoke and the out-of-doors. He smiled. "Or were you hoping for breakfast in bed?"

She closed her eyes for a moment, trying to force herself out of the lethargy morning always brought. It was so difficult to make herself want to be up, to make herself respond. Maybe if she didn't try to deal with anything important...

"Do you remember the miniskirt?" she asked.

"Ah...no," Dane replied. "I *was* around for hot pants, but I was just a kid. Why? Were you old enough to wear a miniskirt when it was the rage?"

She sighed. "I was fourteen and scrawny, but I wore one, anyway." Fourteen. She closed her eyes and considered going back to sleep. God, she felt old. And her muscles felt older. "You eat," she said with a sigh. "I can't move."

"Eggs, corned beef hash, apple nut muffins," he cajoled.

"Save mine," she said. "I'll put them in the microwave later."

"No microwave," he said. "Come on, you'll feel better when you're on your feet."

"No, I won't."

Apparently unwilling to argue the issue, he scooped her off the sofa, blanket and all. Too surprised to struggle, she simply gasped indignantly as he carried her into the bathroom, where a bucket of water still steamed. He put her on her feet in the middle of the small room.

Gathering the blanket tightly around her, she gave him the look that always chilled blood in the boardroom.

"How dare you manhandle me," she said with regal disdain.

He raised an eyebrow as he started to pull the door closed. "If you consider that manhandling," he said laughing softly, "it must be a long time since you last experienced it. Or the man who did it didn't make it very memorable."

She pushed the door closed and heard his soft laughter diminish as he went into the kitchen. She leaned against the door, aware of being very much awake. She could feel her heart pumping, her blood flowing. Every inch of skin on her back and the back of her legs where his arms had touched when he carried her pulsed with life. After several years of near dormancy, the effect was startling.

Impatient with herself, she dropped the blanket and reached for the fresh washcloth and towel he'd placed on the counter. She scrubbed herself quickly, the warm water cooling the moment it touched her in the chill morning air. She toweled herself dry until her skin was pink, but the feelings hadn't diminished one bit. Her body and her spirit tingled. She was awake and alive. That could be good or bad, she thought. It was really too soon to judge.

DANE STARTED POURING her coffee when he heard the bedroom door squeak open. He glanced up as she walked into the kitchen. Her cheeks were still pink and her eyes still sparkled, but he could see that he and his charge were back to the stiffness of their first few hours together. He had ruffled her, and that, apparently, was against the rules. She wore her dignity like a shield.

"Good morning," he said, determined to ignore her attitude. He refused to spend the next few days in an atmosphere of tension. Although that might be easier said than done. In old jeans and a shrunken green sweater that clung lovingly to full, round breasts and a lean midriff, she made him forget that he'd sworn off women, and made him remember how long it had been since the last time he'd . . .

She went to the stove and helped herself to minuscule servings of eggs and hash and one muffin.

"I put your needlework on the lamp table in the corner of the living room," he said, replacing the coffeepot and resuming his seat. "You fell asleep holding it with the needle sticking out of the cloth stuff. I was afraid you'd hurt yourself."

She realized the last thing she remembered during the night was stitching the brim of the groom's top hat. Dane must have gotten up and covered her. His vigilance was a little unnerving for a woman who'd felt adrift and alone for so long.

"Thank you," she said politely, trying not to think about him leaning over her in the night. She just had to get through this ordeal, then life would be back to normal. She'd sell her business, leave on her cruise, and . . . cruise. Nothing else would be expected of her.

She broke open the fragrant muffin and swiped the butter knife over it very lightly. "So, what do we do today?" she asked airily. "Hunt our lunch? Blaze a trail? Make a pet of a bear?"

He sipped his coffee. "We've got our lunch, and we don't need a trail 'cause we're not going anywhere. If you want to cozy up to a bear, though, you're welcome to try. You might fare better than most. Like attracts like. It's a law of nature."

She looked up into his guileless smile and shook her head. "Now, how would you explain it to my father if I became brunch for a bear?"

He shrugged. "Presumably I wouldn't be around to have to explain, having died myself trying to save you."

They were teasing; she knew that. But, suddenly the concept of another human being dying in defense of her life was not something she wanted to consider.

"If it should come to that," she said, her brown eyes dark and grave, "don't you dare."

A little alarmed by her seriousness, afraid he'd lost the thread of their conversation, he asked with a smile, "What? Feed you to a bear?"

"No. Die for me."

He stared at her for a moment, watching emotions chase through her eyes too quickly to be defined. He didn't precisely understand what he saw, but he recognized it. He'd seen it in the eyes of a comrade who'd stepped on a mine in Kuwait and died in his arms.

He didn't try to analyze why she should be wearing that look. He just tried to reach the fear that was causing it.

"The purpose of this whole exercise, Paula," he said, "is that nothing happens to either of us."

"I know." She angled her chin stubbornly. "But I've seen the hate in Hailey's eyes. And the mad genius. He may very well find us."

"If he does," he replied calmly, "we're prepared."

"There are some things for which we're never prepared. If it comes to your life or mine . . ."

"My job is to save yours."

"I won't appreciate it," she said, her voice rising. "And neither will the people who love you."

He looked at her evenly. "So, you do have a death wish."

She lowered her eyes and sighed. "Not really, but I've lived ten years longer than you have. I . . ."

He slapped a hand on the table, making the cups and plates jump. Paula blinked.

"God, here it comes again," he said, impatient with her attitude and just a little frightened by it. "Why don't I just bury you right now and save us both a lot of trouble? The fact that my life's been shorter than yours doesn't make it any more valuable."

"I just meant . . ."

"I know what you meant," he said, angry out of all proportion to the situation. He was aware of that, but was unable to quiet his nerves. "You're going to live, Mrs. Cornell. I don't know what your problem is, but you're not going to throw your life away with help from me. I had a friend die in my arms in the desert. He'd have gladly changed places with you."

Her face paled. "You couldn't save him, so you're going to save me, is that it?"

He studied her a moment, realizing again she wasn't as tough as she pretended to be. He'd had no right to pounce on her like that. "Anyone who's ever been to war," he said quietly, "comes out applauding life, however much it hurts. Buck up, will you? I promised your mother I'd bring you home safely and I intend to do just that."

"Fine," she said quietly. "My point was, I didn't want you to send me home alone. I'd like you to go home, too."

That swamped his anger like water thrown on a fire. He leaned back in his chair and sighed. "Developing an attachment to me, are you?"

She went back to her breakfast with a dry glance up at him. "Not if you're always this grumpy in the morning."

"I was fine," he said, "until you started getting casual about your life."

"I explained that."

"Yes, you did. I apologize." He gave her a quick smile as he pushed away from the table. "You seem to bring out the worst in me."

She shrugged a shoulder, chewing, then swallowing. "It's a gift. I'd say you do the same for me, but I'm always bad-tempered."

He carried his cup and plate to the counter. "Probably comes from being cooped up in a skyscraper in the heart of a crowded city."

She flexed a sore shoulder muscle as she looked out a wide-paned window at the view of trees and sky. "If that's true," she said grimly, "this landscape ought to make me a saint." Then she turned her attention to him. "Where are you going?"

"To work on the roof," he said. "We'll have rain by tonight."

She looked doubtfully at the blue sky beyond the window. "There's not a cloud in sight." She raised a mocking eyebrow. "Don't tell me. You can smell rain."

He picked up an old wooden toolbox near the back door, a grin acknowledging her taunt. "I can listen to weather reports. Rain for the weekend."

"Aren't weathermen always wrong?"

"The hole in the roof's over your bed," he said, pushing the door open. "Want to take the chance?"

Without waiting for an answer, he disappeared.

Paula washed the dishes in the tub of water that had been warming on the stove, and cleaned up the kitchen. Overhead, she heard hammering and other sounds of Dane's industry. She remembered his flash of anger and wondered about it. "Buck up," he'd told her. For a moment she'd been hurt and annoyed by that directive. He seemed to think all she'd suffered had been a minor disappointment.

But he didn't know about that part of her life that had once given it purpose, then finally destroyed it. And there wasn't time for her to consider it at the moment. Her parents' safety was the issue now, and she had promised to cooperate.

With a sigh, she looked around the sun-drenched little room naked of all the conveniences to which she'd grown so accustomed, and hoped she could survive for however long it took the police to find Hailey and neutralize his threat to the Emmett family.

Paula pulled her jacket on, picked up her needlework and went out onto the porch.

Dane's voice, sharp with authority, demanded from somewhere overhead, "Where you going?"

The sun was bright, the birds were singing and the meadow was the most brilliant green she'd ever seen. The beauty of their setting startled her, then transformed her serious mood to one of mild mischief.

"Rodeo Drive for a little shopping," she shouted up, "then the Beverly Hills Hotel for lunch by the pool. Want to come?"

There was a moment's silence, then he said, a smile in his voice, "Park it in the rocker, Paula."

"Right."

An ancient chair made of wooden slats stood in a sunny corner of the porch. Beside it, presumably for a table, was an overturned half barrel. Not exactly the veranda at Tara, Paula decided, but comfortable enough. She went to work on her cross-stitch.

It wasn't long before the perfume of the cabin's wood smoke, the fragrance of sun on grass and leaf and weathered wood, and the thousands of little sounds that brought the silence alive when one concentrated on it completely distracted her. She dropped the hoop in her lap and stared at the meadow.

The play of sun and shadow seemed to change its appearance from moment to moment. Insects and small creatures moved, leaves and branches stirred, a smudge of cloud appeared at the tops of the trees lining the hilltop beyond the meadow. She smiled. Rain by tonight.

She went back to her needlework, aware of a subtle loosening of tension in her fingers and in her back. She crossed her legs and discovered that they still ached abominably.

She checked her pattern, counted tiny squares framed in her hoop and made the three stitches that began the bride's shoes. She was halfway up a diaphanous skirt when Dane's face, upside down, appeared below the porch's roofline.

She put a dramatic hand over her heart. "Eaves dropping, Mr. Chandler?" she asked, separating the words for the sake of her little joke.

"Unoriginal, but cute," he said. "I was thinking about your mention of the Beverly Hills Hotel and lunch by the pool."

She stood up and went to the unadorned four-by-four that served as porch column. "Tell me," she said, looking into his eyes, though upside down, "that you can arrange for a helicopter to take us there."

He shook his head. An inch or so of wiry dark hair fringed it and dangled. "Sorry. I thought maybe you could get them to cater."

She frowned, then tilted her head sideways so he could get the full effect of her expression. She splayed a hand over her breast. "In the person of yours truly, I presume?"

"I did fix breakfast."

She nodded reluctantly. "I suppose I could fill the galvanized tub and we could pretend it's a pool and dangle our feet in it."

His eyebrows quirked. "I guess. If you like."

"I'll get right on it."

"You're a champ."

"CHANGED YOUR MIND about the tub, huh?" Dane asked.

They'd followed the sun and sat side by side halfway down the porch steps, a box of buttered crackers between them. They ate soup from pottery mugs and watched the distant clouds advance slowly toward them.

Paula shook her head. "I decided it just wouldn't be the same. It wouldn't smell of chlorine and you couldn't float an inflatable zebra in it and coast from side to side with your big toe for a rudder."

His eyes widened slightly. Sunlight slanted across his face and she noticed for the first time the spray of silver in the green of his eyes. "You've actually done that?" he asked.

Distracted for a moment, she asked vaguely, "What?"

"Sat in an inflatable zebra and tacked across a pool guided by your big toe. Weren't you embarrassed? I mean, you're so—" there was laughter in his eyes as he considered carefully "—correct," he said finally.

She'd been about to be seduced by his laughter, until the memory reminded her just how much she'd changed. She dismissed the gloom that threatened with a toss of her head.

"That was then," she said.

"When?"

She made a vague gesture with her hand. "Before," she said, and reached into the box for another cracker.

He hadn't expected her to answer. It was none of his business, after all. He was working, and he couldn't afford to allow himself to be distracted by sexual attraction, or the simple concern of one human being for another. But it was happening all the same.

The attraction he could control. The concern was almost harder. Unguarded, her eyes were so soft and so hurt. He thought if he could understand what underlay her careful distance, he'd be better able to deal with her—and she wouldn't be on his mind every moment.

He leaned an elbow on the stair above him and stretched his legs out to the grass. "Where is Mr. Cornell?" he asked quietly.

He saw her brow pleat as she sat up, resisting the answer. Then she sighed, leaned back on both elbows, and lifted her face to the sun. "Taos, New Mexico, last I heard."

"An artist?"

"A lawyer."

"Why'd you leave him?"

Paula turned to him, an indignant exclamation on the tip of her tongue, but he forestalled her with a grin. "Stop me if I'm getting too personal," he said facetiously.

She swatted his upper arm, unable to hold back a little laugh. "Why do you want to know?"

"So I can understand you," he replied.

"My father insists that he can't, and he's known me thirty-nine years."

"Ah, but he's operating at a disadvantage. His perception of you is distorted by the fact that he helped create you. Makes it hard to analyze the facts and be objective."

"But you could?" she asked, apparently unconvinced.

"I seem to be driven to try," he replied honestly.

She shook her head, frowning, as though the subject of her marriage was something she hated to confront. That didn't surprise him. He understood perfectly. But he had to know what motivated her. He had to know she wouldn't give up at the critical moment.

She sat up and stared out at the meadow, her pretty profile set. "I didn't leave him," she said. "He left me."

There'd been times in the past forty-some hours with her when he'd have gladly abandoned her himself if he hadn't promised so many people he'd keep her safe. But there were other times when she seemed so vulnerable, so desperate, he couldn't imagine any man leaving her to fend for herself—particularly one who'd vowed to love her.

"Did you want him to go?" he asked.

She thought a moment. "I guess so. I drove him away."

The obvious question was "Why?" but he thought he'd pushed a little too hard already.

"Well, what do you know?" He sat up, drew his feet up to the stair below him and folded his arms on his knees. "We have something in common."

Paula shook off her painful memories and turned to look at him in surprise. "You've been married?"

"Six years."

She had trouble absorbing this new information. He seemed too controlled to have ever loved someone.

"She walked out on me," he added.

She repeated his question. "Did you want her to go?"

He turned his head to smile wryly. "No. I was mortally wounded. Still am."

"How long has she been gone?"

"A year."

Paula remembered what he'd said about the time he'd spent in the Gulf War, and did a quick calculation. She asked in disbelief, "You mean, she left you while you were in Saudi Arabia?"

He nodded. "She'd been gone six weeks when I got home."

"She left without telling you?"

"She told Kurt," he said. He heard no self-pity in his voice, but the bitterness was strong. "He chose not to tell me."

Paula grappled with that a moment. "Because he was afraid of what the news would do to you?" she guessed.

He gave her a quick glance filled with quiet anger and deep mistrust. "That's what he said."

Completely pulled into his dilemma, Paula didn't realize she'd drawn close enough to him that their shoulders and their knees touched. "Why don't you believe him?"

He sighed, staring at the trees beyond the meadow. The silver in his eyes had darkened to slate. "Because when I met her, she was his girl. But she married me. He's always hated me for that."

Paula shook her head, unable to believe that. "He doesn't talk about you like someone who hates you. Didn't he keep saying over an over at the house that you were the best man he had?"

"Yes," he agreed, "but he has this ability to coolly put everything where it belongs. He wouldn't let his feelings interfere with his work. We haven't spoken since I've been back from Saudi, but he needed someone to take care of you, so he didn't think twice about calling me. That's the way he is."

Paula shook her head. "Dane, I don't understand. What could you have done about it if he had written you? They wouldn't have let you come home, would they?"

He ran a hand through his hair. "No. But I'd have known my life was falling apart. I could have had someone try to trace her whereabouts."

"And maybe while you were worrying about all this, you'd have done something thoughtless and gotten yourself killed. I think he did what he thought was best for you." She put an arm around his shoulder and rubbed, her voice and her touch gentle. "Maybe you're angry with him, because he was here to blame and she wasn't."

Anger flared in him, but quickly subsided when he looked into the concern in her eyes. It had been a long time since a woman had looked at him that way. He felt drawn by it, softened by it and just a little frightened.

"Yeah," he said on a gusty breath. "Maybe."

"When did you two buy this place?" she asked, looking around her at the verdant stillness. "It's so perfect. It would be a shame if you never enjoyed it together again."

"After our mother died," Dane replied. "Kurt had been working on the docks for a couple of years and I had just enlisted. We pooled everything we had and bought this from an old guy Kurt knew who couldn't make it up here anymore." He frowned. "We usually came up here when I got home on leave, though we haven't for the last couple of years." He got briskly to his feet and pulled her up beside him. "Come on. We're going to take a walk and wear you out so you'll sleep tonight."

She groaned. "But my legs are already so stiff I can barely move."

"We've got to limber you up," he insisted. "If we have to run for it, I can't carry you."

She stuffed her cross-stitch into the little fabric bag and tossed it at the chair. "If you insist on taking me on this walk," she warned, "you may have to carry me back."

Holding her firmly by the hand, he headed off toward the trees. "I'll just leave you for the wolves."

She stopped in her tracks. "Wolves?"

He tugged her along. "Joke, Paula. No wolves."

She breathed a sigh of relief.

"Coyotes, though," he said, then dodged as she swung her free hand at him.

THEY WALKED for an hour, through the dense canopy of fir, pine and cedar, by a stream that was lined with aspens and gurgled and sparkled in the waning afternoon light. Pine needles and cones crunched underfoot and birds sang overhead.

Though Dane kept up a casual conversation with her, Paula saw his watchful eyes explore every shadow and thicket, and felt the tensile energy in the arm across her shoulders.

The activity did loosen her cramped muscles, and soothe her nerves. The knowledge of what Dane had been through in the past year upset her. She couldn't imagine a woman abandoning her husband without even telling him, and she particularly couldn't imagine one doing it to Dane. He was autocratic and unafraid to speak his mind, but he was as reliable as the day was long. She recalled the bearded man in the restaurant who'd tried to grab her, first near the lounge, then in the parking lot. Dane had been there in an instant both times. The thought made her smile.

"What are you grinning about?" Dane asked, pushing a low, fragrant pine branch out of her way as they negotiated the edge of the woods.

"I was thinking about the men at the restaurant," she chuckled. "I'll bet they're all still running."

He pinched her shoulder scoldingly. "That wasn't funny. Had I stopped for a pack of cigarettes, you might be a motorcycle mama right now, or the harem favorite of some eastern potentate."

"I suppose you're right," she said. "Both life-styles sound far more demanding than what I have planned for the rest of my life."

"You going to be a celibate pedestrian?"

"I thought . . ."

One moment she was forming a reply, the next she was facedown on the forest floor, pinned under Dane's body. She heard the small sound of movement in the trees ahead of them, and Dane's urgently whispered, "Don't budge."

He braced on one knee astride her back, his gun hand supported on the other as the crashing sounds in the underbrush grew nearer. Paula raised her eyes to the sound, her heart pounding. Already? Had Hailey found her already?

She uttered a little cry and flinched as a browning-gray deer burst out of the undergrowth, velvet eyes wide, graceful head high and poised as it caught their scent and stopped. She stared at its stunning beauty and its curiously prominent ears. Above her, Dane muttered an oath, then she heard the click of the safety as he lowered the gun. The deer bounded stiff-legged toward the stream.

Paula dropped her forehead to her arm with a deep-throated laugh as relief spread through her.

Dane, still kneeling astride her, turned her onto her back. "What's so funny?" he demanded, biting back his own laughter.

She tried valiantly to look serious. "Nothing. I mean if..." She cleared her throat. "If that deer had intended to savage me, you were prepared. Why were his ears so big?"

She saw amusement and playful censure in Dane's eyes. Beyond his head, blue sky was visible through the lacy canopy of leaves and pine needles, but she didn't see it. Her attention was caught by something else in his eyes, something that wiped her smile away and made her heart race anew, as though danger threatened again.

Dane's pulse wouldn't settle down. The danger was past, had never really existed, except as one of the unpredictable possibilities Kurt was paying him to foresee.

Despite Paula's teasing, he knew he hadn't overreacted. It was simply that the threat hadn't been real. So, he'd been willing to laugh with her about throwing her to the ground because of a deer.

He just hadn't counted on what her genuine laughter would do to her—and, ultimately, to him.

It lit her eyes, created a dimple at the left corner of her mouth, and melted the cool dignity that usually stood between them like a wall of ice. It made her suddenly warmly ingenuous, and gave him a glimpse of the woman she must have been before she became the imperious woman he protected. She looked like a teenager, and she made him feel like one.

Unable to stop himself, he reached into her cloud of redwood-colored hair, cupped the back of her head and brought her to a sitting position.

"That was a mule deer—a little different from Bambi. You through giggling?"

He watched her smile fade as amusement diminished in her eyes and excitement grew.

"Yes," she whispered.

"Good," he said softly.

Paula considered it a good sign that her mind continued to function. Dane was going to kiss her. She wanted him to kiss her. But she had her wits about her, and she understood why it was happening. It was all elementary.

Dane, the hunter, the protector, had prepared for a confrontation with danger and been denied it. He needed another target for his store of adrenaline and tautened reflexes.

She, the partner, the protected, had been frightened, then relieved, and now needed to be held, reassured, cosseted. It was all very logical, very scientific, and probably followed established patterns of human...

Her mind shut down abruptly as he rubbed a rough, but gentle thumb across her bottom lip. His gaze roved her features with slow, sharply focused attention, then settled on her eyes. She stared into his, her mind too clogged with sensation for her brain to function.

She grasped his forearms, reaching for steadiness, for solidity. He held her still while he lowered his mouth to cover hers, drawing her deeper into the world of feeling she'd scrupulously avoided for so long.

His lips moved artfully over hers, touching, retreating, then touching and retreating again until she closed the gap between them, wary, but needing to know what he offered.

Dane shifted sideways, bringing her down into the crook of his elbow, bracing it on the forest floor.

She opened her mouth to him and he invaded. His free hand swept her hair back as he kissed her until she felt her bones become liquid. Warmth spread through her. She parried with his tongue and felt his large hand wander over her.

She was aware of the paradox of his fiercely protective embrace, and his darkly dangerous kiss. In that moment, she was grateful that one did not preclude the other.

She kissed him back, looping her arms around his neck, marveling at the little tingle of life running under her skin wherever he touched—her face, her arms, her shoulders, her back.

She was surprised to know that she was capable of passionate response, surprised to discover a greedy little being within herself that would have liked this forest idyl to go on and on. With a little moan of satisfaction, she nuzzled her nose into his throat, prepared to let the world move around her while she clung to Dane.

He swept a hand down her back, then over her hip, pausing to shape its fullness in his hand. Feeling fluttered deep inside her, at the heart of her womanhood, feeling she hadn't experienced in years and hadn't wanted to.

She lay still for an instant, torn between the deliciousness of Dane's touch, and the threat it presented. It could awaken everything she'd so laboriously sedated, everything that made her want to scream with pain, everything that made her want to close her eyes and never open them again. She didn't feel strong enough to take the chance.

She put a hand to Dane's chest and straight-armed out of his embrace.

He dropped his hand instantly, watching her as she sat up stiffly and put a shaky hand over her eyes. He fought a surprising sense of loss. He'd come so close to meeting the real Paula Cornell, the woman behind the mask of cool indifference.

He'd sensed her wariness, but he'd felt eagerness, too. She wanted out of her self-imposed emotional exile.

As he sat up beside her, she dropped her hands to her knees, pushed the hair out of her face and heaved a ragged sigh. She turned to him with eyes that held genuine apology, but carefully concealed everything else.

"That wasn't fair of me," she said. "I'm sorry."

He pushed himself to his feet and offered her a hand up. "Maybe it wasn't fair of me to take without asking."

She put her hand in his and sprang up gracefully in front of him. "You didn't take," she said.

That surprised him. He'd expected her to be anxious to blame him. He was pleased and flattered that she didn't, but concerned also, because it meant he was still no closer to understanding her.

He pulled a pine needle out of her hair. "Then why did you stop me?" he asked.

She withdrew her hand from his grip and folded her arms, shuffling the toe of her old Rockport into the rich earth. It was almost dark in the forest now, and the air had grown considerably cooler.

She tilted her head up at him and smiled thinly. "Because distracting you with sexual awareness would be hazardous to my safety."

"But you keep telling me you aren't concerned with your safety."

"And you keep reminding me," she said, rubbing her arms, "that I should be, for my parents' sake."

"I wonder," he asked, looking into her eyes as he pulled off his jacket, "if you aren't more concerned about your emotional safety. You felt that kiss, Paula. We both did."

"If I did," she said, angling her chin, the distant lady once again, "a short-term affair just isn't in my plans for the future."

He dropped his jacket on her shoulders and saw her eyes react to the touch of it. Was it simply because it provided the warmth she needed, he wondered, or because she responded to his body heat?

"I'm not a man who does anything short-term," he said.

She shook her head, looking tired suddenly. "A relationship with me," she said, "short- or long-term, would be hazardous to *your* emotional safety. Since I'm already a physical danger to you, a smart man should take me at my word.''

He knew asking her to explain further would be futile at this point. She was a woman who posed many questions and offered few answers. Though not patient by nature, he'd cultivated the quality in the military. The five-month buildup in Saudi had helped him hone it to a fine art.

He hooked an arm around her neck and began leading her out of the woods toward the meadow.

''You would argue me to death, no doubt,'' he said.

She laughed softly. ''I would consider it my duty.''

CHAPTER FIVE

THEIR DINNER of canned stew and fruit cocktail was interrupted by a call on the radio.

"Nelson tells me bad weather's coming your way." Kurt's voice was strong despite the crackling reception.

"Right," Dane replied.

"I was just thinking about the..."

"Roof." Dane finished for him. "Fixed it."

There was a moment's silence.

"Everything okay?" Kurt asked.

"Fine."

"Paula?"

"She's fine."

"Tell her her parents are well. I'm into her mother for fifty-seven bucks. Card shark."

Paula leaned over Dane's shoulder and asked into the transmitter, "She suckered you into playing poker?"

"Yes." Dane heard Kurt's voice lighten at the sound of Paula's.

"Want a tip?" she asked.

"Please. Before I lose my house and my boat."

Paula laughed. "If she has a good hand, her eyelashes flutter. If she starts humming, you're in real trouble."

Kurt laughed. "I owe you, Paula."

"My pleasure."

"Food holding out?" Kurt asked Dane.

"Yeah."

"Anything you need?"

Dane raised a questioning eyebrow at Paula. She grinned and whispered, "My body talc? My blow dryer?"

With a wry glance at her he replied into the transmitter, "Nothing. Thanks."

"Any comments? Questions?"

"No."

Another pause. "Thanks for the detail," Kurt said. The impatience in his tone came through the noisy line.

Dane drew a breath. "You want conversation," he said, "see me when this is over."

"Out," Kurt said briefly, and the line went dead.

Dane slapped the Off key and hooked the receiver onto the radio. "Right," he muttered under his breath.

They went back to the table, and Paula reached to the stove for the coffeepot, topping up their cups.

"Want me to heat that up for you?" she asked Dane, indicating the few bites of stew left on his plate.

He pushed it aside. "No, thanks. I'm fine."

"So you told Kurt. Repeatedly." She carried their plates to the counter, took two apples from a bowl and tossed one to the table. Dane stretched out a long arm to catch the wide pitch.

"Don't try out for the Dodgers," he teased.

Paula acknowledged his jibe with a forebearing frown and sat down again. "You don't cut him a lot of slack, do you?"

He raised an eyebrow at her. "You sold out your own mother's poker secrets. Don't get moralistic with me."

She took a dainty bite of the glossy red apple and shrugged a shoulder as she chewed, then swallowed.

"I'd have liked to have a brother. I hate to see you at odds with yours."

"I'd have liked to have had a mother," he returned. He extracted a knife from his jeans pocket and cut the apple in half. "You make do with what you're given."

Paula watched him peel the fruit with exaggerated care and concentration, and wondered about the calm quality of his voice. In the brief time they'd spent together, she'd learned he was at his coolest when he was the most concerned.

She took another bite of apple, considering what his remark had meant. Had he and Kurt been abused? Abandoned? Considering how she'd been loved and spoiled, that possibility evoked sadness in her. But he didn't seem receptive to sympathy at the moment.

"Aha," she said. "You were produced in a robotics laboratory. I knew it."

His eyes met hers for a quick instant, their smoky quality reminding her that no robot had kissed her, but a flesh and blood man. She lost all ability to be clever and keep her distance.

"Did your mother leave you?" she asked gently.

"No, she stayed," Dane replied, slicing a crescent-shaped piece of apple off the pared half. "Drunk, disoriented, useless...but she stayed. They'd take her away and dry her out every once in a while, but she stayed. We'd have probably been better off if she hadn't. She died when I was in high school."

She leaned toward him on her folded arms, feeling as though he had drifted away from her. Suddenly panic threatened to overtake her. After two and a half days of having him so close she was sure he read her mind; his sudden remoteness made her feel more alone than she'd felt since Natalie had died.

"I'm sorry," she whispered.

The look in her eyes brought him back. The fear and loneliness he saw there reflected emotions he'd experienced countless times, as a child and as an adult. No one should ever feel like that.

"So, don't take your mother for granted," he said, suddenly abandoning his efforts with the apple. "She loves you. Lots of sons and daughters in this world don't have that and never will. The love of a mate can give you something to live for—" except in his case "—but it can never replace what you miss when you don't have parental love."

"I know that," she said, leaning back in her chair, her eyes challenging his. "I imagine that's true of growing up with a sibling. You can have friends, but it isn't quite the same. I think Kurt did what he did because he loved you."

He smiled reluctantly. "Easy to live someone else's life, isn't it?"

She nodded, smiling. "Infinitely easier. The peel's the best part, you know?"

He looked back at her blankly.

"Of the apple," she said, pointing to the tidy pile of peel on his paper napkin. "The peel's good for you."

He hadn't even realized what he'd been doing with the apple. Kissing Paula earlier had played havoc with his sanity. Kurt's voice still had the ability to upset his equilibrium, and thoughts of his mother were always disturbing.

He gathered up the napkin and its contents in one fist and pushed away from the table to toss it into the container that held degradable trash. "Habit, I guess. I always peeled apples for..."

He hesitated as he put the bucket under the pump.

Paula knew why. "For your wife?" she asked.

He made a scornful sound and pumped the bucket full. "Joyce would have liked her grapes peeled."

"Ah. An aristocrat?"

"No. Just the opposite, really. Her father was a bum and her mother was a victim." He put the bucket on the stove. The water on the bottom sizzled on the cast iron. "Kurt was called out to their place on a domestic dispute when he was a cop. Her mother went to the hospital and her father to jail. Joyce was eighteen."

"She made a play for Kurt?" Paula guessed.

Dane smiled, drying his hands on a towel. "She didn't have to. Kurt isn't just *my* older brother, he feels duty-bound to protect the whole world. Security isn't just his job, it's *him*."

There was a reluctant fondness in his voice. Paula resisted the impulse to point it out to him.

"I was at Quantico, Virginia, at the time." Dane went on, leaning back against the counter. "He wrote me that he'd put her into a small apartment and helped her get a job. He said she told him she wanted out of that environment. When I went home at Christmas, they were head over heels—or so it appeared to me. I guess, in truth, he was the only one in love."

"Was that when you and she . . . ?" She wasn't sure how to put it.

"No." He stopped in the act of shaking his head, then admitted ruefully, "Well, maybe. She was the prettiest thing I'd ever seen." He sighed and folded his arms, his expression reflective. It seemed free of anger but filled with a poignant sadness. "She was very fair and very small and had a look of injured innocence that just . . . got to me. But I ignored how I felt, and did my best to ignore her.

"Then they came to see me a few months later. The suburban force Kurt was with had to let a few officers go because of budget cuts and he'd been one of the most recently hired." He shifted his weight. "I, on the other hand, had just made captain and was feeling like big stuff. I took them to the officers' club and Joyce asked me to dance while Kurt talked to some friends of mine."

He raised an eyebrow in self-deprecation. "She was very subtle, then. Just a look of longing in her eyes, the slightest pressure of her body against mine that no one else would have noticed, a wistful little sigh that made me willing to slay dragons to make her smile. Stupid, I know, but I admit to not having a brain in gear during that period."

He sighed and went on. "When they were getting ready to drive back home, I'd bought them fruit and candy for the trip and Kurt took them out to the car. She kissed me in a way that assured me those subtle gestures had not been my imagination. And she whispered that she wondered if she'd fallen in love with the wrong brother."

Paula listened quietly, thinking it ironic that big, strong men could deal with natural disasters, sophisticated weapons and powerful enemies, and be felled by a little blonde with big eyes.

"They broke up not long after that. Kurt didn't say much about it, just that it was over. She came to see me and slapped a weekend on me that made me believe I was God's gift to her and mankind." He frowned and studied the floor a moment. "I also have to admit there was a smug satisfaction in having the attention of a beautiful woman who'd thrown my brother over for me. I had a little trouble with self-esteem in those days, and thinking she preferred me to my handsome, efficient, noble brother was pretty heady stuff." He glanced at Paula. "Not a pretty side of me, but there you are."

She shook her head. "No one's judging."

He came back to the table and leaned on the back of the chair, his thin smile rueful. "I hadn't made the correlation then between Kurt having lost his job and my just having earned a promotion and a raise. Anyway, I called Kurt to tell him we were getting married.

"He told me I was a fool. That she wanted out of her environment all right, but she didn't want to work her way out, she wanted a meal ticket. He told me that she'd let three jobs go in the last three months and that she'd come to see me on money he'd lent her for rent. He told me to stop and think, that she'd used him as long as he was useful and then left him, and she'd do the same to me."

"And you didn't want to hear that," Paula said quietly.

"Right. I was feeling invincible. I told him he could come out and be my best man, or he could go to hell."

"And?"

"And he came. That's Kurt. Even in my arrogance, I appreciated what that must have cost him, so I did my best to try to be for him the kind of brother he'd been to me." His mood darkened. "Then Joyce left and he let it happen."

"You had no idea there was a problem?"

He pushed away from the chair and went to the window. "We weren't married very long before I realized that with Joyce there was always a problem. We didn't have enough money, we didn't have enough things, I was away too much, she hated moving. A lot of the problems most service wives are up against but she was a little opportunist." He turned back to Paula. "She'd told me before I wasn't moving up fast enough and if I didn't do something about it she was gone. I guess I should have believed her."

She frowned and rested her chin in her hand. "Has it occurred to you that you're better off without her?"

"That's what Sandy keeps saying."

"Sandy?"

"Kurt's wife."

Paula frowned. "I thought you and Kurt haven't been speaking."

He smiled as he crossed back to the cupboard. "We haven't, but Sandy calls me a couple of times a week. She's a good friend. She keeps telling me that when I stop feeling sorry for myself, I'll consider myself lucky." He reached into an overhead cabinet that held a collection of board games and pulled out a pack of cards. He wandered slowly back to the table. "I guess I can forgive Joyce. She had a grim beginning and I guess she wants insurance that she'll never slip back into that again. She found a guy with bucks while I was gone and took off. Kurt's another matter."

"He forgave *you*," she reminded gently, "and stood up for you at your wedding."

He studied her for a moment with an expression she couldn't read. She half expected him to tell her it was none of her business. Instead, he sat down and asked, "I take it you play poker, too?"

He was telling her that was enough questioning. She had to agree. His life was more complicated than his direct personality made it appear.

"Very well," she said. "Especially when the stakes are high."

"Trying to get my hardware store savings, huh?" he asked.

She laughed as she cleared salt and pepper shakers from the table and wiped it off. "Actually life in the wilderness has distilled the important things for me. I was thinking in terms of gambling for the privilege of sleeping late in the morning and letting you fix breakfast, even though it's my turn."

He resumed his seat and shuffled the cards with a flick of one hand that humped them, cut them, then sprayed them in a showy arc. Her eyes widened as she sat opposite him.

"I take it your experience isn't limited to whist, either?"

He dealt the cards.

She wasn't surprised to discover he played better poker than she did. She was logical, with a good memory of the placement of every card, but he was gutsy and reckless and in the end, he won the luxury of sleeping in.

"I demand a rematch," Paula said, shuffling the cards as Dane got up to make another pot of coffee. "And one of those shortbread cookies I saw you hide in the corner cabinet."

He smiled over his shoulder. "I was saving those for when the rain hits. Something comforting about cookies when it's raining."

As though on cue, the wind rose, and a spray of rain splashed against the kitchen window. They heard it begin lightly on the roof, then grow in intensity as the wind picked up. Dane grinned at her. "Did you arrange that?"

He left the coffee perking and pulled down the box of cookies. "I'd better check the leak. Deal, but don't cheat." He headed off toward the bedroom.

In the cool, dark bedroom, Dane heard no drips. He passed a hand over the bedspread and the pillowcase and felt nothing—but his fingers came away smelling of gardenias. Great, he thought. As though his nerves weren't stretched tight enough already.

He waited a few moments while the wind blew fiercely and rain fell heavily. Still no drips. If he didn't get the hardware store, he might make it as a roofer.

He went back to the kitchen.

The sight that greeted him softened him from the tight center of his being, to all the little nerve endings screaming for some undefined relief.

Paula had fallen asleep, her head pillowed on her arms, her hands still holding a full complement of cards, as though she'd been ready to deal and simply gave out.

He let himself just stare at her a moment. He should carry her to bed, but there was such pleasure in watching her sleep. There was a little pleat between her eyebrows, as though she wasn't quite relaxed, even in sleep, and her free hand was closed in a tight fist.

For the hundredth time since he'd met her, he wondered what could haunt a woman who was so beautiful, so successful, and who appeared to have everything. Since it wasn't likely he'd be finding out in the near future, he put the question to the back of his mind, gently pried the cards from her fingers and lifted her out of the chair.

With a little moan of disapproval, she struggled until he had her up in his arms, then her head fell comfortably to his shoulder.

"Bill?" she asked groggily.

When he didn't answer, but kept walking, unwilling to engage her in conversation and wake her up, she asked, "Dad?"

Still silent, he placed her in the middle of her cool bed. He went to straighten and pull the covers over her, but she caught his face in her hands and said sleepily, "Dane. 'Night." Her hands slid from his face and she curled onto her side.

Longing rolled over him. He tugged the blankets out from under her, removed her shoes and pulled the covers up to her chin. She snuggled into them, making a soft little sound of contentment.

He secured the shutters over her bed, then went out into the living room, giving serious thought to nailing the door closed. It wasn't necessary. He knew himself better than that. At least, he used to.

He washed the dishes, pumped more water, stepped out onto the porch to look and listen. He didn't hear a sound, except those that belonged.

He looked up in the direction of the ridge, though all he could see was inky blackness. Someone on Kurt's team was probably watching him through a night scope as he paced the porch. Satisfied that all was well, at least *out*side the cabin, he went back in, bolted the door, secured the shutters, then stretched out on the sofa and watched the fire die.

HE KNEW THE MOMENT she was awake. He'd fallen into a doze sometime after midnight, but the little sound of distress she always made when she woke up brought him to instant alertness. He wondered about that sound. Most people hated to get up, except a small percentage the rest of the world would never understand, who awoke ready and eager to face the challenges of the day.

But he knew few people, young recruits included, whose first waking sounds expressed pain.

He heard the subtle rustling of blankets being shifted, then another little groan. He raised on an elbow.

"Paula?" he called.

There was a moment's silence, then she replied raspily, "Yes?"

"Something wrong?"

"No." There was more rustling, then another, louder groan.

He got to his feet, grabbed the Coleman light and went to the bedroom door. He found her sitting in the middle of her bed. She had removed her jeans, and was rubbing at one well-shaped calf. He noted that her limbs were very white in the eerie glow of the lantern.

"Cramp?" he asked.

She shook her head. "It's just that everything hurts. I'm used to wearing heels, and my calves and tendons are stretched and protesting." She stopped rubbing her leg to stretch both elbows back. "And my back and shoulders will probably never be the same from the hike up here. I just wasn't meant for life in the out-of-doors."

Dane studied her a moment, then reached for his pack in the corner of the bedroom. This was not going to be easy. In fact, he was almost sure on one level, at least, it was a bad idea. But if she didn't get a good night's sleep soon, she would be useless if Hailey did get through to them.

He pulled out a tube of sports cream and knelt beside her bed. "Put your legs over the side," he said. "This'll help."

Paula complied, exhausted, her mind too caught up in her aches and pains to register concern. Even the warm, sure touch of his hands brought none.

Dane worked clinically, methodically, from her ankle to the back of her right knee, his fingertips probing and loosening, strong palms rubbing soothing circles, then long, relieving strokes.

He squeezed more cream into his palm. "Other leg," he said.

She dutifully raised it, feeling her taut calf muscle relax as he worked over it.

"You've got to get more exercise, Paula," he said, glancing up at her with a grin. "If you're not careful, you're going to be the only sixty-year-old woman without a line in her face, but in a wheelchair."

It was the grin that did it. Until he'd looked up at her she'd innocently enjoyed his perfectly fraternal ministrations. Then he'd given her that same look he'd given her in the forest just before he'd kissed her. And suddenly, as his hand moved up from her anklebone to her knee, she imagined it sliding onto her thigh and higher.

She experienced that little flutter again, that suggestion of awakening that shouldn't come as a surprise to a woman approaching forty, but did. No. She didn't want that! Instinctively she flinched.

Dane held his hands away, looking up at her in apology. "Sorry. Hurt you?"

He read her eyes, even in the dark shadows and the firefly light of the lantern.

"Just hit a knot," she said with a quick, unconvincing smile. "That's much better."

"Good." He stood.

Paula breathed a small sigh of relief.

Then he sat on the edge of the bed behind her and her lungs seemed to collapse with the mattress that took his weight. He wrapped the blanket around her waist and propelled another dot of cream into his palm.

"Pull your shirt up," he directed, "and I'll do your back."

She would have protested, but she had no air with which to speak. She tugged the back of her shirt up and waited for the touch of his hand.

He had to finish this, then she could go back to sleep, and he could go back to lying in supreme frustration on the sofa in the living room, wondering how the hell he'd gotten himself into this fix in the first place.

What was it about her that did this to him, anyway? She didn't like him, and she was everything in a woman he didn't want—or at least, hadn't wanted. She had secrets and so did he. And, anyway, she was a job.

The skin of her back was like silk. He felt the delicate line of her shoulders as he rubbed across them, then the scalloped ridge of her spinal column as he swept down to the blankets he'd bunched around her waist. He'd been wise to do that, he acknowledged with a private smile in the darkness. The need to lower the sweep of his hand was almost overwhelming.

Instead, he ran both hands gently, therapeutically, up and down either side of her spine, feeling her small expulsion of breath which he hoped meant relaxation.

Paula wanted to run screaming into the night. Had she been less conditioned by a mother determined to raise a lady, and by the imposition of her own code of behavior that would protect her from involvement and dependence, she might have done just that.

Instead, she bore Dane's gentle touch stoically. The artful push of his fingertips, the circles made by his palms, the almost-but-not-quite painful working of his thumbs along her spine were chipping away at her defenses. She didn't precisely understand what was happening, but she seemed on the brink of laughter or tears. Emotion ran riot inside her.

Then he stopped and stood, and all the feeling inside her crashed like a computer whose plug had been pulled. Nothing. Back to what she'd been before the telephone call came about Hailey. For the first time in two years, she realized just how really empty she was.

"Want a glass of water?" he asked, drying his hands on the handkerchief in his pocket and capping the tube.

"Please," she said quietly, lying back and pulling the covers up to her chin. She wasn't thirsty, but the dark shadows of her dreams hovered so near, and a glass of water would bring him back into the room.

She sat up and accepted the glass.

"Try to sleep," he said gently, and picking up the lantern, turned to leave the room.

"Dane!" she said, more loudly, more desperately than she'd intended.

He turned in the doorway, an eyebrow raised in question.

What could she say? Please don't leave me? Don't touch me, but don't leave me? I need you, but not too close? I can't get involved, but I can't bear one more moment of being alone?

She took another sip of water and pulled herself together. His job was to keep her physically safe, and he was doing that very well. There was attraction between them, but she was almost ten years older than he was and haunted. After what she'd been through, he didn't need the grief.

She sighed and smiled. "Thank you," she said. "Good night."

"Good night." Dane gave her a protracted, considering look, then left the room with the light.

Darkness and loneliness edged around her and she squeezed her eyes shut. A picture of Natalie tried to form in her mind, but she refused to let it. She tried to picture her mother and her father, cuddled close together and safe somewhere, but the image wouldn't form. Thoughts of her father brought with them thoughts of Hailey. And thinking about her parents always reminded Paula how disappointed her mother was in her.

A sound at the bedroom door brought her upright with a start.

"The sofa's beginning to feel like the Saudi ground," Dane said, his voice light in the darkness. There was the sound of something hitting the other mattress—his pillow, probably. "I need my bed," he said, his shoes landing on the floor. "And it would help me a lot if you'd keep your hands to yourself. I know what a temptation this is going to be for you, but try to be strong."

Paula felt every muscle in her body relax, and a smile form on her lips. The shadows dissolved as she strained her eyes in the dark to watch Dane's form slip into the second bed, chest bare, but jeans in place.

"There are probably only six steps between your bed and mine," she teased, the tension gone despite the nature of the playful conversation. He was being the consummate gentleman.

"Think of it as a moat filled with alligators."

"You know me," she said, snuggling into her pillow. "I could compromise you and have an alligator purse and shoes by morning."

"Mmm," he said with a sigh. "Then we'd have conservationists after us as well as Hailey. Go to sleep, Paula."

There was a moment of comfortable silence. Then she asked, "Dane?" She saw him turn his head toward her.

"Yeah?"

"Thank you."

"Sure. Go to sleep."

He hadn't had to ask and she hadn't had to explain. Curious, she thought. They communicated better in silence than they sometimes did with words. She was afraid to consider what that meant.

CHAPTER SIX

PAULA AWOKE to the ringing sound of silence in the cabin. Outside, the birds sang, but inside was a stillness she didn't like.

Dane's bed was tidily made, as though it had never been slept in. Had she imagined him there last night, she wondered. No. She felt rested this morning because she'd finally slept well, knowing he was only a few feet away.

There was no smell of breakfast cooking, no quiet sounds of puttering to let her know he was performing one of the dozens of chores with which he was always occupied.

Alarm brought her bolt upright. "Dane?" she called. No answer.

She pulled on old black jeans and a ragged gray sweatshirt that barely cleared her waist, and went barefoot into the living room.

"Dane?" she called again, going on into the kitchen when there was still no response. That, too, was empty.

Her heart began to pound. Had he left her? Had he grown tired of being awakened in the middle of the night, of being alternately snapped at and swooned over?

Probably, but even so, she doubted he would have walked away of his own accord. Had something happened to him while she slept? Could they have been found?

That possibility didn't make sense, either. Had Hailey found them, he certainly wouldn't have taken Dane and not her. She stopped in the middle of the living-room floor and considered. Unless he'd wanted to drive her crazy as a stalker often did in old movies. Maybe he knew it would take very little to tip her over the edge.

Her hands shaking, she yanked the cabin door open and ran onto the porch.

She opened her mouth to shout for Dane when a pair of long, jeans-clad legs swung down from the roof. Paula shrank back against the door with a shrill scream as Dane landed lightly on the porch.

"Whoa," he said softly, taking a step toward her. "What's the matter?"

His flesh-and-blood presence brought her such relief, it seemed only fair he be made to pay in some small way for the anxiety he'd caused her. She put a hand to her heart and straightened, drawing a shallow breath.

"I thought," she said sharply, "there was a rule about going out alone."

He looked over the face she knew was flushed with color, then settled on her eyes, his own narrowing as he tried to read her mind. She stiffened, trying to close it to him. Something about that seemed to amuse him.

"It doesn't apply to me," he said with a grin. "Were you worried?"

She struggled to relax. "If it applies only to me," she said reasonably, "I'm still alone, whether you leave me that way, or whether I go off on my own."

He sobered just a little. "You *were* worried."

"What's wrong with the roof now?" she asked, folding her arms, trying to pretend she hadn't come to the brink of hysteria simply because she hadn't known where he was for five minutes.

"I was checking my patch job," he replied mildly. "I thought we'd have breakfast at the stream this morning." He indicated the fishing gear leaning against the porch railing. "You fish?"

"No," she replied, frowning. "Fish for breakfast?"

He handed her a pole, shouldered a pack, then picked up the other pole and the tackle box. "Sure. Best camp breakfast in the world. Come on. You'll like it."

Still annoyed, she stood her ground as he ran lightly down the steps. He stopped at the bottom to look up at her inquiringly.

"Fingering worms at 7:00 a.m.," she said, "is not my idea of a good time."

He smiled winningly. "I'll bait your hook for you."

It wasn't fair, she thought, for a man to have a smile that could dissolve a woman's anger. She continued to resist. "And my idea of breakfast is French toast, strawberry butter and champagne in a restaurant overlooking the beach."

He shrugged a shoulder. "Soon as this is over, I'll see that you get just that."

Something about that had such appeal that she could almost forget they had nothing in common but this surreal situation.

She went slowly down the steps toward him, shouldering her pole. "Don't think I won't hold you to that," she said. "Lead on. I just want to warn you that I'm not gutting anything."

Dane shook his head as they headed off side by side into the trees. "I don't know," he said. "You won't bait the hook, you won't clean the catch. I presume you are willing to hold the pole?"

She slanted him a glance. "This was your idea, remember? If it were up to me, we'd be having toast in the kitchen. Yes, I will hold the pole as long as I don't have to put anything on it, remove anything from it or deal with anything that's been on it."

"Pansy."

"Bully."

PAULA SAT across the small fire, her arms wrapped around her knees, interested in Dane's preparations.

"I'd have reacted differently," she said with a grudging grin, "if you'd told me we were having onions and potatoes and biscuits with it."

He looked up from cutting small chunks of potato into the skillet in which onions already sizzled fragrantly. "You should have trusted me," he said. "Would you pass me the fish, please?"

She picked up the plate beside her and considered the two elegant fish it held, neatly halved and boned and rolled in cornmeal. She looked at him innocently, retaining control of the plate.

"Are you eating?" she asked.

His gaze sharpened suspiciously. "I'm cooking. You'd better believe I'm eating."

"But, you see," she said, indicating the fish, "if you recall, I caught these. You caught the one we threw back."

"Who baited your hook?" he asked.

She shook her head. "But, you baited your own hook and nothing happened. Apparently that isn't where the skill lies."

"Then," he asked, "who cleaned the fish?"

"Had I not caught them," she insisted, "there'd have been nothing to clean. The way I see it, all you get are potatoes."

"Who climbed the tree to untangle your last cast?" he asked. "Who chased your shoe upstream? Who got the hook out of your hair, Madam Outdoor Disaster?"

She frowned at him and passed the plate over. "No need to hurl insults. All right, you can have the smaller one, but then I should get a larger portion of the potatoes."

"Who peeled and sl..." he began.

She rolled her eyes. "Don't start that. Potatoes don't have to be hunted or caught. It's not the same thing."

He laughed, and put the fish into the pan, causing a sizzle that interrupted conversation.

They ate in companionable silence, sitting cross-legged on the bank of the stream. Paula ate everything on her plate and two biscuits, and finally fell onto her back, stuffed.

"Jeez," she groaned. "I'm going to have to change the name of my business to Plump Lady Cosmetics."

Dane glanced at her trim waist and flat stomach and laughed. "That'll be that Ferrante fox's problem, won't it?" he asked. "And your world cruise won't help the calorie cause very much."

"They have spas now, and aerobics classes," she said, dropping an arm across her eyes and sighing content-edly. "It's not like in the old days when the only exercise you could get on a ship was to run around the deck."

"If the classes are before ten," he said, putting their plates into a plastic bag, then back into the pack, "you'll never make it. You're the worst sack rat I've ever seen."

She hesitated only a moment, and he instantly regretted the teasing remark. That little sound she made when she awoke spoke of something that hurt. A frown line came and went between her eyes.

"I'll go to the gym," she said finally. "I'll swim laps."

"You swim?" he asked, his voice exaggeratedly indignant.

She lowered her arm and looked at him in surprise. "Yes. Why?"

"Because *I* waded into the stream after your shoe, that's why."

"Oh, that." She resumed her comfortable position. "I knew you were trying to impress me, so I let you do it. When we get back, I'll be sure your brother knows you went above and beyond the call of duty."

"Thank you. Come on. We're going to take a walk."

"But I'm still stiff from..."

"That's the point." He smothered the fire and put everything back in the pack.

With a groan, she pushed herself to her feet. "You're going to regret this. I'll be all achy and I'll wake you up again in the middle of the night and you'll have to play doctor again..."

The old playful euphemism hung in the air between them, not at all what she'd meant when she'd spoken the words. She turned to Dane and found him grinning as he adjusted the pack.

"I didn't mean..." she began to explain.

"Oh, don't spoil it," he said, taking her hand.

PAULA HEARD THE CAT before she saw him. It was nearly noon, and Dane was in the bedroom talking to Kurt on the radio while she prepared lunch.

The loud, plaintive cry brought her head up from the soup she stirred. She peered through the window, wondering if she'd imagined the sound. It hadn't been strong enough for a wild cat, and there wasn't a residence for miles that could be home to a house cat.

Then she heard it again: a clear, desperate meow coming from somewhere behind the cabin.

It occurred to her that Dane wouldn't like her opening the door when he wasn't around, but she did it anyway. She couldn't imagine what harm could come of her standing in the doorway and looking out.

She pulled on it cautiously, scanning the short space of meadow to the trees beyond. She saw it. A smudge of orange, hunkered down in the grass halfway between the cabin and the woods, let out another cry. A house cat!

Paula went down the steps, as excited as though a host of friends had come to visit.

"Here, kitty," she called, patting the knees of her jeans in a coaxing gesture. "Come on, kitty. Come on!"

The cat called back, took several steps toward her, then backed away again, hunkering lower in the grass.

Forgetting entirely what Dane might think, she started slowly across the meadow toward the cat, calling quietly. "Come on, kitty. Here, kitty. I won't hurt you."

As she drew closer, the cat poised for flight. She saw that he was young, probably a feline equivalent of a teenager, not kittenish, but not full-grown, either. He was pitifully thin and scruffy. He watched her with wide green eyes, every hair tensed to run.

It had probably been lost by campers, she guessed, or abandoned on a country road by some ignorant owner who thought it could fend for itself. She couldn't imagine how far it had walked to find its way up the mountain. It looked hunted and desperate.

Paula felt a kinship with the poor little beast and moved closer, suddenly finding it very important that she cuddle it and feed it and let it know somebody cared.

It ran to the edge of the woods, stopping once to look at her before disappearing into the trees. Without a second thought, Paula ran after it.

DANE SMELLED SOMETHING burning when he walked out of the bedroom. He went into the kitchen, a teasing remark on the tip of his tongue about women who couldn't even heat something out of a can without burning it.

When he found the kitchen empty, and the soup bubbling and sticking to the bottom of the pan, his heart gave an uncomfortable lurch. When he saw the back door open, it leapt into his throat.

He removed the pan to the counter and ran to the door.

"Paula!" he shouted as his gaze swept over the quiet, empty meadow. Oh, God. She was gone.

He fought an unfamiliar sense of panic. *Come on,* he chided himself. *Straighten up. Think!*

He went down the steps and around the house. It couldn't have been Hailey. He'd just talked to Nelson on the ridge, and he hadn't seen anything. And Campbell was at the head of the trail and he'd just reported to Nelson that all was well.

Paula must have gone out on her own. And left a pan burning and the back door open?"

Okay, that didn't compute.

When he saw nothing in any direction, he began to lose his grip on the panic. And it had nothing to do with what Kurt would think, or how Paul Emmett would react. It was all very personal. He'd lost her!

The wit he was beginning to know, the charm under the icy shield, the smile he'd seen all too seldom. Her touch. Her kiss. God!

"Paula!" he shouted, and heard his desperation as though it belonged to someone else. He'd always had a warrior's mind-set. The worse the situation, the calmer he became. When the options thinned, only a cool head could pick the right one. He'd always used his fear to tighten his focus, to look the situation full in the facts and deal with it.

He seemed to have lost the skill. Now fear was a debilitating thing that scrambled his brain and rolled over his emotions like an M-1 tank. He'd read Hailey's bio. He knew what the man was capable of.

"Dane!" Paula's voice shouted. "Dane!"

Dane spun toward the woods, drawing the pistol he'd carried at his back for days. Relief at the strong sound of Paula's voice was swamped by deepening fear. She'd sounded frightened, and that frightened him because she'd been remarkably brave so far.

He ran into the disorienting shelter of trees, stopping a moment to get his bearings.

"Paula, where are you?"

"Here!"

He ran forward toward the sound, deeper into the woods, trying to look left and right as he ran. He could be racing headlong into a trap. He could—

He stopped abruptly, staring. In a little clearing, Paula hung sideways from the lowest branch of a sturdy cedar. One arm and one leg dangled, the others held on for dear life.

"If you let me fall on my head," Paula said, her tone strangled, "I'll tell my father not to pay you!"

Dane uttered a pithy oath, quickly holstered his pistol and positioned himself under her. Anger erupted in him, full-blown, but he put it aside.

"Let go," he said.

"I'll...smash you," she stammered worriedly.

"No," he said evenly. "I'll catch you, then *I'm* going to smash *you*. Let go!"

"All right." She sounded doubtful, but she complied.

He braced himself, took the first, strong impact of her falling weight then held her tightly and let it carry them to the ground.

He felt the breath leave him as he hit and heard her little scream. She rolled off him instantly, kneeling over him and demanding, "Dane! Dane? Are you okay?" She grasped his shoulders and shook him. "Dane! Say something!"

He dragged in air, and with the gradual return of oxygen through his system came the anger he'd put aside to get her down. It filled every corner of his being, sharpened his awareness and renewed his strength. He pushed her away from him and sat up.

Paula felt the anger in him, though he didn't touch her. It darkened his eyes and made a pulse tick in his jaw. She sat back on her heels, judging it wise to put that little bit of distance between them.

"What," he asked with ominous quiet, "were you doing in a tree?"

She smiled sheepishly. "Bird-watching?"

He didn't move a muscle or blink. She expelled a sigh and accepted that it wasn't funny, and that she was responsible for frightening him. A corner of her mind not occupied with gearing up to cope with what would undoubtedly be a scene, wondered why she hadn't given one thought to the possible consequences of running out of the cabin to chase the cat. The cat had seemed so important at that moment. She had an elusive notion why, but she didn't particularly want to explore it. And now wasn't the time.

"I came after the cat," she said without excuse or apology.

He looked at her as though she'd spoken Swahili. His eyes still deadly, he asked, "Cat?"

She pointed to the branch above the one from which she'd hung.

Dane looked up at an orange-and-white-striped cat watching the action. It appeared half-starved and ready to bolt. His mind immediately turned to the possibilities. A collar. A transmitter. But it wore nothing but thin, mangy fur and a hunted look. He tried not to consider what might have happened had it been otherwise.

He turned to her, temper barely held in check. "You scared me out of ten years of my life," he said quietly, "because of a cat?"

That was about it. It couldn't be put otherwise. "Yes," she said. "I'm sorry."

"Well, I'm relieved to hear that," he said, his voice still darkly quiet. He sprang to his feet, the sudden movement making her start. He yanked her to hers, his hand holding her arm in a biting grip. "Had Hailey been out here and slit your throat from ear to ear, it would have relieved me *and* your parents to know you were sorry!'' The sound of the last few words rose in intensity until he was shouting at her. ''What in hell is wrong with you? Don't you get it? The man wants to kill you!''

''Well, he isn't here . . .'' she began reasonably.

He grabbed her other arm and shook her. ''The point is, he could have been!''

''All right!'' she shouted back, on her tiptoes to try to relieve the pressure of his hold. ''I *get* the point. Do you have to grind my bones to powder?''

Dane dropped his hands, as angry with himself as he was with her for having let her out of his sight. But he still had a lot to say. He pointed toward the meadow. ''We'll finish this in the cabin.''

She held back when he tried to usher her out of the woods before him. ''First, I have to get the cat,'' she said. She knew how Dane would react, but she didn't care. The cat had become critical to her sanity.

''The cat,'' he said, on the brink of mayhem, ''climbed the tree to get away from you.''

''Because he thinks I want to hurt him. He's probably been dumped, or lost and is scared out of his mind.'' She pointed up at the cat, who sat up, as though indignant that she should do so. ''Look at him. He's starved! I'll bet he's been alone for a week!''

''If he's that hungry,'' Dane said, ''he'll follow us back to the cabin.''

She folded her arms and gave him her best CEO stare. ''If he doesn't, I'll only come back for him.''

He put his hands on his hips and took several steps toward her, wearing the look that once made every man in his command eager to follow orders to the letter.

"You do that to me once more," he said, "and you will never wear that superior look again."

It was all she could do not to take a step back. "I'm not leaving without the cat."

"You're going back to the cabin."

"If you'll get the cat."

"If you go back to the cabin, the cat will follow."

"If he doesn't, I'll..."

"Go!"

Paula went, tears streaming down her face. She wasn't sure what was responsible for them. Temper, certainly, because she wasn't used to being bested in a battle of wills. She also was unused to being intimidated. She didn't need the details of his you'll-never-wear-that-superior-look-again crack to worry about it.

Then there was self-recrimination for stupidly leaving the cabin in the first place; humiliation at having been found hanging upside down in a tree; hurt feelings because he was angry even though he had every right to be angry.

This is what comes of letting your feelings come to life again, she thought, storming into the kitchen, throwing the door back until it slammed against the wall and bounced back on her. She'd let herself enjoy things, little things, and it made her forget how ugly life could be. So, now she was angry, humiliated, hurt and filled with self-recriminations. Emotional sleep had been so much more comfortable. Well, now she knew better.

Several paces behind her, Dane watched her stiff back as she marched to the cabin. There'd probably been a better way to handle that, he thought, but he was still too angry to try to rectify the situation.

Men were so much easier to handle. Even young or stupid ones could be made to understand and respect the magnitude of a problem. Women, on the other hand, saw only what they wanted to see, and presumed what they couldn't deal with would have the grace to step out of their way.

Joyce had been that way. "What do you mean, we can't afford it? Charge it. Quit the army so you can make some decent pay. Go to work for Kurt, he's always asking you."

He didn't want to think about that now. His brains were scrambled enough as it was.

The kitchen door flew back on her as she punched it open, but she elbowed it aside and went to the counter. As he followed her in, he saw her find the pan with soup gummed and stuck to the bottom.

Stiffly she checked the fire, put the pan aside and took down another can of soup. She bounced a quick, empty glance off of him.

"Lunch in ten minutes," she said.

He reached back to push the door closed. A blur of orange raced across his feet and hid under the table.

"Lunch for three," he said.

She looked up. He pointed under the table. The cat was as far back as he could go, but looking interested.

Paula began to smile, then glanced at him and changed her mind. She turned her attention to the soup.

Shaking his head, Dane went into the living room.

Paula made a face at his back as she opened a can of tuna. She wasn't crazy about adding being wrong to the long list of today's frailties.

She plunked a mug of soup down in front of him on the trunk that served as a coffee table and dropped a spoon into it.

He looked up from a two-week-old copy of *Sports Illustrated*. She turned on her heel and walked into the kitchen. She didn't return.

Later, he carried in his empty mug and found her sitting under the table, petting the cat, who ate with complete concentration. His gut seemed to have expanded several inches.

Dane reached into the cupboard for the shortbreads. "Want a cookie?" he asked, "or are you still pouting?"

He wasn't surprised when that brought her out from under the table. She bounced up beside him, bristling.

"Okay," she said, "let's talk about that."

He put the cookies aside, thinking he might very well regret this. He should have just let her be. But he wasn't the type to endure long silences and endless intrigues. He said what he thought, and respected that in someone else. It was just that she was unlike any adversary he'd ever had.

He folded his arms and leaned a hip on the counter. "Go ahead."

She looked momentarily startled, then squared her shoulders. "All right. I do not appreciate being yelled at, I do not like being ordered around, and when I do something wrong, I'm usually smart enough to recognize it so I don't have to have it pointed out."

"That was not just wrong," he said reasonably, "that was stupid. It could have cost your life and mine."

"I apologized."

"That would not have comforted your mourners."

She growled impatiently. "You don't give an inch, do you?" she asked. "Is that a power thing, or what?"

"I don't give an inch," he said clearly, "because I give a *damn*. A number of very unpleasant things could have happened to you. Had you waited two minutes until I was finished on the radio, I would have helped you with the cat.''

"Oh, sure," she said, making a broad gesture toward the animal still eating, though watching them suspiciously. "Like you helped me in the woods." She folded her arms and mimicked his voice. " 'You scared ten years off my life for a cat?' What? If it doesn't wear army boots, or know what size nut fits what size bolt it isn't worth saving?''

He drew a breath and asked quietly, "Who told you he'd follow us back to the cabin? At the time, I was considering your life over his. Maybe that was a mistake.''

She tried another tack, still mad enough to chew nails. She heard her own analogy and wondered distractedly if hardware was going to be the death of her.

"If you order me around," she warned, "or shout at me one more time, I'm out of here and *you* can explain to your brother and my father what happened.''

"You continue to behave like a forty-year-old brat," he said, leaning down until they were nose to nose and she got the full impact of his deadly serious green eyes, "and I will continue to shout at you. I will order you around until you are out of this mess and you will do as I say because I am bigger and you'd do well to remember that.''

Though he saw trepidation in her eyes, she didn't flinch. But, then, he hadn't expected her to.

"That makes you a bully," she said.

"That makes me the man who's going to bring you back alive. If you want to throw away the rest of your life, you can do it when you're no longer my responsibility. Now—'' he picked up the bag of cookies and offered it to her "—if we're finished discussing who's in charge, do you want a shortbread?"

Paula was frustrated beyond endurance, but she'd built a company by knowing when to push and when to retreat. And maybe, she admitted to herself, at the moment there was just a little comfort in knowing her life was dependent on someone even more cussed than she was.

She reached into the bag for a cookie. "I'm a thirty-nine-year-old brat," she corrected him, and with a glance that told him not to grow too complacent with his success, walked away.

CHAPTER SEVEN

IN THE AFTERNOON, rain beat against the roof and the windows. While Paula worked on her cross-stitch in a corner of the sofa and Dane read in the rocking chair, his long legs stretched out until his feet were propped on the trunk, the cat sat in the main room's wide window-sill and looked out at the torrent. The silence was companionable, the morning's tension forgotten.

Then the cat jumped down and walked around the room, peering into things, sniffing corners, swiping at a bouquet of dried grasses Paula had brought in from one of their walks.

"Peaches," Paula called, patting her lap invitingly. "Come on, Peaches."

Dane looked up from his book with a raised eyebrow. "Peaches?" he asked. "What kind of a name is that for a guy?"

The cat had turned to look at her.

"Look," she said softly. "He likes it. He turned when I called him."

"You'll notice he isn't coming to you," Dane said.

Paula rolled her eyes. "Well, what are you calling him? Sarge? Schwarzkopf?"

"I'm not calling him anything," he replied, snapping his fingers. "Maybe he just needs to be incognito for a while."

To Paula's consternation, the cat leapt onto Dane's knees and looked into his face. Dane rubbed between the orange ears and the cat closed his eyes. His purr was audible from the sofa.

"You ungrateful little beast!" Paula laughed.

Dane gave Paula a mockingly superior look. "Male bonding. Females just don't get it."

"He certainly didn't mind taking tuna from these female hands."

"Oh, women are good for some things."

He was teasing, but Paula didn't bite. She felt too comfortable. And there was something satisfying about watching the cat ease its half-tuna body on one of Dane's thighs and rest his head on his knee.

Paula gave up on her needlework when the sun set. She lit the lamps and added a log to the fire. Then she stopped in front of Dane's chair, arms folded, and surveyed man and cat, who appeared quietly content with each other.

"I imagine you've forgotten it's your turn to fix dinner," she said.

He smiled winningly. "You wouldn't want me to move the cat, would you? I mean, he's obviously a mass of insecurities. He's probably been dumped or lost or..." He repeated her earlier litany of the cat's woes.

She put a hand up to stop him and looked down at the limp animal. It opened its eyes to slits, considered her, apparently dismissed her as a threat and went back to sleep.

"A real bundle of nerves," she said dryly. "This means you fix breakfast tomorrow."

"I fix breakfast every day," he said with a superior turn to his smile. "However, you do deserve a bonus for this. I'll make popcorn tonight."

She felt genuine enthusiasm. "Really?"

He noted the little spark in her eyes and was touched by it. "Really. There's a popper in the utility closet. I'll scrub it out after dinner. We'll pretend we've got an old movie to watch."

"Yeah." She sighed and looked longingly at the corner near the fireplace that would be a logical place for a television set. "You and Kurt really should consider a satellite dish."

He laughed. The cat stretched but never opened his eyes. "No electricity for the television. And anyway, the point of coming here is to get away from all the little tyrannies of nineties life."

"I suppose," she agreed, turning thoughtfully toward the kitchen. "But I can't imagine significant life going on anywhere without the knowledge of what's happening on *L.A. Law.*"

PAULA RETURNED to the living room while Dane cleaned the kitchen. She found the cat stretched out to twice his length before the fire. He lay on his back, forelegs reaching over his head, and back legs stretched *en pointe* like a feline Pavlova.

She smiled at his obvious hedonism. It didn't take long, she thought with sudden, sharp perception, to identify what was missing in one's life. If one was fortunate enough to find it, it took even less time to become unable to live without it.

It's happening to me, she thought with a little frisson of panic. I have time to think, I have time to feel, I have time to study a man up-close and personal. I have time to want.

Paula sat Indian-style beside the cat and told herself firmly that life would never be the way it had been. She used to be one of three. She used to be friend and lover, adored mother and playmate. She used to be needed. Life had been cozy and full and she'd been confident in how necessary she was to their happy little circle—and then she had failed.

Blackness threatened to smother her as if a heavy blanket had dropped over her, tightened around her. For an instant she couldn't breathe, and she rose to her knees with a panicky little gasp.

The cat, startled by her sudden movement, rolled onto his feet in a flash, prepared to run. She caught him around the middle and tried to pull him to her.

He swiped a paw at her face and scrambled over her shoulder and into the kitchen to hide under the table.

Dane was beside her in an instant, setting the popcorn popper on the hearth as he knelt to inspect the long red parallel scratches on her cheek. Her eyes were hurt by the cat's reaction, but the pain in them was compounded by something far deeper, something he guessed she'd sought solace for in the sleeping cat's company.

As was becoming habit, he felt her pain. He couldn't identify it and didn't understand it, but that didn't prevent his feeling it. For somebody who'd refused to feel his own, it was a curious situation.

"I've got something for that," he said gently, and went into the bedroom for the tube of antiseptic cream in his pack. He sat knee to knee with her before the fire and applied the antibiotic cream with the tip of his little finger.

She had pulled herself together and was eyeing him wryly as she sat still under his ministrations. It amazed him how well she did that, considering the depth of the pain he'd seen in her eyes from time to time. She'd be in complete misery one moment, then draw a breath and be, for all appearances, perfectly functional the next.

He'd always considered himself a man in control of his emotions and his reactions, but he'd be willing to admit there were times she had him beat.

"You're not going to tell me I was stupid to grab him like that?" she asked, wincing as he hit a sore spot. "That he could have put my eye out, further diminishing my usefulness to you and proving once again that I was stupid to chase after him in the first place?"

He grinned and capped the tube. "You told me when you did something wrong you were smart enough to recognize it and didn't need it pointed out." He pinched her chin and tossed the tube to the trunk. "Seems you were right."

She made a self-deprecating little sound. "You're not going to rub it in?"

He pretended surprise at that suggestion. "You told me not to order you around or shout at you. You scared me."

"Really?" She looked pleased with herself. "I've tried hard to cultivate a scary look." She sat cross-legged beside him as he knelt and reached the long-handled popper into the fire. "When I first went into business, I was just a young housewife with an idea and a famous father. Everybody treated me like an airhead. At the time, my father was playing Peter Costain on *Broken Dreams*. That was before he moved to the *Phantom Lake* soap. Ever see it?"

He glanced down at her in time to see her smile fondly. He shook his head. "Sorry."

She made a wry face. "You were probably still in high school at the time."

"How long ago?"

"Fifteen years."

He calculated, then laughed. "I was. Okay, so I was scratching my head over geometry and you were on your way to becoming a tycoon. How did Peter Costain figure in this?"

"According to the storyline, he was chairman of the board and his upstart, illegitimate son was trying to unseat him. I watched faithfully, and one night I saw him give the boy a look." She looked up at Dane very seriously for a moment. "That's Dad's forte, you know. The look. He can say more with his eyes, with a quirk of his cheek or the slant of a glance than most other actors can say with words. And the look told Damian Costain that it didn't matter what tricks he played, how many friends he had, how many diplomas, or connections, or ruthless plans. Peter was a better man, and they both knew it. So, I just worked with it a little. I didn't want my people or my competitors to think I thought I was better than they were, but I wanted them to see that I had confidence in my plans, in my product and in myself."

"Apparently you did."

She thought a moment, then smiled with satisfaction. "Yes, I did."

"Was your success too much for your husband?" He hadn't intended to ask the question, it just came to mind and with the mellow mood between them it had tripped off his tongue without his giving it a second thought.

She sighed. It wasn't precisely a withdrawal, but a careful sidestep. "No, he was a very successful attorney, and it had nothing to do with business. At least, not in the beginning."

The popcorn began to pop. Reluctantly he turned his attention to it. He knew there was something more to the story, something that was the key to understanding her.

She got to her feet. "Want me to make coffee?"

"How about cocoa? I've got butter melting on the stove for the popcorn. Want to bring it out, and the big bowl on the table?"

Dane poured the popcorn into the bowl; Paula drizzled the melted butter over it with an "Mmm!" of anticipation, then went back to the kitchen for the cups of cocoa.

They sat side by side on the sofa, feet resting on the trunk, the pan balanced on his left leg and her right.

"What movie will we pretend to watch?" she asked.

"What's your preference? Adventure or romance?"

"Romance."

"Groan."

"A romance with sex and violence?"

"Keep talking."

She shook her head pityingly. "Men are so predictable."

"*Texas Chainsaw Massacre?*" he suggested. "*Barbarella?*"

She rolled her eyes. "How about a Bogey movie? A romantic adventure with exotic locales and bizarre characters?"

"Most of those are so old."

Paula elbowed Dane viciously. His handful of popcorn sprayed into the air, showering down on them like bulbous confetti.

"I meant," he said, "that they're old even for someone ten years older than I am."

"Nine," she said.

"You know, it's interesting that you keep correcting me on that." He took another handful of popcorn and tossed a piece at the cat, who had come cautiously around the edge of the room to give them another chance. He pounced on it, investigating it with deliberate care. Dane turned to look at Paula. "I think isolation is making you feel younger. At first, you kept insisting you were pushing forty. Now, if I even mention forty, you insist that you're thirty-nine." He grinned. "My boyish charm is getting to you, isn't it? Go ahead. You can tell me. I promise not to use it against you."

"Generous of you," she said, blushing. "Holding on to your youth is a very feminine quality. I just never believed in trying to . . . to hold time back before."

"And now you do?" he pressed.

She looked into his eyes with an expression that remained cautious despite her smile. "I guess I'm just not in a hurry to run through the rest of my life. About the movie."

Fine. He could be a patient man. "Okay." He stared at the window as though it were a TV screen. "A Bogey and Bacall thing."

"No, a Bogey and Bergman thing," she insisted. "His movies with Lauren Bacall had a lot of sizzle, but those he did with Ingrid Bergman had class."

He looked resigned. "You're walking me into *Casablanca,* aren't you?"

"You don't like it?"

"I've seen it a dozen times. Let's just throw popcorn at the screen and pretend we're sitting in the balcony where it's dark and very private.

She bit back a grin and tried to look severe. "Mr. Chandler, are you suggesting we . . ."

There was not just mere suggestion in the kiss he gave her, it was forceful, decisive, sure—and absolutely delicious. It occurred to her to protest. Then it occurred to her that that would be stupid.

CHAPTER EIGHT

IT BEGAN as all the other mornings, except that when she awoke, she was almost happy to do so. She'd had to call a halt to the balcony fantasy over Dane's protests because it developed too quickly into something neither could control—or seemed to want to. She just wasn't ready for intimacy.

But he did have a way about him that thrilled and confounded her, and made her wonder as no man ever had, even Bill, what she truly wanted out of life.

She could smell the coffee, hear the fire crackling in the main room and rain still beating on the roof. She had slept well and she stretched with an unfamiliar sense of well-being. If she disregarded the fact that their lives were in danger, she was enjoying herself for the first time in two years.

She dressed and went into the kitchen to find Dane at work on French toast. At his feet, the cat lapped up something from a saucer. She watched from the doorway as the cat licked the saucer clean, then leapt up onto the counter to inspect Dane's work.

"Ah, ah, Peaches," he said, hooking the cat in one arm and leaning down to drop him to the floor. "I know you think you've reached the promised land, but we have to observe a few rules here. No cats on the counter. You need more milk?"

He squatted down to pour powdered milk into the saucer from a small pottery pitcher. As the cat lapped it up greedily, Dane stroked him with an absent smile.

"Peaches?" Paula asked, walking into the room.

Man and cat turned to look at her.

She reached down to stroke the cat, and he went back to the serious business of breakfast with a loud purr.

"I thought you wanted to name him Alexander, or General, or something," she teased Dane as he straightened and turned the French toast onto a plate. "I thought Peaches was an affront to his maleness."

"So did I until I got up this morning and found him sleeping beside you with his head on your pillow." He carried her plate to the table with an easy smile. "I don't think he's cut out to be a military man. I think he's a marshmallow like you."

Paula didn't take offense. She knew it wasn't an insult, but simply a statement of fact. "Marshmallows are important, too, you know. You can't make S'mores without them. Or do you even know what those are?"

He looked mildly indignant at the suggestion that he didn't. "Of course I know what they are."

She took the jar of jam from the cooler. "No offense intended," she said. "It's just that unless you've been a Boy or a Girl Scout, or gone camping with children, you wouldn't know what they are. I mean, I'm sure you didn't learn about S'mores in the Marines."

He concentrated on removing the last two pieces of French toast onto a second plate. "How do you know I wasn't a Boy Scout?"

"I don't," she said, pulling her chair out. "It's just that from what you said about your mother, I didn't think she'd have thought of...you know..." She didn't know how this had begun, and she wished she knew how to stop it. There was something here he didn't want her to touch, and she was anxious to respect his wish.

He looked at her and she had to finish.

She sighed. "I didn't think she'd have thought to put you in that kind of a program."

He put his plate on the table and sat opposite her. "She didn't," he conceded. "We spent six months in foster care when I was eleven and Kurt was fifteen. Our foster family were ardent campers. That's where I learned about them."

His tone was defensive, and she said gently, "You think that diminishes you, don't you?"

His first reaction was anger because she was right. It was hard to live the formative years of your life with a drunk and grow up with any sense of self-esteem. It was ugly to watch someone self-destruct, and it was almost impossible for a young boy not to conclude that he was somehow responsible.

Then he saw the compassion in Paula's eyes and realized why he was so defensive about it at this moment: because he'd seen her family, so caring and concerned for one another and knew instantly she'd had everything he and Kurt had only dreamed about—love, cuddling, comfort, support.

It occurred to him with a sharp sense of sadness that he could never give her anything she hadn't already had—emotional or material. And a relationship couldn't exist without both parties having something to give to it. He'd learned that from Joyce. He'd thought he could give to her indefinitely, but learned that in the end, everything he had would never be enough. One had to get something back to replenish the ability to give.

"Yes," he admitted quietly. "I guess I do."

She sat straighter, her tone stiffening. "Well, *that's* stupid, Chandler. I presume, by the rules you've set down, I have the right to point out your stupidity to you?" Before he could offer an opinion on whether she did or didn't, she went on, leaning toward him and waving her fork in a manner that made him lean back for safety's sake.

"You survived, damn it! You came out of a depressing, demeaning hole and made yourself a worthwhile human being. More than worthwhile. Important. I had everything on a plate, and I still messed up, so don't get that look of diminished worth when you talk about your childhood, or we'll just see who can make who wish he'd been left to Hailey's mercy." Her diatribe delivered, she spooned jam onto her toast and passed the jar across the table with a smile. "Want some?"

The call came while she was cleaning up the kitchen. Dane headed for the bedroom, then hesitated in the kitchen doorway. "If anything calls or cries, or even if there's a clap of thunder and a deep voice overhead says your name, *don't* go out without me."

She grinned over her shoulder. "Got it."

"Good." He disappeared.

She noticed that the conversation lasted longer than usual, but she wasn't concerned. He'd spoken to Kurt just last night and reported that her parents were fine and there'd still been no sign of Hailey.

The kitchen sparkling and rain still falling in torrents, Paula went into the living room, set the lantern up on the trunk and settled in the corner of the sofa to work on her cross-stitch. Peaches sat in Dane's rocker, his body curled into a ball, a paw across his nose.

She heard Dane's footsteps come out of the bedroom.

"What's Kurt into my mother for now?" she asked. "She must have the house and the boat and be working on his IRA.'

She felt the tension in him before she even saw him. He walked around the back of the sofa and sat beside her. She continued to make x's in the pink flowers of the bride's veil, afraid to look up. Her heart was beginning to pound. Something was wrong.

Dane took the fabric and the needle from her fingers and put them on the trunk. Then he turned off the bright light. There was nothing but the storm light from the window, and the dancing light from the fire.

She drew a breath and turned to Dane. His eyes were sympathetic, reluctant. A gulp rose in her throat. "Is it my parents?" she demanded in a strangled voice. "Tell me."

He shook his head quickly. "No, your parents are fine."

"You're sure?"

"Positive."

"Then . . . what?"

He put an arm on the back of the sofa, and a hand on the ones knotted in her lap. "Your house burned down during the night."

She stared at him dumbly for a moment.

"To the ground," he added, as though he'd had to make himself say it. "We don't know if it's Hailey or not, yet. The police will be in touch with Kurt."

To the ground, she repeated to herself, and tried to feel something. In her mind's eye she went from one beautifully decorated room to another, from antiques to paintings to Limoges china with a distinct lack of emotion. When it had been Bill and Natalie and her, the house had been so important, a home they were creating together, a space that rang with their laughter and their dreams.

But in the past two years it had been just a collection of rooms—filled with lots of things that no longer mattered to her.

Mentally she climbed the widely curving staircase to the dove-gray carpeted second floor. She saw the wall of books on the landing, and the gray-and-rose-upholstered chair under the reading floor lamp with its jewel-colored Tiffany shade.

She went through Bill's study where she now stored Pretty Lady stock, through her bedroom that had once been their bedroom, and was now where she did all the work she brought home. She kept the drapes closed, and the room lacked air and light and anything else that would have made it a comfortable place to sleep. That was no loss.

In her mind, she stopped at Natalie's door. Terror flooded her as memory reached for the knob. She was vaguely aware of her name spoken in a man's voice, but she couldn't turn her attention to it. Every energy was directed at the doorknob to Natalie's room—at preventing her mind from opening it. That was the one place that could still hurt her. That was the one place in the house that remained the same.

"No," she whispered, drawing back as the knob turned and the door opened. "No."

She'd walked into the room every day for the past two years. She'd pull Benny, the one-eared teddy bear, wearing Natalie's outgrown pink newborn's T-shirt out of the rocker and sit on the edge of the canopied bed with him and rock him back and forth. In the yellow-and-white room with its mural of a farm, complete with animals and birds and smiling sun that she and her mother had taken days to paint the month before Natalie was born, she would tell Natalie how much she loved her, how much she missed her and that she was sorry.

She would tell her she was taking good care of Benny, because Natalie loved Benny so much.

She would imagine Natalie sitting beside her, curly dark head leaning against her, wrapping her arms around her, patting Benny. Telling her she was forgiven.

The door in her mind's eye opened but there was no yellow-and-white room. There was no ceiling, no bright mural on the wall, no bed, no rocking chair—only ashes. She could see daylight all around, and everything else was black. The wind swept through, and a pile of ashes where the little rocking chair had been blew away. There was no Benny. Nothing to bring Natalie back.

She heard herself scream. The shrill sound and the vicious clarity of the picture in her mind brought her back to the awareness of utter desolation.

Dane's arms were around her. She was sobbing, she realized in surprise.

"I know it's a blow," he was saying gently, "but in the end, they're just things. Your parents are safe. You're safe. Your insurance will..."

She yanked away from him, shaking her head. "You don't understand! Benny was in there!"

Dane was beginning to understand there was more here than the loss of a home. While that was certainly major, in light of a number of other things that could have happened, it was an acceptable casualty. And he knew she understood that. This horror in her eyes was something else.

"Benny," he repeated, proceeding carefully. "A pet?"

She shook her head, her eyes seeing something invisible to him. She huddled into the far corner of the sofa, brought up her knees and wept into them, deep, gulping sobs.

Dane leaned forward to touch her arm, wrapped around her knees. "Paula, who is Benny?" he asked.

She raised tearful, miserable eyes to him. For the first time since he'd known her, she looked her age. He saw lines at her eyes and mouth he'd sworn hadn't been visible an hour ago. "A teddy bear," she said, her mouth contorting. "Natalie's teddy bear."

An awful premonition crept along his spine. "Who is Natalie?" he asked.

"She was my daughter," she replied, and dissolved into hysterical weeping.

SHE WAS MY DAUGHTER. Past tense. Dane went to the kitchen for the bottle of brandy, feeling as though he'd been slapped by a mailed hand. He poured a generous measure into a juice glass and carried it back to the sofa.

She was huddled in the corner, still sobbing. Every nerve in his body pulsed, feeling her pain. *He should have poured a glass for himself,* he thought. He had a feeling he was going to need it. He was going to get all of this out of her if it destroyed both of them.

He sat near her, took one of the hands wrapped around her knees and put the glass in it.

She shook her head, trying to give it back to him. "I hate brandy."

He pushed it back. "This is medicinal brandy. Drink it."

She took three sips, then drew in a breath and tried to pull that magic act that always restored her equilibrium when she came close to losing it. Only this time she'd crossed the line, and she couldn't quite go back.

Her lip quivered and a large tear fell, though her sobs had quieted. "I'm okay now," she said. "It's just a house." She reached over to put the glass on the trunk. "I'm sorry. I'm okay."

"Tell me about Natalie," he said gently.

She shook her head adamantly, closing her eyes. "I can't."

"How long ago did . . . did you lose her?"

Her brows knitted tightly and her breath came out in a high gasp. "Two years."

"Tell me."

"I can't!" She tried to swing her legs over the side of the sofa to escape him, but he put a foot out to the trunk, blocking her in.

"Then tell me about the bear."

She let her head fall sideways against the back of the sofa, anguish in every line of her body. "It's burned now. It's gone. Everything's gone."

"You're here." He put a gentle hand to her face. "I'm here."

She pulled his hand away and looked into his eyes. All the pain he'd ever seen in her brown gaze was distilled in that moment into profound agony. "It was my fault," she said flatly.

"Tell me," he insisted.

She warned him with that look of misery. "I'll come apart."

"I'll hold you together," he promised.

She expelled a ragged breath, then drew another, as though she were in the middle of Lamaze classes—as though she'd tried to bury the memories so deep, speaking them aloud required a rebirth with all its attendant pain.

"Start with Benny," he suggested softly, tucking her hair behind her ear.

Her eyes lost their focus, and a reminiscent smile formed on her lips. He'd lost her, he knew. She was on her way back to where everything hurt so much, and he felt a jarring sense of helplessness. She was somewhere he couldn't follow and he felt cruel suddenly for having encouraged her to go there. He'd promised to hold her together, but she had to do this part alone.

"Bill bought Benny when Natalie was born," she said, her voice quiet, but a little high. "It was twice as big as she was—soft and fuzzy with big button eyes and a bow tie. It played 'Teddy Bears' Picnic.' We were so proud of Natalie. It took us seven years to have her. My tubes are scarred from a ruptured appendix when I was a teenager. Then, finally..." She smiled brightly. "Like a miracle I...I conceived Natalie and she was born perfect." Her smile softened and she shook her head. "She loved Benny. He went everywhere with her...even—" her brow furrowed and her eyes widened "—even that day...I found Benny first."

She raised a hand in her lap to something she saw in her mind, something she tried to reach and couldn't. He captured it gently in his own and pulled it back, holding it between them.

"What happened, Paula?" he prompted in a whisper.

He didn't think she'd heard him; she just went on relating what memory played out.

"She'd had the chicken pox," she said with an absent little frown. "Bill was out of town on business and

I'd been up with her five nights in a row. I'd hardly slept. Then, the afternoon of the fifth day, she was suddenly much better. She was sleeping soundly, so I lay down on the sofa to take a nap."

She shifted fretfully and closed her eyes.

Dane was ready to back out. Though he didn't know precisely what had happened, his heart was already bleeding for her. But he couldn't reach her. She was with Natalie.

"It was August in Topanga Canyon," she went on evenly, like a narrator somehow remote from the action. "It was dusty and hot and the air conditioner just wasn't keeping up. I opened the front door to let some air in through the screen." She heaved a great sigh, still focused on the past.

"My neighbor called to tell me she'd be bringing over a casserole in a little while so I wouldn't have to cook." Paula smiled fondly. "She was a good friend. We watched each other's kids and had Sunday barbecues." Her expression changed, and the hand he held gripped his with the strength of anguish. "I unlocked the screen door so that she could let herself in if I dozed off. We ran in and out of each other's houses all the time."

Her voice dropped in pitch and tightened. "I fell asleep. Sally let herself in and put the casserole in the refrigerator." She began to gulp for air and he pulled her closer, trying to calm her, rubbing soothing circles on her back. But he knew nothing could ease what she was reliving.

He knew she wasn't even aware of him. She just went on because now there was no way back. She'd let the past become real again, and she had to see it through.

"When Sally left," she said, "the screen door didn't latch. Natalie woke up, and climbed out of her crib." She shook her head, tears falling freely. "She hadn't been out to play in five days, so she went straight to the door and opened it."

A sound that was part sob, part scream rose from her throat. "A car hit her right in front of the house. The rosebushes on the walk were taller than she was and . . . and the woman didn't even see her. Benny was thrown back onto the walk, but Natalie . . ." The sound again and a gasp for air. "Natalie lay in the middle of the road as though she were asleep. I heard the brakes, then people screaming. I ran outside and . . ." The gasps grew more rapid, but she was limp in his hold. "She looked just like she was asleep. There was no blood and no bruises. Her hand was curled up near her face. And I thought, 'That's not where I put her down. I put her down in the crib.' Sally was sobbing, and the woman who hit Natalie wouldn't stop screaming."

Paula turned to Dane, her unfocused eyes still filled with the horror. "I didn't lock the door. She'd never opened it before, but I should have known. At that age children learn something new every day. I should have known. I should have locked the door. Natalie died because I didn't . . ."

"Paula," Dane whispered, his own voice choked with emotion and the ravages of her grief. His ability to feel her pain had walked him through what she'd told him as though he'd been beside her at the time. He knew the black depth of her grief. He pulled her close and she fell limply against him, lifeless. "Paula," he said urgently, "it wasn't your fault. It was one of those ugly accidents no one can explain and for which no one is responsible. Don't blame yourself anymore. It wasn't your fault."

"Mothers are supposed to second-guess things like that," she said with sudden, startling calm. He held her away from him and saw that she'd crossed into some kind of waiting place. She'd brought out the pain and confronted it. That was behind her. But she couldn't walk away from it until she accepted it. The guilt somehow bound her to Natalie in a way that would always keep her close. "I should have known that would happen."

"How?" he demanded. "How could you have known? You're not the only one this has happened to. Good parents lose children because it's a fact of life that they're quick and impulsive and inexperienced."

"That's why they have mothers," she said. "To protect them."

"They have mothers to love them and do their best by them, but love can't save anyone from the unforeseen. The world turns anyway. Things happen. Babies die."

He didn't know if she'd heard him or not. Her eyes were on him, but not focused, as though he were simply a screen for whatever it was she saw. "The worst part," she said, her voice tightening with emotion again, "was that I saw her and felt her all the time. Bill and my mother told me I had to get over it, I had to pull myself together, and I tried."

Her gaze narrowed on him at last and he knew she'd come out of her private hell to share this with him. He circled his arms around her and listened, his eyes stinging, his throat so tight he could scarcely breathe.

"But I'd waited for Natalie so long," she said, a tear spilling over. "And I lay in bed for five months so that I could carry her safely. I felt her inside me and talked to her all the time. When she was born, we looked at each other, and we were already old friends. I saw it in her face. She knew me. She was my baby. My—baby!''

The last words erupted in a scream. ''I couldn't forget her!'' she shouted. ''I could see her in her crib, and in the playpen in my office. I could feel her at my breast and in my arms. I could hear her baby babble and she called me the way she always did when she woke up. I heard her every morning. Every morning! But when I get up...'' She began to sob, deep, tearing, painful sobs that abraded his throat just listening to them. ''She . . . she isn't there.''

''Oh, Paula.'' He pulled her into his arms and let her cry. All the hackneyed, bracing words of comfort came to mind. *She's dead and you have to accept that. Life goes on. She's in a better place.* It was all true, but there was precious little comfort in it.

He held her for what seemed like an eternity. She wept most of the time and finally sagged against him, her hand clutching a fistful of his sweater. ''I'm so tired,'' she said.

He leaned back until his shoulder hit the corner of the sofa, and propped her against him, pillowing her head on his chest. He covered them with the afghan and smoothed the hair out of her face.

Peaches leapt up to investigate and curled up on Dane's stomach, leaning back against Paula's chest. She moved the hand holding Dane's sweater to hook it around the cat, locking her thumb in Dane's belt loop.

''We had a cat,'' she said wearily. ''A white Persian named Puff. Bill took it with him when he left.''

Dane stroked her hair, just listening.

''It wasn't his fault,'' she went on, her voice growing slower, thicker. ''He . . . wanted to get on with our lives and I just couldn't. My life...was over. Like a road that isn't finished, or the end of a pier. There was just nowhere else to go."

He leaned down to plant a kiss in her hair. "Maybe you'll have to learn to swim," he said.

"Maybe..." She sighed and yawned. "I'm afraid of the water."

"There are boats, jet skis, sailboards, surfboards, inner tubes, water wings..."

But she had fallen asleep, and he wasn't completely sure in the state he'd been in since Joyce left that he could keep someone else afloat, anyway. Then she sighed contentedly in her sleep, the first easy breath she'd taken since he'd told her about her house, and he knew he'd better learn. He'd already made the choice.

PAULA AWOKE feeling as though she'd fallen from a high precipice, or scratched her way out of a deep hole. Everything hurt—her neck and shoulders particularly. Her throat and her eyes felt scraped.

She opened her eyes to find herself nose to whisker with Peaches, who was still sound asleep.

She knew an instant's disorientation, then became aware of the hands on her upper arm, the solid muscle that cushioned her body, the heartbeat under her cheek.

She lifted her head and looked into quiet green eyes. She saw the compassion there and remembered everything. She dropped her forehead to his chest with a sigh. "I'm sorry," she said.

She felt his fingers weave into her hair. "For what?" he asked. "For loving your child and grieving for her?"

"Bill thought I grieved too long. He loved her, too. I know he did. But when it was time to get on with life, he was able to, but I wasn't. I broke the love between us. Even my mother got impatient with me."

"Because you're living a half life," he said gently. "The other half is devoted to guilt, and that's destructive. She loves you. She wants you to be happy."

"If I had locked the door..."

"It wasn't your fault, Paula." He pushed her to a sitting position, pulling up beside her. Peaches leapt down with a whine of protest. Dane held her arms firmly and looked into her eyes. "You're using your guilt as a way to hold on to Natalie. It gives you a good excuse to dwell on her day after day. But she's gone, and you have to put something else into that part of your life."

She shook her head and said gravely, "I don't want anything else there."

His training and his own personality led him to scorn surrender of any kind. But retreat had its place and its purpose. He dropped his hands and looked out at the still stormy, darkening afternoon.

"Since we missed lunch, I'll fix dinner a little early. Want something light?"

The thought of food held little appeal, but she knew it would do her no good to insist she didn't want to eat. "Eggs and toast?" she suggested.

"You got it." He pushed her back down and covered her with the afghan. Peaches leapt up again immediately, kneading on her stomach and purring. "Rest a little longer. I'll call you when it's ready."

After dinner, Paula cleaned up and made a fresh pot of coffee while Dane brought in more wood. She felt limp from her emotional outburst and just a little embarrassed.

Paula Cornell never lost it. She was always controlled, always in charge. But the call on the radio had changed all that, and she'd been stripped emotionally naked in front of a man who interested her a great deal—even though he was almost ten years younger than she was.

Dane added wood to the fire, consumed with guilt for all the times he'd teased Paula about getting up late, about being bad-tempered and spoiled, about making herself old before her time.

He'd thought Joyce had made him suffer, but he couldn't imagine what it would be like to lose a child. That would be beyond bearing—and yet, Paula had had to bear it. He wanted to ease that pain for her, but knew he was powerless to do so. At least, for the moment.

She walked into the living room with two cups of coffee. She looked hollow-eyed and a little limp. She had tied her hair back, and her exposed jaw gave her a look of vulnerability.

Dane straightened to take the cup from her. "I want to apologize," he said, "for all the times I've teased you about…things. I had no idea what you were up against. If I ever call you a marshmallow again, you can hit me."

She smiled. "That isn't necessary, but thank you. May I use a blunt object?"

"By all means."

She sobered and sighed, her expression suddenly sad and just a little wistful. "I think your wife was crazy to leave you. There'll be a dozen women waiting to fill her shoes."

He raised his eyebrows, amused. "A dozen? You're sure?"

"At least."

"Well. Maybe I'll have to line up help."

"Now, now." She curled up in a corner of the sofa and grinned at him as she reached for her needlework. "Don't be modest. A man who makes his living in combat survival should be well equipped to handle twelve women."

He frowned and took the opposite corner of the sofa. "I don't know. My record isn't great so far. One's divorced me, and one's giving me fits."

It took her a moment to grasp what he meant. "Certainly you aren't referring to me."

His gaze was steady. "But I am."

She tried to maintain a teasing air. "You can take comfort in the fact that I'm only temporary."

Over the rim of his coffee cup, his eyes scolded her gently for pretending. "The situation is temporary," he corrected her. "What's developing between us isn't."

She made a production of untangling her embroidery floss. "We're coming to like each other," she said, "that's all it is. The... other is just... enforced proximity, close quarters, cabin fever."

"The other," he said, leaning down on the sofa until he could rest his head on the back, and his coffee cup on his flat stomach. "That's an interesting way to put it. Almost as interesting as all the excuses you have for it." He rolled his head sideways to look at her. "They don't apply, you know. You're deluding yourself. You're falling in love with me."

"No, I'm not," she replied mildly, rethreading the needle she'd just fumbled loose. "I don't want that anymore. I'm going to cruise the world, and—"

"Afraid?" he asked quietly.

She looked him in the eye and answered honestly. "Yes. I don't ever want to be responsible for another child's life. I know, I know..." She raised a hand to stop him when he would have protested once again that she wasn't to blame for what had happened. "Whether I was directly at fault or not, Natalie's little life was my responsibility, and—" she drew a breath and finished pointedly "—she's dead." The pain in her eyes was joined by a touch of wry, self-deprecation. "And I can't imagine many men wanting to trust a woman like me with their offspring."

Carefully she fitted the hoop over her work. "I'll be beyond childbearing years pretty soon anyway...."

"Paula...God!" Dane sat up, banged his cup on the trunk and turned to look into her startled expression. "That's absurd, and you know it. You're not punishing yourself, you're punishing life because it didn't play fair with you. You'll show it. You'll just throw away the rest of yours. That's spoiled and selfish."

She stiffened, her eyes hardening. "It's going to get me through."

"Maybe it'll get you *by*," he corrected her, "but it'll never get you *through*. You think you can retire from womanhood and live? You're crazy."

"It's my choice," she said coolly.

"The hell it is. It was a gift to you. Look at you." He waved a hand the length of her. "You're about as perfect a specimen as God ever made. He gave you beauty and grace and intelligence, and he gave you a family. Do you have any idea how many people would kill for a week of what you've had?"

She held tears back through strength of will. "But I don't have them now, do I?"

"No," he conceded. "You're alone, and you're the only one who knows how that happened. Natalie's loss was just an awful accident, and maybe Bill could have tried harder to understand what you were going through, and maybe he did all he could—I don't know. But I do know that you're equipped with everything it would take to start over again.

"I'm sure there's a man out there who wants a home and family, and would fall all over himself in a minute if you gave one interested look in his direction. In a year, you could be on your way to family number two, with life opening up for you all over again. If you weren't in a permanent pout."

"That isn't fair!" she shouted at him. "You have no idea what I've been through. You just apologized..."

"You're absolutely right," he said. "I don't know what you've been through because I've never had a fraction of the family life you've known. I was born to a drunk, and married to a bitch. But that empowers me to sympathize with your loss because in a way, I've lost that, too, by never knowing it." That muscle ticked in his jaw.

"But when you start whining about giving up life, and about your childbearing years being over, you lose me as a champion. I've held you in my arms, remember? I know how much of a woman is in there. You're just giving up. And that's a crime."

"And hating your brother isn't?" she demanded, getting to her feet and stalking to the fire. She reached the hearth and rounded on him, arms folded. "If you're so into going on heroically, why don't you forgive and forget?"

She had him there—sort of. He got up and went to the window. "When he didn't tell me Joyce had left," he said, staring out at the moonless black night, "he prevented me from guiding my own life. He made the decision I should have made."

"Seems to me Joyce made the decision. And if we apply your principle to you, I'm sure there's a woman out there who'd anxiously bear your children if you asked, and *you* could start all over. You've got a whole decade on me."

Dane rolled his eyes, picked up his half empty cup and went to the kitchen. Paula followed him to the doorway.

"Time's a shaky standard," he said, throwing out the cold coffee and pouring fresh. "Who knows how much time anybody has. Want some?"

She went back to the trunk for her cup and brought it to him. "Generally speaking," she said as he poured, "you haven't even hit your prime yet, and I've already peaked."

He looked up from the coffee and into her eyes at that, something subtly dangerous in his gaze. For an instant, time seemed to stop. Then he put the pot on the stove, and his cup on the counter, the steady look in his eyes unsettling her. She took and instinctive step back.

He reached a long arm out to take her cup from her. The strong aroma of rich coffee swirled around her, along with the pungent alder burning in the stove.

"You're sure?" he asked, taking a step after her. She retreated. He advanced steadily.

"About...what?" She glanced over her shoulder, saw wall and angled right, to back into the living room.

He followed. "About having peaked."

"Well . . . sure." Halfway into the room, she decided to hold her ground. "I was married for more than ten years. I had a child. I built a business. All the..." She swallowed when he stopped with a hairsbreadth between them. He put a hand to her face. "All the . . . the climbing is over," she said, her voice sounding fragile. "It's downhill from here."

His touch at her cheek caused a riot in her chest. She gave up ground and backed away again. He followed relentlessly.

"That would be possible," he said quietly, "if you followed the course you had planned. The cruise. A life of retirement."

"I intend to."

"Because you're afraid of the options."

"Because I don't want the options."

"Because you're afraid of them," he said again. "Because you don't want to start over. All you remember is the effort and the pain." He reached out again and she tried to move away, but came up against the back of the sofa. He snaked a hand around the back of her neck and pulled her into his arms. "You need someone to remind you what else life has to offer. And to show you you're still climbing. You haven't peaked by a long shot."

She didn't want to know that. She was desperate not to know that. She wanted to push out of his arms and lock herself in the bedroom. Yesterday, she thought with a sense of fatalism, she might have been able to do that.

But tonight, she'd told him about Natalie and her sturdy shield against the world had crumbled. She'd spent the past few hours trying to pretend it was still in place, but it wasn't.

She felt Dane's every touch with the intensity of involvement. She knew when he looked at her, even when her back was turned, and she felt the touch of his eyes as if it were the stroke of his hand. His voice spoke inside her, even when he was silent. She loved him.

The realization pinned her in place. Though common sense told her this was foolish and could never work, something else had taken control of her and common sense seemed suddenly of little consequence. She was alive to feeling now, and she'd experienced so much of the dark side of it today that the light his arms offered was stronger than her sense of self-preservation.

Dane read the uncertainty in her eyes and pressed his advantage. He lowered his head, lips parted and slipped a hand under her sweatshirt.

CHAPTER NINE

HE HADN'T INTENDED to make love to her. He'd wanted to kiss her senseless, to make her tremble, to remind her that she was still alive and had so much to live for.

The surrender in her eyes sabotaged him. She wasn't submitting to his kiss; she was submitting to him. She was putting aside the pain and the grief, and trusting him to bring her something else.

As he closed his mouth over hers, he knew he was setting himself up for potential failure, and he hadn't quite recovered from the last one. But in four short days she'd become everything to him, as important to his emotional safety as he was to her physical one.

Plans were already forming in his mind that he knew she would reject, but that didn't matter. He wouldn't let her quit, and he wouldn't let himself give up on what he'd wanted so long and finally found. He had more against him than his age, but he wouldn't think about that now.

At this moment, he wanted to love her. He wanted to show her what he could give her now that she'd shared her horror with him and shed her shell.

Paula was frantic with feeling. He was showing no quarter. His lips delved and probed and taunted until she abandoned every last vestige of reserve she'd tried to hold in place.

His warm hand against the flesh of her back made her muscles leap in response. He traced her waist, her spine, smoothed over her bra to her shoulders, then down again. With one hand, he pinched the clasp of her bra until it unhooked and fell loose. He splayed his hand across her back and pressed her against him. Her nipples beaded in response and her entire body awakened.

Two years of emotional sleep, and his artful, insistent efforts to resurrect her made her respond with eager desperation. She'd known she needed him, but she'd had no idea how much until she let him make contact with the trapped woman inside who'd silently awaited rescue. Everything in her reached out to him.

Dane lifted her in his arms and carried her to the fire. He laid her down near the hearth and stretched out beside her, reaching to yank the pillow from the rocker and place it under her head. Peaches watched from a perch on the back of the sofa.

Dane nudged her sweatshirt up, planting kisses in the silky hollow of her waist and stomach. He inched it up higher, and his lips followed the jut of her ribs. He heard her little gasp and felt her fingers tighten in his hair as he nuzzled the underside of her breast. He circled it with his lips, reverently kissed its pearled tip, then took it in his mouth.

Paula felt sensation blot out everything else. Under Dane's touch, she lost contact with the past, and even part of the present. She forgot that anything had ever hurt. She even forgot Hailey.

She felt the warmth of the fire on her flesh as he pulled her sweatshirt off, and as his eyes swept over her, she saw a glow in them that heated her to the marrow of her bones. Her blood warmed and thickened.

His hands went to the zipper of her jeans and life fluttered at the heart of her womanhood. This time, she was no longer afraid of where it would take her.

Dane tugged the zipper down, placing a kiss on the exposed V of black silk panties. Then he slipped his fingers between her flesh and the silk and tugged jeans and panties down. The flutter in Paula increased in strength as he swept them off and tossed them aside. He ran one hand over her knee and along her thigh and she felt herself begin to smolder.

Dane watched her in fascination as she rose gracefully to her knees and urged him onto his back. She pulled his sweater up and off, then lowered her mouth to his pectoral muscles.

Her dark red hair caught flame highlights from the fire and he felt as though he might ignite as the fragrant cloud of it fell over his face and throat. She kissed and nibbled down the center of him to the waistband of his jeans. She worked her way slowly back up again to his throat, his ear, his eyes. She stopped at his mouth, drawing all the leftover anger and bitterness out of him, infusing sweetness and promise with a womanly generosity he'd never encountered in his life. He drank them in.

As she worked her way down again and unbuttoned and unzipped his jeans, he caught fire. He raised his hips to help as she pulled the briefs and denims off him. He pulled her down until she lay along his body as if she were a length of silk against his heated flesh.

She made little sounds of pleasure, little movements that told him she felt as he did: flesh to flesh wasn't close enough.

Dane pulled her thigh up, then followed the line of it with his fingertips to the source of the now mad flutter inside her. She heard her own little gasp, felt everything inside her stop and wait for his touch.

It came with a gentle but possessive sureness that made her wrap her arms around his neck and hold on. She understood he was not simply going to make love to her, but that he was going to make her his.

A little part of her mind that continued to function outside the overwhelming sensations said, *Paula, this is crazy. He's almost ten years younger than you are. Your life-styles are miles apart. He's just beginning and you're about to...*

She lost coherence even in that little corner of her brain as she began to feel the tightening circle of pleasure. Everything inside her began to constrict, and the instant before climax stretched into a taunting eternity.

Then the tension burst, flinging her out of the past, out of captivity, out of time. As pleasure broke over her, she seemed to lose all relationship to anything earthbound.

She floated free like a leaf on the wind, no longer spring green, but caught forever in the air, destined never to fade or fall. She clung to Dane as her body pursed then opened, then pursed again, drowning in feeling both physical and spiritual.

As she finally began to drift to earth, Dane turned them, cushioning her in his arms then entering her with that same sureness that spoke of possession.

Her body accepted his as a part of itself, welcomed him, enclosed him. She felt as though twenty years had been pared from her life and it all lay ahead of her, fresh and new.

Caught in the fist of passion, on the brink of the kind of physical satisfaction he knew would be perfect even

before he experienced it, Dane was surprised to enter-
tain a thought that had nothing to do with his body.

Buried deep inside Paula, feeling her body tighten
and pulse around his, he felt the comfort and rightness
of homecoming. He felt her love and her generosity,
and her surrender that had nothing to do with submis-
sion. She wanted him, and not simply because he'd
given her pleasure. She wanted him because she loved
him.

As she clasped her legs around him and her hips made
slow, sinuous circles under him, his last thought as he
abandoned sanity was to wonder if *she* knew.

HER HEAD pillowed on his chest, Paula stared into the
fire. Dane combed his fingers through her hair from her
scalp to the tips made gold by the firelight. There was a
little tension in her, and he didn't like that. "What are
you thinking?" he asked softly.

She crossed her arms on his chest and propped her
chin on a wrist, smiling into his eyes. "I can't think. My
brain hasn't recovered yet. What are you thinking?"

He ran his fingers through her hair again and let it
slip from his grasp like copper rain. Then he shaped her
head in his hands and looked steadily into her gaze.
"That you feel tense, and I'm wondering if you're already regretting making love to me."

She moved her hands to plant a kiss on his chest, then
crossed them again and sighed, smiling. "On one level,
it was like being attached to life support, or like being
given new blood. I feel alive for the first time since my
daughter died."

He could identify with that. He'd never felt the enthusiasm he had for life at this moment. As a child, he'd
clung to it out of stubbornness, and as a soldier, he'd

gripped it as an example to his men, and because it was certainly better than the alternative. As a man trapped in a bad marriage, he'd held on to it because he'd had other responsibilities—but there'd been times then, when he'd realized his mistake in loving Joyce, when he hadn't really cared whether he awoke or not.

But life flowed through him now; he felt renewed and revitalized. He wanted every dream he'd ever owned and that included Paula. The problem was going to be convincing her.

"On another level..." she went on carefully, "the very depth of what you made me feel scares me."

That was promising, he thought. "Why?"

She sat up, reached for her sweater and pulled it on. She put her hands under her hair to pull it out of the sweater's neck and it tumbled around her shoulders alive with fiery color and movement. He could die of wanting her.

She handed him his clothes and he dressed while she pulled on her jeans.

"It's complicated," she admitted with a glance at him as she knelt to fasten them. "And it's going to annoy you."

He stood, bare-chested, and zipped his jeans. "If you mention age," he warned, "I'm leaving you to Hailey."

Her eyes widened, and he said quickly, regretting the idle threat, "Paula, come on. It was a joke."

She shook her head, getting to her feet. "I know that," she said, her eyes still big. He realized now that it was wonder in them and not fear. "I'd forgotten him," she said in amazement.

His sweater hanging from one hand, he reached the other out to catch the back of her neck and pull her toward him. He kissed her slowly, lingeringly. "See how good I am for you," he whispered as she sagged against him, her arguments dissolved for a moment.

"That's the point," she finally said, pushing her hands against his chest to wedge a space between them. "I wouldn't be very good for you."

He looked heavenward in supplication. "Paula, that's true in that *I* almost forgot Hailey. You could make me crazy. Do you have any idea how long I've waited to feel the kind of love you just gave me? And I don't just mean that it was the greatest sex I've ever had. I mean that I felt it in my heart."

She nodded, dropping her arms to wrap them around him. "I know." She hugged him hard, then stepped back from him. "Don't you see that it's already too important?"

He studied her, trying to determine precisely what that meant. He finally shook his head in confusion. "Too important for what?"

Without answering she walked into the kitchen, taking the full cups Dane had placed on the table before he'd backed her into the living room. She poured the cold coffee down the sink and poured fresh from the pot still warming on the stove.

She handed him a cup. "Too important," she said, "for two people who have nothing else in common."

"We have love in common," he insisted quietly. "Nothing else matters."

She pulled out a kitchen chair and sat. "Dane," she said patiently, "that isn't true and you know it. Maybe if we just wanted a fling, nothing else would matter. But I told you I just can't do that at this point in time."

He sat opposite her. "And I told you I don't do anything short-term. Paula, I want you to marry me."

She looked shocked at first, then her expression softened, as though considering that possibility touched and moved her. Then she became stern. "You don't know what you're talking about. Obviously love is essential to marriage," she said patiently, "but you have to be compatible on many other levels also. What you like to do in your free time, how you like to spend your money. Children."

He put the cup to his lips and asked calmly, "Children?"

"Yes. You're only thirty," she said reasonably. "Undoubtedly you'll want children. But even if I hadn't made a personal vow never to have another child, I probably couldn't if I wanted to. Natalie came only after years of trying and failing." Her brow furrowed and she shook her head. "That's very hard on a couple."

He nodded. "I imagine it is," he said evenly. "But children aren't a problem for me."

She put a hand over his, which was resting on the handle of his cup. "Maybe you think so now, but the day will come when you'll want a son to take over the hardware store." She smiled sadly, leaning toward him. "And I won't be able to give him to you."

He threaded his fingers in hers, then leaned his chin on his other hand. "Do you hate the idea of the hardware store, is that it?"

Paula closed her eyes, frustrated that he didn't seem to grasp the gravity of what she was saying.

"I mean," he went on, "small-town life can be as relaxing as a cruise, though considerably less glamorous. But I suppose a coastal Oregon town would be a comedown from Topanga Canyon."

She straightened and drew her hand away, glaring. "Thank you for that shallow view of my character."

He smiled. That indignation was just what he'd wanted to see. "I'm just trying to present a realistic picture. Just like you are."

"I've been spoiled rotten," she admitted, "and I've done things the average person will never have the opportunity to do, but I'm not the kind of person who needs a thrill a minute to feel fulfilled, or a Beverly Hills address to be happy. In fact, I would probably be an asset when you do get that hardware store because I know a thing or two about business you've probably never imagined."

He couldn't help the smirk of self-satisfaction. That had worked precisely as he'd planned. "Then, that's a yes?"

Paula scraped her chair back and got to her feet. "No, it's not a yes! Aren't you listening to me?"

He watched her as she paced across the room, his expression amusedly perplexed. "I am, but what you're saying doesn't seem to be coming to a firm point. Our relationship is too important for you to marry me, you can't have children and that doesn't bother me, you wouldn't mind your life revolving around a hardware store in a small town. In fact, you might even have some ideas for it, but you're still turning me down. Is that it, or did I miss anything?"

She stood at the window and glared at him over her shoulder. "You're being deliberately difficult."

"No, I think you're being arbitrarily difficult." He went to stand behind her and wrapped his arms around her waist. He put his lips to the side of her neck. "I love you and you love me. We're great together. You just need a little more convincing to see it my way."

"My mind is made up, Dane. I won't..."

He had swept her up into his arms and was striding toward the bedroom.

"Sex is *not* the answer," she said in a tone that sounded comically proper, even to her.

"It may not be the answer," he said, standing her on the edge of his narrow bed. "But it's a damned good argument."

She clung to his shoulders on the bouncy mattress as he unbuttoned and unzipped her jeans again. She felt his fingertips inside the waistband of her panties, then the rub of his knuckles against her flesh and the slow descent of undies and jeans down her legs. She lost all rationality.

As he lifted her against him to toss the jeans aside, eager anticipation swelled inside her, making a mockery of every argument she had against their building a life together. He swept a hand over her bare hip, down her thigh to her knee, then cradled her to lay her down on the mattress.

What caution could possibly stand against this delicious sensation and this deep, emotional satisfaction? she wondered. Common sense tried to tell her it would be safer if she tried to find an answer to that question, but feeling overrode all thought.

As she pulled Dane down beside her and divested him of his clothes, she ignored everything but her body's reaction to his touch, and his to hers. They came together like volatile substances, their earlier tenderness replaced by a desperate hunger. As they exploded together, Paula clung to Dane's shoulders, flung out once more as if she were a leaf that could float forever. She closed her eyes and simply let the moment be.

SHE CAME OUT of a formless but frightening dream with a start, struggling to sit up. She had a sense of being pursued, of having left something critical in her well-being behind. She opened her eyes to the darkness, an anxious cry on her lips.

"Paula," Dane said gently, sitting up beside her. "What's the matter?"

His arms came around her, his hand grasping her shoulder and tipping her against him. She felt the heat of his chest, and the bristly rub of his chin against her temple. The unnamed fear subsided and the bad dream was pushed aside. She wrapped her arms around him and nuzzled into his neck.

"I...I'm not sure," she whispered. "Just a dream." She held him a little tighter, remembering their love-making. He made her feel as though nothing existed in her world without him—as though she'd been reborn into a world completely different from the one she'd known because he was in it. "I'm glad you're here."

He lay back against the pillows, pulling her with him. He settled her on his shoulder and tugged the blankets up.

With a small sigh of contentment, she hooked a leg over his and let herself relax against him.

"I'm glad you're here, too," he said, kissing the top of her head. "But I wish we were here on a fishing trip."

She laughed and curled even closer to him. "I don't bait or gut, remember?"

He, too, laughed. "But you do catch pretty well. You're sure you've had no previous experience?"

"I've picked out my own lobster at a seafood restaurant, but that's about it."

"Well, you have natural abilities. We'll cultivate them on our honeymoon."

"Dane..." she warned halfheartedly. Now, in the middle of the night, wrapped in his arms, a relationship with him wasn't so frightening a prospect. But, marriage? She simply hadn't the courage for that.

"We'll go to some sleepy Mexican village," he said, ignoring her tone. "We'll eat tortillas and exotic fruit, and fish all morning, sunbathe all afternoon and make love all night."

He conjured up an image on which it was easy to focus. She made a little noise of pleasure and kissed his collarbone. "That would just be too good to be true."

"I don't think so," he said, tracing the point of her shoulder with his fingertips. "I think it's well within our reach if we make up our minds it's what we want."

"And when we come home from the honeymoon?"

"A lifetime ahead of us," he replied simply.

She sighed and said nothing.

That worried him. "If you're out of arguments," he teased, "you can just capitulate. I can be a gracious, generous winner."

"I have lots of them," she said. "I just can't quite organize them right now. What time is it, anyway?"

He raised his wrist. "Three-seventeen."

"What do you suppose my parents are doing?"

"Probably wondering what you're doing."

The feeling with which she'd awakened from her nightmare crept over her again. "You're sure they're all right?"

"We talked to Kurt this afternoon, remember? He told us they were fine, and he now owes your mother his retirement fund."

"How much longer, do you think, before they find Hailey?"

NO RISK, NO OBLIGATION TO BUY ... NOW OR EVER!

CASINO JUBILEE
"Scratch'n Match" Game

Here's how to play:

1. Peel off label from front cover. Place it in space provided at right. With a coin, carefully scratch off the silver box. This makes you eligible to receive two or more free books, and possibly other gifts, depending upon what is revealed beneath the scratch-off area.

2. You'll receive brand-new Harlequin Superromance® novels. When you return this card, we'll rush you the books and gifts you qualify for, ABSOLUTELY FREE!

3. If we don't hear from you, every month we'll send you 4 additional novels to read and enjoy before they are available in bookstores. You can return them and owe nothing, but if you decide to keep them, you'll pay only $2.96* per book, a saving of 43¢ each off the cover price. There is **no** extra charge for postage and handling. There are **no** hidden extras.

4. When you join the Harlequin Reader Service®, you'll get our subscribers-only newsletter, as well as additional free gifts from time to time, just for being a subscriber!

5. You must be completely satisfied. You may cancel at any time simply by sending us a note or a shipping statement marked "cancel" or by returning any shipment to us at our cost.

> YOURS FREE!
>
> *This lovely heart-shaped box is richly detailed with cut-glass decorations, perfect for holding a precious memento or keepsake—and it's yours absolutely free when you accept our no-risk offer.*

CASINO JUBILEE
"Scratch'n Match" Game

CHECK CLAIM CHART BELOW
FOR YOUR FREE GIFTS!

YES! I have placed my label from the front cover in the space provided above and scratched off the silver box. Please send me all the gifts for which I qualify. I understand I am under no obligation to purchase any books, as explained on the opposite page.

(U-H-SR-08/92) 134 CIH AFPC

Name _____

Address _____ Apt. _____

City _____ State _____ Zip _____

CASINO JUBILEE CLAIM CHART		
🍒🍒🍒	WORTH 4 FREE BOOKS, FREE HEART-SHAPED CURIO BOX PLUS MYSTERY BONUS GIFT	
🍒🔔🍒	WORTH 3 FREE BOOKS PLUS MYSTERY GIFT	
🔔🔔🍒	WORTH 2 FREE BOOKS	CLAIM N° 1528

HARLEQUIN "NO RISK" GUARANTEE

- You're not required to buy a single book—ever!
- You must be completely satisfied or you may cancel at any time simply by sending us a note or a shipping statement marked "cancel" or by returning any shipment to us at our cost. Either way, you will receive no more books; you'll have no obligation to buy.
- The free books and gift(s) you claimed on the "Casino Jubilee" offer remain yours to keep no matter what you decide.

If offer card is missing, please write to: Harlequin Reader Service® P.O. Box 1867, Buffalo, N.Y. 14269-1867

"It's bound to be soon." He rubbed her arm and asked gently, "Getting scared?"

"Yes," she admitted, hearing the surprise in her own voice. When this had all begun, her parents' safety had certainly concerned her, but she hadn't been afraid for herself. Now, she just wished it was all over and she were back in her office.... She waited for comfort to wash over her at the thought. It didn't. She frowned into the darkness. Since Natalie's death and Bill's departure, her office had become home. She arrived early and stayed late and had most of her meals there. It now seemed to represent what she was: workaholic businesswoman. Was she going to lose that small comfort, too?

"I mean," she said, thinking aloud, "when all this started I wanted my parents to be safe, but I was more interested in my deal with Ferrante than my own personal safety. I think I'm going coward on you, Dane."

"That's not what it means," he said.

She raised her head to look into his eyes in the darkness. "What *does* it mean, and how do you know?"

"It means," he said softly, "you've found something to live for that makes each day suddenly more important than business." He pulled her face down to kiss her with slow, artful concentration. She emerged trembling and disoriented. "And I know," he added, "because what you've found is me."

She dropped her head on his chest. "No wonder I'm scared. You know, don't you, that when this is all over you'll take a second look at me and decide this was all some very predictable bodyguard/woman-in-danger syndrome and you'll wonder what you ever saw in me."

"Mmm," he said, "and oxen will fly."

She raised her head again. "Oxen? Isn't the expression 'pigs will fly'?"

He nodded. "But to really express the absurdity of your suggestion, I thought it should be something bigger. Go to sleep before I get really annoyed with you and send you to your own bed."

She snuggled into him again. "You wouldn't do that," she said confidently.

He wrapped both arms around her and gave her a squeeze. "You're lucky I have no strength of character. Good night."

A small meow heralded Peaches's arrival into the room. It was followed by four feet landing on Dane's chest and Paula's arm, walking across Paula's face then back again to curl up under her chin. Peaches purred loudly. Paula wrapped an arm around the cat, feeling ridiculously content.

Dane stroked both of them until they went to sleep.

DANE HEARD THE SOUND just as they were about to sit down to a breakfast of pancakes and fruit. He caught it when it was just a distant drone, similar to the annoying buzz of an insect. It grew louder, becoming a growl, closing in on them. He grabbed Paula's breakfast and threw it into the trash, and cleared her place of utensils, putting them into the bottom drawer.

She stopped in the middle of floor, a bottle of syrup in her hands, watching him throw away her untouched breakfast.

"What are you...?"

He took a look around the kitchen, and apparently satisfied by whatever he saw, he grabbed her arm in a biting grip and walked her into the bedroom.

"Dane..."

In the bedroom he took hold of both her arms and gave her a small shake to ensure himself of her attention. "Listen. Hear that?"

She heard the loud sound of a motor. "It's a bike, or something, but what..."

"We didn't get a call from Nelson," he said, lifting the lid on the old campaign trunk that stood at the foot of his bed. "He was supposed to call me if they let anyone through. He didn't."

"You mean something's wrong?" Her heart was pounding as he lifted her into the trunk, pushing on her head until she was curled up inside it. He leaned down to kiss her quickly, then stuffed a blanket in on top of her. "Don't move or make a sound," he said. "I'll have you out in a couple of minutes, but if they get inside..."

"If they get inside," she said, her voice high and muffled by the blanket, "it'll be because they got by you, won't it?" She tried to stand. "Dane, I want to help. I don't want you to..."

He pushed her back down and readjusted the blankets. "You do as I say," he said firmly and dropped the lid.

Paula heard it fall with a bang and felt herself completely enclosed in darkness, unable to budge. She moaned quietly, straining her ears to hear as Dane's footsteps went back into the living room. She prayed that no latent tendency toward claustrophobia would rise to thwart her.

Even through the trunk, she heard the roar of the motor as it pulled up, probably directly in front of the cabin.

WHEN THE TWO MOTORCYCLES approached, Dane stood in the doorway, drinking a cup of coffee, the Smith & Wesson a comfortable weight at the back of his waist.

The two bikes held three men. The one that rode singly wore leathers and a helmet with a swastika painted on it. His face was concealed by a lowered face shield.

The driver of the second bike weighed probably three hundred pounds. His leathers were studded, and his greasy head of blond hair was covered by a stained blue kerchief knotted at his nape.

His passenger wore jeans and a denim jacket and no helmet. He was thin and had a Charlie Manson look in his eyes.

Dane would have bet his offer on the hardware store the big guy in the kerchief packed a gun in his jacket. The single rider's left leg covered a scabbard strapped to the bike.

"Morning," Dane said genially, saluting the trio with his mug. "Out early."

"Beautiful day," the man in the denims said with a personable smile. "This your place?"

"That's right."

The man looked toward the woods across the meadow, then back at Dane. "Lonely spot."

Dane shrugged. "Suits me."

"Nobody for miles."

"You're here."

The three men exchanged a look of amusement. "We're lost," the man in the bandanna said. "Can't find the road back to the highway. Spare a cup of coffee?"

Dane shook his head regretfully, holding up his mug. "Last cup. Sorry."

The men exchanged another look, this one less amused. The man in the denims got off the bike and walked toward the porch. He stretched dramatically, walking back and forth in front of it, studying the cabin.

"Nice place," he said.

"It's comfortable," Dane replied, calmly sipping coffee while every nerve ending begged for the opportunity to react. He forced himself to remain still. There was more at stake here than the excitement of confrontation after so many days of waiting.

"All the comforts of home. Could even bring a woman up here." The man in denims stopped at the foot of the steps and squinted up at him.

Face-to-face in the clear early-morning light, Dane knew he wasn't Hailey. He bet on the man behind the shielding helmet. He smirked. "Scares the fish away."

Denims started up the steps.

"That's far enough," Dane said. He put the coffee cup on the windowsill.

Denims stopped on the third stair, his hand on the railing, his expression darkening. "Not very neighborly."

"That's the way I am," Dane replied quietly. "That's why I'm out here."

Denims took one more step up. Dane moved indolently to the brink of the porch, hands loosely on his hips. "Don't," he said simply.

He looked into Dane's eyes, his own dark and fathomless and frighteningly vacant. Dane stared him down, letting him see his lack of fear.

Denims held his gaze another moment, then chuckled. "You got unresolved hostilities, man," he said, backing down the stairs. "Oughta see a shrink."

"Appreciate the advice," Dane said. "Follow the logging road you came in on down the hill. You'll pick up the road to the highway on the other side of the stream."

The single rider revved his bike while Denims climbed onto the back of the other. "Obliged to you," the big man in the bandanna said.

Dane nodded. "Sure."

He watched them coast past the porch, turn wide and head back slowly. Then he saw the movement he'd been waiting for, the nonchalant reach of the mysterious single rider toward the scabbard under his leg—Denims reaching into his jacket.

Dane drew and dove behind the rocker in a corner of the porch as automatic weapons fire sparked over his head and into the pillar next to which he'd been leaning just an instant before. He fired and the single rider shouted, blood spurting from his shoulder.

The second bike made another pass, Denims firing a lethally compact Uzi. The top half of the back of the wicker chair fragmented and the cabin window behind it shattered. The bike made a turn and started back. Dane tipped the chair and pushed it to the railing, balancing his gun hand in the other over the back. He aimed at the driver, who chose that moment to give a burst of speed. Denims blew off the back of the bike as though he'd been hit by a low-hanging branch.

The driver made a turn to go back for him, but he appeared to be unarmed, and Dane fired again, the bullet angling off and shattering the deflector.

The single rider roared off down the logging road, and the man in the bandanna followed, hunkered low over the handlebars and the jagged remnants of his windshield.

PAULA FEARED her heartbeat, and not the trunk, would suffocate her. She heard sounds of an indistinguishable conversation, the unmistakable staccato sounds of gunfire and bikes roaring in the yard. She heard several cries and the cymbal crash of the living-room window shattering.

That was it. She didn't know what she could do, but she wasn't going to cower in the trunk while Dane faced whatever was happening alone.

She climbed out of the trunk and crawled on her stomach toward the living room.

By the time she reached the sofa and crept up to her knees, using it as a shield, the roar of the bikes was moving away and Dane was hauling a body onto the porch. Not a dead body, she judged by the sounds of the man's screams.

"Dane, are you all right?" she demanded, running to the doorway. She saw the man had been shot in the leg, and the thigh of his jeans was already drenched with blood.

Dane gave her a quick glance as he rifled through the man's pockets. "Get our jackets, and whatever food you can stuff into my pack."

She turned instantly to do as he said.

"Who told you where we were?" she heard Dane demand of the man now moaning in pain. She slung Dane's pack over her shoulder and ran into the kitchen.

"We just . . . knew."

"Who?"

"I don't know."

"I could fit my fist right into your thigh and maybe cut a few things or shove them around."

Paula fought nausea as she stuffed the small frying pan into the sack, and reached up for cans, unmindful of what they contained.

"Hailey got...to one of your...your brother's men," the man said. "It's over...buddy. We got you. And we got her."

"All *you've* got," Dane said in a hard, cold voice Paula had never heard before, "is a big hole in a main artery. If your buddies come back for you, maybe you won't bleed to death."

The pack full, Paula shouldered it, slumping under its weight. She dropped it to the floor and dragged it into the living room where she carefully skirted the man on the floor who was pleading with Dane to apply a tourniquet to his leg. Dane ignored him, loading the man's weapon with shells he'd found in his pocket. Paula grabbed their jackets and skirted the man again.

Dane handed her the Uzi. She took it, admitting candidly, "Dad bought me a little revolver I keep in my bedside table, but I don't know anything about..."

"It's okay," he said. "The safety's on. I'll give you a crash course in its use later." He straightened, shaking off Denims's grasping hands.

"Come on, man," Denims pleaded. "I could bleed to death before they get back."

Dane nodded amiably. "Yeah, you could." He grabbed Paula's arm and pushed her toward the back door. He grabbed the rifle leaning in the corner.

"Wait!" She stopped, resisting his efforts to push her through.

"What?" he demanded.

"Peaches," she said imploringly. "We can't just leave him here."

"Where is he?"

"I don't know." She tried desperately to think. She hadn't seen him since their aborted breakfast, when he'd been sitting under the table ready to beg from them. "Let me look..."

She tried to pull out of his grasp, but he held fast, stepping out onto the back steps and pulling her with him.

"Paula, there's no time for that now," he said as reasonably as he could manage. "Either he ran off when he heard the gunfire, or he's hiding somewhere. Either way, we don't have time to look for him. Hailey'll be right back with reinforcements."

She followed him at a run across the meadow toward the trees because she couldn't break free of him, and because she knew what he said made sense. But she couldn't shake the guilt that she'd lured a poor, starving cat into their cozy cabin only to place him in worse danger than he'd been before.

In her haste to try to keep up with Dane's much longer stride, she tripped and fell, going down with a little scream.

Dane yanked her to her feet, then stopped, turning an ear toward the same faraway drone that had transformed one peaceful, sunny morning into one fraught with terror.

"Come on." He tried harder to shorten his steps this time as he pulled her toward the woods.

He was aware of the drone growing louder, becoming a growl and then a roar as the shelter of the woods seemed to recede from them.

She was gasping for air, and he half dragged her the last few yards to the rim of the trees. He dropped her behind a fat fir and crouched beside her. He could see the front, back and side of the cabin as five bikes with a total of six riders approached and rode around it, shouting taunting, graphic threats.

Paula watched over Dane's shoulder in fascinated horror. It reminded her absurdly of western movies of Indians circling a solitary wagon. It also occurred to her that Hailey must truly hate her to have involved six other men in his vengeful pursuit of her. She wondered what he'd told them to make them willing to help him commit murder.

They heard the shouts of the wounded man on the porch as his friends circled. They finally stopped in front in a neat line, as though lining up in a night-club parking lot. The man with the bandanna got off his bike and ran up the porch steps, tossing Denims onto his shoulder and carrying him down. He laid him beside the bikes, taking the bandanna from his head and tying it above the wound.

Denims's complaints could be heard clearly.

Paula watched them aim their weapons at the cabin, thinking they meant to walk into it and search for them. Instead they opened fire.

She stared, openmouthed, as the other window shattered, the wicker chair splintered and the half timbers that composed the cabin were shaved and then sliced by the lethal spray of the six weapons.

The sound went on and on, and she covered her ears, leaning her face against Dane's back to blot out the sight and sound of the destruction of the safe harbor of the past four days.

She felt his tight muscles and the anger in every line of him. Then she remembered that not only had the cabin been an idyllic hideaway for her, but it was also the place Dane and his brother had bought together, the place where they'd learned to understand each other, where they'd grown together out of the mire of their childhood and become productive human beings. She wrapped her arms around him, her eyes still shut tight against his back, trying to comfort him in the only way she knew how.

The firing went on and she imagined the furnishing inside reduced to stuffing and springs, shards of glass and kindling wood. Then suddenly it stopped.

She lifted her head to see three of the men go inside while the other three remained outside, looking around, focusing on the woods. One man pulled off his helmet, and Paula saw the sun glint off shaggy platinum hair. As he turned in a circle, probably looking for some telltale movement of his prey, she saw the black eye-patch. *Hailey*.

"That's him!" Paula whispered to Dane.

She fought off a cold, heavy fear. Then she prayed that Dane had been right about Peaches, and that he'd run off when the noise first began.

In a moment smoke began to roll out the back door and the three men who'd gone inside ran out onto the porch. Smoke followed them, then flames became visible through the broken windows.

Paula dropped her forehead against Dane's shoulder. "I'm sorry," she whispered. "I'm sorry."

He was still one more moment, then he rose to a crouch, grabbed her hand and pulled her after him, deeper into the woods. Paula did her best to keep up, knowing the six men would be right behind them.

CHAPTER TEN

"OH, GOD," Paula groaned, pulling Dane to a stop to gasp for air. "Tell me this isn't poison oak," she said, trying to push away the undergrowth that rose high around them between the tall firs and cedars, choking off light and air and room to move.

He had his anger under control now and his mind on the job. He gave her a grim smile. "I wouldn't worry about a skin rash when your tush is in serious danger."

She drew a deep breath and returned the smile. "Good point. Okay. I can go on."

He noticed that she carried the Uzi he'd given her tucked under her arm. He slung his rifle over his shoulder, took the gun from her and looped the sling over her head.

"Even if you can't use it," he said, "it might still give them pause if you aren't carrying it like a purse."

"Purse," she said, grimacing, holding both hands out in dismay. "I didn't bring it."

"It's okay," he assured her. "We aren't likely to encounter a Neiman Marcus."

She made a face at him. "I was thinking of my lip definer and my eye cream." She sighed. "You're about to see what I really look like without my paint."

He pulled her to him, kissed her quickly and led the way on, pleased and a little surprised by her matter-of-fact reaction to running for her life. Of course, it was early yet. Bravado could easily peter out given cold, rain and sufficient time. It had even happened to him, and he was a seasoned veteran.

"Jeez!" she complained, pushing branches out of her face. "It's getting almost too thick to walk."

"If it's too thick to walk," he said over his shoulder, holding a springy branch of vine maple out of her way, "it'll be too thick for their bikes."

"Oh," she said. "Right."

Paula followed without a complaint for better than an hour, until what had begun as a stitch in her side grew into a pain she couldn't ignore. She pulled Dane to a stop again and doubled over, digging her hand into her side.

"I know, I know," she said breathlessly. "I'm a marshmallow, but I need a minute."

He sat her down under a tree. "Stay there. I'm going to see how close they are."

Nodding while she dragged in air, Paula watched him disappear into the thick green through which they'd just come and tried hard to ignore the fear engendered by having him out of sight. She closed her eyes and leaned back against the tree, concentrating on breathing normally. *You're in trouble now, girl,* she told herself. *Six men are trying to kill you and you're in love with a man almost ten years your junior. Not to mention that a multimillion-dollar deal that would have set you up for life is probably down the tubes by now.* She tried to care about that point and couldn't muster the will.

Everything important to her at the moment had distilled into the fact that Dane had disappeared into the woods and she wasn't sure where he was.

He returned from behind her, startling her. "Come on. We've got to keep moving." With one hand he pulled her to her feet.

"Are they right behind us?" she asked, allowing herself to be tugged along as if she were a wagon with a bad wheel.

"Close enough. We've got a few minutes on them."

"I don't mean to present a negative note," she said, already breathless again as she dodged a vine-maple branch, "but how're we going to fight off six of them?"

"Right now," he replied, "there're only three. Watch the hole."

Paula leapt over a wide-mouthed burrow. She preferred not to consider what occupied it. "What happened to the other three?"

"They're looking for us in the woods in front of the cabin, I imagine," he replied. "They couldn't be sure which direction we took, so they split up."

"How long before they decide we didn't go in that direction?"

"If they're good trackers," he said, "they've already turned around. If not, we might get a couple of hours on them."

Dane paused to help her over the hollowed-out fallen skeleton of a tree.

"So for the moment, it's just two against three?" she asked.

He smiled as he lifted her down because he could see that she was serious—the woman who carried an Uzi under her arm like a purse.

"Right," he replied. "Not bad odds at all."

"I know what you're thinking," she said as they ran on again.

"What's that?"

"That I'll be useless." When he turned to glance at her as he kept up the pace, her look dared him to deny that was true. "I'll show you," she said. "Watch out!"

He turned back to the trail and found himself two inches away from collision with the trunk of a ponderosa pine. He stopped abruptly with an oath and Paula slammed into him, knocking him against it anyway.

Her body off balance and pressed against his, she grimaced. "I'm sorry. Maybe we should talk later."

This close to her he saw the near panic behind the cavalier manner and took a quick moment to wrap his arms around her. "It'll be all right," he promised gravely, "if you trust me and do everything I say."

She laughed softly against him. "I'm too old to fall for that line, sailor."

He wanted to make her stop the one-liners and admit to the fear, and he wanted to make her understand that as bad as it looked it wasn't hopeless. But they hadn't more than five minutes on Hailey's men.

Instead, he took her hand and ran on, concentrating on the trail and looking for a thicket full enough to hide her.

It came a quarter of a mile later in the form of a tall, tightly clustered fern. Only yards from a cedar with a low enough branch, it was perfect.

He stopped and pulled her back when her momentum propelled her forward. He stuffed her into the fern, handing her the pack.

"There could be something in here that doesn't want company," she protested though she crawled into it and dragged the pack in with her. She looked at him worriedly when he began to pull the tight fronds around her. "Where are you going?" she asked.

"Just stay absolutely still," he ordered, afraid to take the time to explain. "Don't make a sound, no matter what happens."

Paula hunkered down in her leafy bower, trying to peer through the screen of leaves as Dane slung his rifle around his neck and leapt at the low branch of a tree. He disappeared almost immediately.

Panic tried to take over. Dane was out of reach and out of sight, she suddenly felt itchy everywhere and she hadn't liked the sound of his last caution. *"Don't make a sound, no matter what happens."*

She pulled up the collar of her shirt and stifled a scream when a spindly spider fell off in her hand. The sudden sound of crashing in the underbrush claimed her complete attention.

She had a mental flash of the time she and Dane had walked to the creek and been startled by a deer. She remembered the touch of his mouth in vivid detail, the touch of his hands down her spine and over her hip.

It was gone in an instant when two pairs of legs stopped on the trail just beyond the thicket.

"I don't think they came this way," a man said in a gravelly tone, which Paula would have considered a whine had his voice not been so deep. "We should turn back and find the others."

"They're right in front of us, I tell ya," said another man in a breathless voice. "Where the hell's Briggs?"

"He swung wide in case they tried to cross the creek."

"He swung wide to suck his flask, you mean."

"Do I look like his mother?"

"Look, if this Cornell broad gets away from us, Hailey's gonna be ticked. You find Briggs, tell him to get his butt back here with us or he's gonna be short some body parts."

Legs passed so close to Paula's thicket she could see the laces on a pair of well-used hiking boots.

She hadn't drawn a breath since the conversation had begun, and she needed desperately to gulp for air. Certain she'd be heard while the second speaker stood in the middle of the trail, waiting for his partner the whiner to find the apparently alcoholic Briggs and return with him, she didn't budge or draw breath, praying that her lungs enjoyed some lingering effects from her years on the high school swim team.

Her head was beginning to spin when she heard a loud thunk, a sharp cry and saw the man's legs crumple on the trail. Dane dropped down beside him as though out of the sky and she heard another sharp crack and then complete silence.

She expelled air in a rush, then drew it in again in a gasp when a long arm reached into the thicket and grabbed her. She resisted, until her face cleared the leaves and she saw the tight planes of Dane's face.

"Hurry, Polly," he whispered. "We've got to get him in there before the others come back."

Yanking the pack out, Paula helped him stuff the man's inert body into the thicket. He wasn't very tall, but a considerable girth at the waist revealed a propensity for beer or doughnuts or something that made him difficult to move around.

"What if he wakes up?" Paula asked, rising beside Dane as he shouldered the pack.

"We'll be long gone. Come on."

Paula ran behind Dane for what seemed like hours. She wondered what had happened when the whiner and Briggs had returned to the trail and found their partner gone. Had they instituted a search for him, or continued after her and Dane? Or maybe the second man had awakened and there were still three men in pursuit of them. There seemed to be no alternative that could be considered an improvement over their previous circumstances.

Her lungs were beginning to burn, her throat was tight and closed and her head was pounding. She remembered her earlier boast. She was going to show Dane, all right. She was going to show him what it really meant to care for a woman almost ten years older than he was. It meant she wouldn't be able to keep up. It meant her vital body functions were about a decade older than his and far less dependable.

Then a thought completely unrelated to her self-flagellation occurred to her. He had called her Polly. No one had ever called her Polly but her father, and that had been when she'd been very small. Tears stung her eyes and she had an overwhelming urge to burst into noisy sobs.

But Dane was still running and she had to concentrate to keep up with him. There would be time to become hysterical later—if they lived long enough.

They ran on. Life seemed to be composed exclusively of dragging in air and blowing it out, of having her arm tugged until she thought it might come out of its socket, of pumping her legs until she felt as though her socks were lead weighted and her shoes were concrete. It felt as if there were a knife in her side, cutting its way out just above her right hipbone.

Dane looked over his shoulder to check on her and stopped abruptly. She literally fell into him, gasping loud. "What's the matter?" she demanded in a kind of stupor as he supported her full weight. "I'm fine. I can keep going. I can."

"Yeah," he said briefly, a sort of flat disbelief in his tone. He dragged her off the trail.

"I can't walk if...if you drag me," she said, helplessly suspended from the arm around her waist.

"I'm dragging you because you aren't walking," he said quietly.

"It's 'cause I'm older than you are."

"It's because you eat junk and don't exercise."

"I wish we could go home," she said with a sigh. Then she remembered. He eased her to the ground and leaned her against the trunk of a huge fir. "But I don't have one, do I?"

He took the gun from around her neck, slapped a clip into it and cocked it. "No," he replied. "Sit still. I'm going to see how far behind us they are." He handed her the gun. "If anyone shows up, release this." He worked the safety, then slid it back into place. "And pull this." He placed her hand on the trigger. "I'll be right back."

He disappeared again and Paula put the gun down between her knees. Her house was gone. Benny was gone. Either she was too tired to feel the desolation she should have experienced, or one more crisis on top of the teetering pyramid of tragedies of the past two years made little impact.

Dane was back in an instant. "You're supposed to be holding the gun," he scolded, pushing her down onto her stomach and forcing the Uzi into her hands.

"I was thinking about my house," she said.

"We've got other things to worry about now."

She made a nonchalant gesture. "Easy for you to say. You've only lost your vacation home. I'm out on the street."

He stopped her from pointing the gun toward herself to study it more closely. "It's loaded," he said firmly, taking her chin in his hand and looking sternly into her eyes. "Listen to me, Paula. The only thing that matters at this moment is that you know how to use this."

She frowned at him. "Where are you going?"

"They're right behind me," he said. "I'm going to try the same trick again, but there're two of them. If one of them gets by me, use it."

"Dane..."

"Do it!" he whispered harshly, already at a run for the trail.

Her heart pounding, panic threatening again—even more strongly this time because she was so tired she wanted to burst into tears—Paula tried to spot Dane through the thick undergrowth. He disappeared into a tall cedar right beside the trail.

It was a few moments before she heard a familiar voice, and a second one that probably belonged to the troublesome Briggs.

The first man sounded even more exhausted than she felt. He drew in air in sustained gulps.

"To hell...with Pickett," Briggs said. Paula saw both men bent double in the middle of the trail, a good dozen yards from Dane's tree. They'd apparently chosen that moment to catch their breath and regroup. Briggs was a big man with a blue bandanna on long, greasy blond hair. She felt a shudder of revulsion go through her. "Who cares what happened to him? He's nothing but an ass kisser, anyway. Who cares about the chick? She ain't done nothin' to me. Come on, Sledge. Let's double back to the bikes and get the hell out of here."

"Sure. And have Hailey on our butts till he blows us away some night in an alley?"

"He won't find us."

"That's probably what the chick thought."

Another shudder went through Paula. This one meant fear—pure, high-gloss fear.

"Well, I ain't stayin'," Briggs said. "I didn't roll drunks every night for months and save my money to spend my time jogging through the woods like a freakin' elf. I'm goin' down to the creek and double back. I'm outta here."

"You're crazy."

There was a snicker. "Yeah."

Briggs turned off the trail and ran through the trees, heading straight toward her.

DANE WATCHED the big man head off directly toward where he'd left Paula at the stream, and he felt a spasm of fear grip his stomach. She had the gun, he reassured himself. If she'd at least have the sense to point it at him, she could hold him at bay long enough for him to deal with the little guy now about to pass directly under the tree.

He gripped the heavy branch on which he knelt, dropped the lower half of his body and kicked with all the strength of legs that had walked across Kuwait.

Sledge dropped like a stone. Dane gave the man's M-16 a wide toss, then slung his rifle over his shoulder and took off at a crouching run toward where he'd left Paula.

He stared at the base of the tree. Grass, fallen pods, a mushroom—no Paula. He continued to stare as though doing so would conjure her up. She'd have screamed if Briggs had grabbed her. He'd have heard her. Briggs had come this way just a moment ago. He couldn't have dragged an unwilling woman away in that amount of time.

He heard the slide of a bolt behind him and had two thoughts. The first was that she'd hidden as some kind of warped joke and had sprung out behind him to tease him. He was going to kill her. The second was that he'd lost his edge. He shouldn't have dropped his guard and spent precious seconds wondering where the hell she'd gone. He cared too much. He could never live this life again.

He turned slowly and confronted a grinning Briggs, an Uzi aimed at his gut. "Gotcha," Briggs said, extending his long index finger toward the trigger.

He wondered how many rounds Briggs could have in him before he got the M-1 off his shoulder. He calmly prepared to reach for the sling when Briggs asked, "Where is she?"

For a moment, Dane simply stared at him. He didn't have her?

Briggs took a step closer, the short barrel of the Uzi ready to cut Dane in half.

Suddenly Dane saw everything with new perspective. She'd gotten away. After an instant's euphoria, he remembered what she was like on the trail, remembered she'd have no idea how to get to the car, remembered Hailey was still out there somewhere.

God. He had to find a way out of this. Stalling for time to think, he gave Briggs a puzzled look and asked with what he hoped was genuine sincerity, "Who?"

Briggs raised the gun, his lip curling menacingly.

Dane took that instant to reach for the sling over his shoulder. But before he could cradle the M-1 and shoot, he caught a glimpse of something that froze him in his tracks.

Paula stood behind Briggs with the Uzi he just couldn't get her to use correctly. She was holding it by the barrel and swinging it at the back of his head. She was a foot shorter than the burly man, and her blow connected with a crack that glanced off the side of his neck.

The man cried out in surprise, still upright, but he was startled long enough for Dane to land a fist in his stomach, then one to his jaw. He finally fell, still looking surprised.

Dane looked at Paula, the pile of Briggs between them. He wanted to scream at her for taking that chance instead of shooting, for hanging around when she'd managed to evade him and should have run.

"I saw him coming," she explained, her voice tight and high, her face as white as paper. "I hid. He...he stopped over there—" she pointed to the base of a gnarled pine "—to relieve himself and heard you hit the other guy. He started to go back, then he saw you coming this way and ducked back behind the tree."

She indicated the gun she held, then realizing she still held it by the barrel, shrugged guiltily and held it the way he'd showed her. "I wasn't sure I'd be able to use this without hitting you." She ended with a sigh. "You're still going to yell at me, aren't you?"

"No." He stepped over Briggs and pulled her close with one arm, kissing her with all the relief he could allow himself to feel now that it was over—this part, anyway.

She responded eagerly and finally pulled away, slumping against him. He felt her boneless exhaustion.

He tucked her under his arm and started down to the stream. "Come on," he said. "We're going to find someplace to spend the night."

"I vote for the Beverly Hills Hotel," she said wearily.

He squeezed her shoulder. "You're not getting me in a pool with an inflatable zebra."

"You could sit on a chaise longue and watch me," she suggested.

That notion was suddenly more appealing to him than any option offered him for as long as he could remember.

HE FOUND a hollowed-out cedar several yards back from the edge of the creek. Paula looked at it worriedly as he dropped the pack to the ground and pulled out a plastic tarpaulin. The woods were almost dark now, though it was only midafternoon. He couldn't see the sky for the density of trees, but he guessed it would begin to rain before he had a fire built.

"What do you suppose lives in there?" Paula asked.

He smiled. "Oh, snakes, large hairy spiders."

She swatted the top of his head. "Smart-mouthed kid!" she accused with a grin.

He hooked an arm around her knees and tipped her off her feet and neatly into his waiting arm. She fell with a little cry that turned into a laugh, then disappeared when her eyes locked on to his.

He saw love for him in her soft brown gaze, the sweetness of it turning to smoldering desire even as he watched. "I'd have never believed this could happen," she whispered, putting her fingertips to the side of his face. "If it hadn't happened to us."

"Love?" he asked.

"Love that makes absolutely nothing else matter," she said with an awed little shake of her head, her eyes going over him feature by feature in a kind of wonder. "Someone is trying to kill us. We could be moments away from being found by Hailey, and all I can think about right now is what it would be like to make love to you in the woods at dusk."

He leaned down to kiss her, taking the thought from her and adding his own embellishments. "Tell you what," he said softly, holding her to him. "I promise you'll find out, but in the woods outside of Heron River."

"Heron River?"

"That's where my hardware store is."

She sighed and smiled, letting herself believe that could be. "I can hardly wait."

He stood, steadying her to her feet. A melodic patter began on the high overhead leaves, changing almost instantly to a rapid drumming. Rain.

Paula looked upward and groaned. "Oh, come on."

Dane wrapped the tarp around her and stuffed dry leaves into the bottom of the hollow tree. Then he pushed her into it. He pulled cups out of the pack and filled them at the creek, handing her one, then downing the other.

"Champagne never tasted this good," she said after gulping it down. "I'll bet if you bottled water from here you could make a fortune."

He probed the pack for something they could eat without heating it. He found fruit cocktail, beef barley soup, baked beans, chicken and noodles, and stew.

"Cold baked beans?" he asked.

She looked disappointed. "Cold?"

Even as he prepared to explain that the rain would soon penetrate the sheltering canopy of leaves, making a fire impossible, it did.

"Cold is great," she said, opening a wing of the tarp for him to join her. "Come in here before you get drenched."

He put the guns under the tarp, pulled the pack as close to them as he could and squeezed in beside her, can and opener in hand.

She laughed softly. "Just like one of the best booths at the Copper Quiche."

He glanced at her as he worked with the opener. "Say what?"

"It's an exclusive little place in Hollywood, famous for elegant cuisine and snobby patrons. During the lunch hour, you have to share a booth if there are only two of you. My secretary and I used to love to go there to people-watch."

Dane imagined the charmed, upscale life she had lived and tried to relate it to the woman he'd come to know in a cabin in the Oregon wilderness. He couldn't make it compute. That life-style was as far removed from his as Earth was from Mars, and he'd come to think of her as such an important part of his life that picturing her in any other setting seemed unreal.

"I thought you were a hard-driving executive," he teased, removing the lid from the can and dividing the beans into their cups, "and didn't have time for society lunches."

"I considered it business," she said, taking her cup from him and handing him a spoon she'd pulled out of the pack. "Thank you. I studied the makeup on all the elegant ladies and wondered what I'd do to make them more attractive."

He frowned in surprise. "Can you tell your makeup from, say, the Ferrante woman's stuff?"

"Well, I just presumed all the most beautiful women were wearing mine." She took a spoonful of beans and closed her eyes, moaning approval. "This is even better than the Quiche's Black Bean Vinaigrette."

"I know," he said, assuming a modest air. "They call me the Graham Kerr of Glendale."

She turned to him, laughing in surprise. "Is that where you live? It's hard to think of you as a suburbanite." Glendale was a pretty foothills community just north of the Los Angeles city limits. "And how do you know who Graham Kerr is, anyway?"

"When I first came home from Saudi and found Joyce gone, I logged a couple of weeks in front of the television." He hesitated, afraid she'd ask why. She simply nodded, apparently considering that behavior reasonable.

"There's nothing like a good soap," she said, "or a cooking show with instructions you can't follow, to make you realize your life isn't as bad or as complicated as it seems." She swallowed a mouthful of beans and smiled at him. "Did I mention that I can't cook, and that I'm really not very domestic at all?"

"Trying to scare me off?"

"I dislike housework. I do like to garden, but nothing seems to survive for me. Even geraniums."

He grinned down at her, his heart swelling with love. "I couldn't care less about geraniums."

He struggled to get an arm around her in the tight space as rain fell torrentially around them and he felt better than he ever remembered feeling in his life. He put their empty cups on the ground outside the tree, then held her close, pulling the tarp around them.

"Do you have a garden?" she asked, snuggling into him.

"It was dead when I came home."

"I'm sorry."

"It's okay. I'll put in some rhodies, some pansies, and ranunculuses when we get to Heron River. What would you like?"

"Those little bell-shaped things that grow near the cabin." The cabin. She wished she hadn't brought it up. Every time she thought about it, she wanted to cry.

"That's bleeding heart," he said. "We'll find some."

Paula closed her eyes and leaned into him, trying to will the feeling to pass. She didn't know what was happening to her. She felt herself swing from jocularity one moment to near hysteria the next. On one level, she treasured this time with Dane because she knew that, one way or the other, their idyll in the woods would soon be over. But on another level, she was absolutely terrified at the realization that they had this time together in the hollow of a tree because Hailey had found them and was tracking them with merciless determination.

For two years she hadn't cared if she'd lived or died, but that had all changed suddenly and forever. Now she wanted desperately to live.

The thought of walking away from him when this was over was almost more than she could bear. She leaned harder into him, trying to lose herself in his embrace and forget past and future. She wanted to live only in the here and now for as long as they had it.

Dane felt the small shudder in her as she leaned even closer. He kissed her forehead and gripped her tighter.

"Scared?" he asked softly.

She nodded against him.

"They'll have to get past me, you know," he said, intending the words as reassurance. But she burst into tears and wrapped her arms around his neck, sobbing.

For a moment, he didn't know what to do. "Hey," he said gently, rubbing up and down her spine. "That isn't going to happen. We're doing all right so far, aren't we?"

Everything she'd been worrying about since Hailey's men had first shown up at the cabin spilled out of her. "There are still three men after us," she wept, leaning back to look into his face. He looked alarmingly calm and indulgent of her hysteria and she wanted to shake him because he just didn't see. "God knows what they've done to your brother's men. I mean, if they were still alive, they'd have found us by now, wouldn't they? No, he's going to get us, then he's going to find your brother and my parents, and we'll all meet somewhere—" she made a broad gesture with one hand, cracking her knuckles against the side of the tree "—over the rainbow where..."

Dane put a hand firmly over her mouth. "Stop it," he said quietly.

She yanked his hand down with both of hers. "There's no need to protect me from the truth," she said fiercely. "I've faced worse—"

"The truth," he interrupted, putting that hand over her mouth again when she tried to interrupt him, "is that we're alive, and as long as we are, we have a chance. We don't know what happened to Kurt's men, so speculating is useless. Right now, we have to concentrate on ourselves."

Paula's sobs abated, the mere release of them seeming to allow her to think more clearly. "Overnight, the three men you knocked out will have time to connect up with the other three."

"And Kurt's men will have time to find us."

"If they're alive."

"If they aren't and they haven't reported to Kurt, he'll be down here himself to find out what happened." He grinned. "And we've got lots of ammunition. You didn't waste any on Briggs."

Reluctantly she gave him an answering grin. "And to make it all worse, I'll bet my crow's-feet are showing."

He studied her face seriously, then looked into her eyes with an expression so loving she felt every fear melt away.

"Your makeup's pretty much gone," he said honestly.

She straightened in distress. "So, you can see them?"

"Yes. A little."

Because she'd expected him to lie gallantly and tell her she still looked perfect, she frowned. "Are they a turnoff?"

He laughed softly. "No." Then he pulled her to him and kissed her right eye, and then her left. "Now, while I insist we're going to get out of this, the situation really doesn't allow us to worry about your makeup, okay? Let's talk about what we're going to do tomorrow."

CHAPTER ELEVEN

PAULA AWOKE to a paralyzing pain in her hip. She groaned, trying to sit up, realizing she'd had it—and the rest of her body—drawn tightly against Dane for hours. She was parched and hungry, and wanted nothing more than a mouthful of the delicious water from the stream.

The darkness of the woods had taken on a different quality, as though beyond the canopy of trees it might be dawn.

She shrugged the tarpaulin off her, and moved carefully, pushed her half of the blanket onto Dane. She got onto all fours and tried to crawl out of the tree.

Dane grabbed a fistful of the back of her jacket and held. "Where are you going?" he asked.

She smiled over her shoulder. "Doughnut shop. Want anything?"

He pulled until she fell backward into his arms. "What were you groaning about?"

"My hip hurts," she complained with a little laugh. "I know you don't feel these things at your age, but I have these little aches and pains now when I get up in the morning."

"Which hip?" he asked.

"The right one."

He pulled her against him and began to rub it. Physical relief and sexual excitement began instantly and simultaneously. She should protest. This was not the time, but his hand felt so wonderful, and the feelings it inspired reminded her that she had a life beyond the fear that had enclosed her for the past twelve hours or so.

His large hand ran over the swell of her hip and down, stroking, rubbing, applying pressure.

"It's my...turn..." she said drunkenly "...to fix breakfast. And I was going...to get water."

He nuzzled her ear. "I owe you the rest of this rub-down another time."

She sighed, half relieved, half disappointed when he stopped. "I'll hold you to it."

"I'm going for the water," he said, easing out from inside the tree. "You stay here until I tell you it's clear." He picked up the M-1, looked around the already lightening woods, then picked up the cups he'd put out in the rain the night before and went to the stream.

Paula opened the can of fruit cocktail while he washed out the cups and came back with them filled with water. After they drank, Dane folded the blanket into the pack while Paula divided their breakfast.

"We'll have to eat quickly," Dane said, taking his cup from her.

"How far are we from the car?" she asked. The fruit felt wonderful against her tongue and throat.

"We're not heading there."

"Why not?"

"Hailey'll have someone waiting there."

Of course. If he knew where they were, he knew where Dane's car was and that the obvious way out of here was to head for it. "Then where are we going?"

"A fire tower about half an hour away."

She looked at him steadily. "Do you think we'll make it?"

"Of course," he replied with confidence.

Paula wanted to believe him, but he hadn't looked into Hailey's eyes and she had. He was close. She could feel the cold fear inching up inside her, growing teeth and talons. She helped Dane pack up, concentrating carefully on each little task to get it done.

She picked up her gun and followed him across the stream and through a thinner growth of trees. Walking was easier, she noted, but they were far more visible now.

"They'll be able to see us," she pointed out to Dane's back.

"We'll also be able to see them," he said over his shoulder.

That made sense. The only problem, as she saw it, was that sense had little to do with this whole thing.

It didn't take Paula long to realize they were climbing. The calves of her legs, which still hadn't recovered from the walk up five days ago, began to feel the strain.

Paula caught up with Dane and grumbled good-naturedly, "Couldn't you have had a fishing retreat in Kansas or Manhattan?"

He stopped to put a hand to her forehead. "You're not losing it on me, are you, Polly?" he asked. He looked her over for signs of fatigue. Her cheeks were pink and her eyes bright, but she was no jock.

She yanked his hand down and gave him a forcedly jocular roll of her eyes. "No, I'm not losing it. I just wish there weren't so many hills in your life."

He pulled her along beside him. "Loosen up. I told you we were going to make it."

She looked up at him, her eyes frank with fear. "He's close," she said. "I'm sure. And I'm not climbing one more hill just to—"

A shot rang out, splintering a raggedy branch of cedar right beside them. Dane dropped, yanking Paula with him.

"I told you," she said, pinned to the ground by his weight.

"Thank you," he said. "Do these sensors tell you where he is?"

"Don't be smart."

"Stay down," he directed, pushing on the middle of her back for emphasis, "and don't budge from here."

"I'm also tired of you leaving me!" she whispered loudly as he ran, doubled over, into the thicker firs far to the right. Paula dropped her forehead on her folded arms and thunked it against the gun she always carried but ignored. Her heart pounding, her fear threatening to claw her from the inside out, she tried to remember what Dane had said about the safety and released it. A satisfying click reassured her. Now she could shoot someone. Great.

She heard a spate of gunfire from the trees into which Dane had disappeared. There were shouts and a scream. She tried desperately to isolate the sound of the scream. *Had it been Dane's voice? It'd been too high,* she told herself. *Screams are always high,* she argued silently, trying to make herself deal with a possible reality. She decided there was no point in wondering.

Paula got to her knees, then rose slowly and ran, crouched over as she'd seen Dane do, in the direction he'd taken. She was terrified, but she was getting a little tired of being a passive participant in this bizarre game. The action was some distance ahead of where she came into the grove. She slid to the ground behind the cover of a thick fir and tried to assess what was happening and where Dane was.

OUT OF THE CORNER of his eye, Dane saw movement from the direction in which he'd left Paula. Knowing he'd hit one of the two men shooting at him, he allowed himself an instant's distraction to turn to see what was happening.

He swore fluently, as he watched her run for the grove in a military crouch. She held her Uzi to her chest as though it were a baby. God. He had to watch her make it to the grove before turning back to the source of the gunfire.

He wasn't entirely surprised to see a bald, brawny giant in leathers running toward him, firing an M-16. It occurred to him as he drew a bead on him that he'd almost waited too long. Had Paula taken two more seconds to make it to the grove, the man would be on top of him by now.

He swore aloud as he took a bullet in his upper arm, falling backward with the impact of it. For a millisecond, pain blurred his instincts and he thought he'd been wrong—he *had* waited too long. Then his brain engaged again, he took quick and careful aim and got his opponent as he ran into the clear to finish him off. He fell with a scream, clutching his thigh with both hands, the weapon tossed away as he landed. Dane headed for Paula.

"WELL," a low, smooth voice said just above Paula. "If it isn't Mrs. Cornell, soldier of fortune."

On her stomach under a tree, her complete attention focused on the gunfire ahead of her, Paula absorbed the sound of the man's voice and felt everything inside her freeze. *Hailey.*

No, no, no! Her mind screamed the denial. They'd almost made it.

But if she'd learned anything in the two years since Natalie died, it was that denial brought nothing but more grief. Reality, however ugly, had to be faced.

Paula rolled onto her back and looked up at the tall, slender man with the wild platinum hair and the eye patch. She was going to die, she thought with a curious calm. But she was going to take him with her. He wasn't going to get to her father and mother. It was stopping here, with her.

He wore camouflage, and a baseball cap, his sighted blue eye wild and bright with hate. He pointed a handgun at her face. Paula inched the fingers of her right hand toward the Uzi.

Hailey whipped the hat off and raised the patch onto his forehead, revealing an ugly pucker of scars and bright red skin.

"They wanted to give me another eye," he said, leaning over her as she drew back, "but I didn't want it. I didn't want to forget what you did to me. I wanted to be able to show you when the time came."

With a swift and brutal kick that caught her hand and the Uzi, Hailey sent the gun skittering along the ground, out of reach.

Paula cried out in pain, fear returning with stunning, debilitating force—not for herself, but for her parents. And for Dane. Where was he? Was he safe?

Hailey placed the gun against her temple. Terrified, she felt the cold steel against her flesh. "The time is now," he whispered.

Dane had a bead on him. In a second he could have shot Hailey through the temple without batting an eye. But Hailey chose that moment to grab the front of Paula's shirt and pull her to her feet until they were nose to nose—head-to-head. He could have done it on the practice field; he knew he could. But his heart was involved here, and it was beating with enough force to shake his body. He didn't dare try. He just had to pray and make himself wait for his moment.

Hailey pulled back the trigger and put it to Paula's temple.

"No!" Dane shouted.

As he walked slowly toward Hailey, the M-1 held harmlessly away from him, he knew the shout had been only part tactic, though it had worked. The pistol was now trained on him. The other part reflected clearly what he felt—a deep-down, gut-level need for her that erased a lifetime of reacting like a Marine.

His eyes locked with hers, saw the bittersweet apology in her sad smile.

"I have no problem with killing you first," Hailey said calmly.

Dane readied himself to slap the rifle into his left hand and fire at Hailey's left shoulder, praying Paula didn't move into his line of fire, and that the surprise was enough to put Hailey's aim off. It was a slim chance, but all he had.

But he was the one surprised the next moment when Paula brought her knee up with frightful precision to Hailey's groin, raising his gun arm at the same time so that the resultant shot was in the air.

Dane was on them instantly, knocking Hailey's feet out from under him so that he fell backward, his face still contorted in pain, his hand clutching his groin, his mouth wide open and gasping for air.

Paula leaned over him and said angrily, "Well, I sure as hell have a problem with it!"

Dane pulled her back, his heart lurching when he saw two of the three men they'd escaped the day before walk into the clearing. It took him a moment to realize they held no weapons and were followed by Kurt and several of his men and half a dozen park rangers.

Kurt holstered a Beretta and ran to Dane and Paula as the rangers cuffed Hailey and took him away. He looked from one to the other in guilty concern. "Are you two all right?" he asked.

It took Dane a moment to realize it was over. He was all adrenaline and fringed nerve endings and burning pain. Now that the crisis was over, he could deal with how and why it went wrong. Pumped for battle, he turned on Paula. "What in the hell did you think you were doing?" he demanded.

Her eyes brimming as the past few minutes played over in her mind, and she saw Hailey train his pistol on Dane and begin to squeeze the trigger, she faced him, planting her feet, primed to take him on. "Saving your butt!" she shouted at him. "What did you think I was doing?"

"My butt wouldn't have been in danger," he roared back, "if you'd stayed where I left you!"

"Well ex*cuuu*se me for trying to lend a hand!"

"You almost got yourself killed!"

"Well, you weren't doing so hot yourself until I . . ." It was then Paula noticed the darkening smear of red on the outside of Dane's sleeve. "Oh, God!" she cried, clutching his arm, turning to Kurt with a desperate "He's bleeding! *Do* something!"

She took the M-1 from Dane and placed it on the ground, gingerly pulling off his jacket. Kurt reached carefully into the hole the bullet had already made in Dane's shirtsleeve and ripped. Dane winced as the action jarred the wound.

"Be careful!" Paula said, elbowing Kurt aside. "I'll do it."

Dane and Kurt exchanged grins over the top of her head, the first friendly communication they'd shared in almost a year.

"Oh, yuck," Paula said, her voice sounding breathless and high. "It's really...I...Oh..."

Dane caught her in his good arm before she sank to her knees. Kurt took her from him, easing her to the ground. "Nelson, bring some water!" he shouted. "And the first-aid kit."

"I'M NOT STAYING," Dane insisted to the doctor putting the final touches on his bandage in the hospital emergency room in Klamath Falls.

The doctor, an older man, gave him an amused but harassed look. "You're not the kind of patient we like to keep," he said candidly. "You'd be disruptive and uncooperative."

"You got that right," Kurt said feelingly.

Paula laughed.

Dane gave each of them a glare before turning his attention back to the doctor. "You can go home, but you've got to promise me you'll go easy on this for a few days. The bullet tore a neat little line right up your bicep. You're going to feel this, and the arm won't be much use for a little while."

"We'll hire somebody to cook and clean up for you for a couple of days," Kurt said.

Dane glared at him again. "No, you won't. I'm not incapable of—"

"I'll go home with him," Paula said, feeling as surprised as they looked to hear the words come out of her mouth. Dane didn't look as pleased as she'd hoped. *Oh,*

God, she thought. *It* was *just a two-people-stuck-in-the-woods kind of affair.*

Dane hadn't been sure how he was going to handle things now that they were no longer bodyguard and client. But her moving in as his nurse hadn't been a consideration. He needed time to explain, time to prepare her, time to...

He saw the flash of hurt in her eyes, then the sudden easy distance she could put between herself and whatever caused her pain. She patted his good shoulder. "Relax. You won't owe me anything, I just figured I owed you. And I don't have a home to go home to, remember? I'll stay with you until you can do for yourself."

Dane made himself smile. There was a certain pointed humor to the whole thing. Time to explain and prepare probably wouldn't make a whole hell of a lot of difference anyway. "Good," he said. "Good."

Paula didn't think she'd ever heard a less sincere affirmative in her entire life. But she kept her cool and turned to Kurt. "Can I borrow a quarter to make a call from the pay phone to my office? I have to know if my deal with Ferrante is down the tubes or not. And I should call my insurance agent about my house."

Kurt shook his head. "No need. You can make the call from the plane your father's sending to take us all home." He smiled from Dane to Paula. "A little Lear with all the amenities. Belongs to the network boss, I understand."

"But, the Scout," Dane said. "I left it off the road at the foot of the trail to the cabin."

Kurt nodded. "One of my guys'll drive it back."

"There you go." The doctor stood, kicked aside the rolling stool on which he'd sat and helped Dane into his shirt. He handed two prescriptions to Paula. "You can fill these right across the street before you guys jet back to Hollywood. You movie stars?"

Kurt laughed, shepherding Dane and Paula to the door. "Their life stories may show up on the screen after this. Thanks, Doc."

KURT WALKED out of the pilot's compartment into the Lear's plush cabin and took the empty high-backed, upholstered chair next to Dane's.

"How you feeling?" he asked.

"Not bad," Dane replied. He stared moodily at the far end of the cabin where Paula sat at a little table, talking on the telephone.

"Take your pain pill?"

"Yeah."

There was a moment's silence, then Kurt asked quietly, "You want to talk about those four days in the cabin?"

Dane turned to look at him. The concern in the features so similar to his own brought back a flash of memory from his childhood. He remembered that same expression on the face of a much younger boy leaning over him when he'd retreated to his bed in despair at about eight years old. He'd brought a friend home from school and his mother had been out cold in the middle of the living-room floor.

Dane had run for a neighbor, who'd called an ambulance. He remembered vividly his fear that she was dead. The friend had left in a panic, and his mother, revived by the medics, had screamed at him for causing a scene.

Kurt, then twelve, had tried to joke Dane out of his despair, then had physically pulled him out of bed.

"She's not taking me down with her," he'd said adamantly. "And she's not taking you."

As an adult, Dane often wondered if he'd have made it through his childhood had Kurt not been there. Even now, he found himself wanting to share his feelings for Paula, and his concerns about how she would react when he got her home. He'd kept his own counsel for a year now, through the trauma of rebuilding a home without a woman in it, of starting over outside of the military, of enduring the long, lonely nights.

But over that mental playback of how important Kurt had been to him, his mind slipped into the memory of coming home after all those months in the Gulf to find Joyce had left him and Kurt hadn't bothered to let him know. He just couldn't put that aside.

"No," Dane replied evenly. "You want to tell me what the hell happened to your foolproof scheme to keep us safe?"

Dane felt instant satisfaction when guilt flared in Kurt's eyes. He was a man who took every responsibility and his ability to cope with it to heart; failing was more difficult for him than for most people.

"I'm sorry," Kurt said sincerely.

Now Dane felt instant remorse. It hadn't been his fault. Even the most brilliant strategist couldn't foresee betrayal.

"Wasn't hard for Hailey to find out we had her," Kurt explained, "because we've provided security for a lot of big names in Hollywood. We expected that. We didn't know he had a friend who could tap into our staff files to help him find something on someone he could use. They found Harriman—he was one of the four men on the ridge with Nelson. He had a daughter at Boise State, just a few miles from where his friends are headquartered. They picked her up and got word to him that she was dead if he didn't get them in to you and Paula." Kurt shrugged. "He was scared. He didn't stop to think that if he'd told me what happened, we could have found them and it would have all been over before it started. But they had his daughter. I guess I can understand."

Dane nodded. "So how'd he get them by?"

Kurt shook his head, looking embarrassed. "Absurdly simple. Harriman was in charge of morning coffee. He drugged it. When nobody checked in with me, I called the park headquarters, left Paula's parents with Buck and lit out here."

"Where were you?"

"Just outside of Vegas. By the time I got here, the rangers had found my guys, most of them as sick as dogs, and had picked up your trail, but it was dark. We had to wait until morning to make any headway. Along the way, we found a couple of Hailey's men with major headaches lost in the woods."

Dane smiled wryly. Yesterday seemed as though it were an eternity ago.

"Mr. Emmett is very grateful," Kurt said.

Dane shook his head, then wished he hadn't. It was beginning to ache abominably. "In the end she saved herself with a kick to the groin," he said, closing his eyes and leaning his head back. "So much for my training and your high tech."

"That's not the way she tells it."

"Really?"

"She told me you put yourself out in any and every way possible, even at times when she was rude and uncooperative. She says you were the epitome of chivalrous and heroic gallantry."

Dane winced without opening his eyes. "Keep it to yourself. I'll be ruined."

"She sounded," Kurt went on, "very much to me like a woman..." He hesitated. Dane rolled his head toward him against the plush chair back and opened his eyes, waiting. "Like a woman in love," Kurt finished with a frown.

Dane rolled his head back so that his gaze rested on Paula, now hanging up the phone. "What she is," he said, "is a woman who doesn't know all the facts."

"I don't understand," Kurt said.

"Neither do I," Dane said quietly. "I'll explain later."

Paula was smiling as she made her way toward them. Dane studied her, trying to determine if it was the phony smile she'd worn since she shocked him with her offer to go home with him, or the genuine smile that lit her face whenever he kissed her.

He couldn't tell. He was too tired and headachy and generally in pain to read her accurately. She did look happy, but she had an uncanny ability to do that, even when she wasn't. He had to be at the top of his form to tell the difference.

"Guess what?" Paula said as she sat in one of the deep chairs opposite them.

"The deal's on?" he guessed.

"Yes!" She waved a sheet of notes she'd taken while talking on the phone. "Not only that, but Giulia Ferrante is willing to give me a week to help you recover before I have to be in L.A. to sign the papers."

He found it hard to dredge up the enthusiasm he was sure she wanted from him. The days in the cabin were over. She could look at things from the perspective of safety and the life she was used to living. She could see him for the ex-Marine he was with nothing to give her but life in a little town in Oregon and the living from a hardware store. She could decide to take her cruise.

"Great," he said. Unfortunately the word came out sounding as insincere as he felt.

She had leaned toward him in her excitement and now leaned back, giving him the same confused look she'd given him earlier in the hospital. Kurt frowned from one to the other.

He stood, reached into an upper compartment and handed Paula and Dane a blanket. "Get some rest," he advised. "We've got another hour until John Wayne Airport."

Dane didn't want to comply, but seemed to have no choice. The painkiller coupled with exhaustion was putting him to sleep. Paula complied, because she didn't want to continue to watch that reluctant look in his eye.

CHAPTER TWELVE

STILL WEARING THE JEANS and sweater she'd put on the previous morning, Paula accompanied Dane and Kurt up the flagstone walk of Dane's pretty little split-level in Glendale. It was late afternoon on a sunny day, and bright yellow geraniums lined up at two-foot intervals against the front of the brick-and-redwood house like clumps of sunshine.

She drank in the sight of them. While Kurt explained that Sandy had said she'd meet them at Dane's, Paula wondered about Dane's excessively quiet mood. Part of her wanted to believe the painkiller had subdued him, but another part of her believed she'd truly frightened him. She'd assumed too much. She'd misunderstood his behavior at the cabin. Still another part of her wondered how one could misunderstand a proposal of marriage.

Her confusing thoughts fled when the front door flew open and two little children burst out of the house, shouting "Daddy! Daddy!" Paula smiled, turning to Kurt to tell him how beautiful his towheads were. But she stopped in her tracks when they ran to Dane, who was down on his knees, arms open, to welcome them.

She stared, her mouth as wide as her eyes, while a little boy, about two, stood on Dane's thigh, hugging him fiercely. A little girl, probably four, with straight blond hair and a neon-green bow in it that matched her shorts and shirt, rested her head on his other shoulder.

"You didn't know?" Kurt asked gently.

She shook her head, still dazed.

Then Dane rose and turned to her, the little boy in his good arm, the little girl holding the hand of the other. He met Paula's eyes with an expression that was both apologetic and faintly aggressive.

"Polly, I'd like you to meet my children. This is Sam." The little boy smiled, then shyly put both chubby hands over his face. "And Paige."

Paige leaned against Dane's leg, rocking the little Reebok on one tiny foot from side to side. "Hi," she whispered.

Paula swallowed, panic rising in her. This child was the age Natalie would have been . . . She swung her eyes to Dane accusingly, silently promising at the first opportunity she was going to do him severe bodily harm.

He looked back at her intrepidly, then smiled down at his daughter. "Tell Paula what Aunt Sandy's been teaching you to do this summer."

Paige looked doubtfully into Paula's eyes. Paula's long-undirected but still sharp maternal instinct told her Paige had read the look in her eyes and misinterpreted it as dislike for her.

Paula squatted down on the flagstones, putting herself on the child's eye level. She smiled. "What are you learning to do?" she asked.

Paige looked her over with bright blue eyes that had the same sharpness as her father's. She apparently reconsidered and said distinctly, separating the words, "Cross—stitch."

Paula resisted the impulse to send another glare at Dane. The child would only misunderstand and he'd

probably just look back at her with the same baldly innocent expression. So she played into his hands on this
one issue, determined to be out of there within the hour.

"I do cross-stitch, too," Paula said, remembering the
half-finished wedding sampler that had undoubtedly
burned with the cabin. "But I...I lost the one I was
working on. Would you show me yours?"

Paige smiled. "Do you want to see it now?"

Paula stood and held out her hand. Paige looked up
at her father. Paula did not.

"Go ahead," he said.

Paige took Paula's hand and led her toward the house
and the pretty, very pregnant brunette holding the door
open. Sam wriggled out of Dane's arms, unwilling to be
left out.

"You didn't tell her you had children?" Kurt demanded the moment Paula was out of earshot.

"It's a long story," Dane said wearily.

"You're in love with a woman, and you forget to
mention you have two small children?" Kurt insisted.
"What did the two of you talk about for five days of
isolation?"

"Back off, Kurt," Dane said stiffly, quietly. "All I
want's a little peace and quiet for a couple of days."

Kurt snorted. "Judging by the look on her face when
the kids ran out, I don't think you're going to get it.
Hey, Babe." He opened his arms as the brunette greeted
him in the doorway. He kissed her soundly then rubbed
his hand over her ripe stomach. "How are you and my
son?"

"We're fine," she replied, clinging to him an extra
moment then leaning back to look into his eyes with an
adoration Dane grudgingly admitted to himself he envied. She reached her other arm out to Dane, and he

leaned into her with genuine affection. She looked dryly from her husband to her brother-in-law. "I see you two are still finessing each other."

Kurt glanced wryly at his brother. "You don't sincerely expect harmony between us? Where's Nancy?"

"I left your daughter with Mom," Sandy said.

"*My* daughter?" Kurt asked. "What's she done now?"

"Locked Paige and herself in the tiny bathroom in Mrs. Gillespie's trailer. We had to call the locksmith."

Kurt closed his eyes and groaned. "Where did this little spawn of mischief come from?"

Dane laughed. "Seed of your loins, brother."

"Come on." Sandy stepped aside to let them in. "I've got a pitcher of margaritas waiting for you. Have you had anything to eat?"

The afternoon took on an almost familiar naturalness as Sandy served drinks, and the mouth-watering aroma of a roast wafted around them. Paula came downstairs with the children, taking the opposite corner of the sofa from where Dane sat while Paige and Sam crowded onto his lap.

"Paula, this is Kurt's wife, Sandy," Dane said, pouring and passing her a drink.

"Yes," she said pleasantly. When she bounced a glance off him, her eyes were anything but. Then she smiled at Sandy. "Paige introduced us. She showed me her cross-stitch," she said to Sandy. "She's doing beautifully. I must have half a dozen projects half-finished."

Sandy laughed. "Me, too. Kurt keeps threatening to build another room for all the projects I start and don't finish."

"You should have let me do it," Kurt said. "Now we'd have it for the baby."

The small talk continued for half an hour, Paula neatly sidestepping all Kurt's subtle attempts to get her to speak to Dane. Even Sandy was beginning to watch her with some perplexity.

Paula felt tense and angry, as though she'd swallowed a giant, emotional knot that was suddenly pulling so tightly she thought she might choke. Sam had fallen asleep in Dane's lap, and Paige lay drowsily in his arm, eyes growing heavy.

"Why don't you put them to bed," Sandy suggested, gathering up glasses. "I'll turn the roast off and set the table and you two can have a nice quiet dinner."

Paula looked up in worried surprise. "You're not staying?"

"No," Sandy replied. "I just came over to bring the kids back and put dinner in the oven. And Nancy's anxious to see her dad."

"Nancy?"

"Our daughter. She's six." Sandy, hands full, inclined her head toward the kitchen. "Come on. I'll show you where everything is while Dane's putting the kids down."

Dane expected Paula to protest but she followed Sandy docilely into the kitchen, though she gave him a look over her shoulder that told him she'd settle with him when the children were asleep.

In a roomy blue-and-white kitchen with a cozy breakfast nook and a preparation island in the center, Sandy checked on the roast and showed Paula where to find plates and utensils. Then she looked at her in concern. "Are you okay? When Kurt called from Klamath Falls to tell me he was bringing you and Dane home, he told me some of what you've been through, but it's my guess—'' she smiled, her expression apologetically frank ''—even he doesn't know everything.''

Paula tried to relax but couldn't. But it was easy to smile at Sandy, anyway. "No, he doesn't." Then she remembered the curious look Kurt had directed at her and then at Dane several times that afternoon. "That is, he might. I'm not sure." Paula sighed and sagged against the counter, realizing she made no sense.

Sandy folded her arms and leaned against the counter beside her. "You're in love with Dane," she guessed.

Paula looked her in the eyes, her own brimming with tears and anger. "I'm going to kill him."

Sandy bit back a smile. "Kurt says you saved Dane's life."

Paula put a hand to her aching head, felt the grimy, matted texture of her hair and shuddered with disgust at herself and her situation. "He saved mine over and over," she said, "but..."

When Paula winced and expelled a sobbing breath, Sandy put an arm around her shoulders and prodded gently. "But?"

Paula sighed. Sandy would never understand, but she said it anyway. "He didn't tell me he had children."

Sandy considered her for a moment, then said softly, "They're lovely children. I know. When their mother left they stayed with Kurt and me till Dane came home. He's doing a good job with them all by himself."

Paula nodded, drawing deep breaths. "I'm sure of that. It's just that I...I..." She couldn't say it. The way she felt she'd lose her composure, and she had so many things she wanted to shout at Dane before that happened.

"I'm older than he is," she finally said as Sandy waited for an explanation. "Almost ten years."

Sandy shrugged. "That doesn't matter much today, does it?" Then with sincere feminine interest she leaned closer and studied Paula's face. "You're forty?" she asked incredulously.

Paula laughed lightly, tears receding. "Close enough. I'm thirty-nine until October seventh."

"How come you haven't any wrinkles?"

"I do," Paula insisted. "I'm just too caked with dirt at the moment."

Sandy shook her head, still examining Paula feature by feature. "I don't see any. A few tiny little lines at your eyes when the light's right, but that's it. But your business is makeup, isn't it?"

Paula nodded.

"Speaking of lines . . ." Sandy grimaced and patted her large tummy. "I've got stretch marks the size of the New Jersey Turnpike."

"I've got a great cream for that," Paula said. "I'll see that you get some."

"Does it work on faces?" Sandy put short-nailed fingertips to a round, pink-cheeked face with a few flattering laugh lines and a warmth in her eyes and her smile that made whatever she found unattractive about herself invisible to anyone else. She laughed at her own joke, then added, "I brought you some things to wear until you can go shopping. Kurt told me you had to leave everything. There are a few pairs of jeans and a couple of shirts I won't get into again for some time."

"Thank you," Paula said, touched by her thoughtfulness. "I can't wait to change into something clean!"

Kurt and Dane walked into the kitchen, talking about Kurt making another trip to the cabin. Sandy's ear picked up on it instantly though the men stopped talking the moment they stepped into the room.

Sandy's shoulders sagged visibly. "When are you going back?"

"Tomorrow morning," Kurt said, holding his arm out to her. She went into it with a frown and he squeezed her to him, kissing her forehead. "I'll be back before nightfall, I promise. I've got to take pictures of the cabin for the insurance company, and pick up a few things we left behind."

"I get left behind all the time," Sandy said, turning a playfully frosty glare on him, "and you never rush back to pick me up."

In a swift movement, Kurt swept her up into his arms, undaunted by her protruding tummy. She squealed in surprise, but wrapped both arms around his neck. "Oooh," she said in a low, seductive tone. "Where are we going?"

"Home," Kurt replied. "We're going to have dinner with Nancy, read her the required bedtime story then sedate her so we can have a night of unbridled lust."

Sandy smiled at Paula and Dane, then said goodnight and, with a sigh, settled herself against Kurt's shoulder. "I'm ready," she said.

Dane and Paula followed them to the door, Dane reaching around to open it for them. He looked worriedly from his pregnant sister-in-law to his brother. "You going to make it to the car?"

"Easy," Kurt said, heading down the path. "Call you tomorrow night when I get home," he shouted back, then leaned down to say something to Sandy, who giggled loudly in the twilight.

Dane pushed the door closed, locked it, then turned to Paula. There were emotions in her eyes he didn't un-

derstand, but the anger was unmistakable. He didn't
blame her for it, he simply hadn't known what else to
do.

"I presume," he said, "that a night of unbridled lust
isn't in store for us."

She folded her arms and glowered at him. He braced
himself for a vitriolic tirade. She even opened her
mouth to deliver it, but was sabotaged by tears welling
in her eyes. She closed her mouth and, stiffening further, sniffed the tears back. "You Lothario!" she accused in a low voice, then stormed back to the kitchen.

He raised an eyebrow at her back, rooted to the spot
by a confusing urge to laugh. Lothario? He followed
her into the kitchen. She had pulled the roast out and
was carving it into surgically precise slices. Noting her
skill, he kept his distance.

"Lothario?" he asked.

"Roué," she snapped over her shoulder. "Seducer of
women." She put the knife down and turned to him,
adding, "Liar!"

"I did not lie," he said calmly.

"You said children weren't an issue!" she shouted.

"They aren't," he insisted reasonably. "I already
have them."

She glared at him, momentarily silenced by that logic.
"You know what I mean." She turned back to the roast.
He took plates and a bowl down from an overhead
cupboard. "When I said that, you were concerned
about being unable to conceive a child. I said children
were not an issue for me."

She spun around again as he placed the bowl beside
her for the vegetables. "You knew they were an issue for
me!" she said, a tear spilling over. "Why didn't you tell
me?"

He put the plates down, keeping his distance. He knew if he reached for her she'd draw away.

"Because I knew if I told you," he replied honestly, "you'd run in the other direction before we ever had a chance to make it work."

"So you let me walk in here in complete ignorance," she went on, her face crumpling, "and come face-to-face with a beautiful little girl the same age Na—" a sob broke the name; she gasped a breath and went on "—Natalie would have been, and with a little boy who looks so much like you, expecting me to just take it in stride!"

"It didn't kill you, Paula," he pointed out gently. "You're still here. Completely undiminished, by all appearances."

"Well, I'm not here for long," she said, snatching up the bowl he'd put on the counter. "I need a spoon."

He opened a drawer and handed her a slotted serving spoon. She scooped up vegetables with the finesse of a clam digger and dropped them into the bowl. "I promised Sandy I'd serve this up, then I'm leaving."

He struggled to keep his voice down. "Where are you going?"

"I'm calling my father."

"He isn't home."

She looked up at him with venomous suspicion.

Dane shrugged. "Kurt had them in Vegas. When he told them you were coming home with me for a few days, they decided to stay and play the tables."

That was reasonable, she thought. *Inconvenient, but reasonable.* Her mother did love to gamble.

"Then I'll call a cab," she said. She speared slices of roast with the serving fork and slapped them on top of the vegetables.

"What are you going to pay him with?"

She banged the fork on the counter and fixed him with her favorite boardroom stare. He parried with a look that kept a hundred trained and restless troops under control. Love, he decided, was a lot like combat.

"Considering you're responsible for this," she said, "you should feel obliged to lend me cab fare."

"I don't."

"Then I'll walk."

"In two-day-old clothes, with your hair like a camouflage helmet? You know tonight's the night the *Enquirer* will be out, looking for front-page stuff. They'll have a ball speculating what you've been up to. You want to skunk your deal after all?"

"Sandy brought me a change of clothes," she screamed at him. "And anyway, public humiliation would be preferable to staying here with you!" She headed for the door.

He followed.

"Financial destitution would be preferable to staying here with you!" she added, reaching for the knob. "*Baldness* would be prefer—"

"I've got the idea," he said, shoving the door closed and pulling her out of the way to lean his weight against it. He was tired and frightened, too, and he wanted her to stop shouting and try to understand. He held her forearms and gave her a light shake. "Paula, listen to me."

She struggled, but he only strengthened his grip.

"That was a cruel thing to do to you, and I'm sorry. But I didn't know what else to do." He spoke quietly, calmly, desperate to reach her. "I wanted you to meet my kids before you decided you couldn't bear to live with them. I wanted you to spend some time with me without people trying to kill us so that you could see what we can have with just a little effort.''

"You wanted things your way," she said, unbending.

"If we do things my way, we have a future, and my kids get back some of what they lost when their mother left. We do things your way, my kids are still motherless, for me the loneliness goes on, and you get a cruise. What'll you do the year after that, and after that, and forever? It doesn't excuse my not telling you, but it explains it, doesn't it?''

She didn't want to admit to him that it did. She didn't want to admit to herself that it did. She sidestepped the issue entirely.

"Your arm is bleeding again," she said coolly. "And you're supposed to take a pill in ten minutes."

"You promised to help me until my arm was better," he said, shamelessly resorting to guilt manipulation.

Her eyes, more hurt than angry now, cut a ragged hole in him. She squared her shoulders and was suddenly all dignity. "Is a hot shower too much to ask?''

"Top of the stairs," he said, feeling his panic quiet. "To the right." He dropped his hands from her and she walked away.

He wrapped the food and put it into the refrigerator. He washed the roasting pan for something to do, holding it with his bad arm while he scrubbed with his right hand. The wound was beginning to ache again, but he felt so generally miserable, the pain seemed to belong.

He rinsed the pan under the stream of water, then watched the water pressure diminish as the upstairs shower was turned on. He put the pan aside to drain

and turned the taps off. He looked upward to the sound
of rushing water and tried to decide what to do.

Much of his life he'd been powerless to affect the
turns his life took. As a child he'd been pretty much at
the mercy of the choices his mother made, and those of
the state agency that tried in vain to help her and her
children.

When he married, he'd been at the mercy of a selfish
young woman and his own arrogant stupidity. When
she left him, he'd been halfway around the world and
unable to stop her. At that moment, he wondered for
the first time if he would have.

Almost a week with Paula had taught him what love
could be like. He didn't have to forge the life he wanted
out of something one-sided and unsatisfactory. He
could have the home and family he'd dreamed about for
as long as he could remember. He just had to make
Paula see it.

PAULA SOBBED and scrubbed her tangled hair, railing
against the fate that had placed the perfect man in her
path, then made him almost ten years younger than she,
gave him a life-style one hundred and eighty degrees
opposed to hers and then gave him two beautiful little
children.

She dropped her head under the rushing water, trying to wash away the resentment she felt that things
couldn't be different. But she couldn't mother two little children no matter how much she loved Dane. She
couldn't. She was adjusting to the age difference, and
she knew she could be as happy with him in a hardware
store in a little town in Oregon as she'd ever been in
Topanga Canyon. But she'd make herself and then him

crazy if Paige's and Sam's lives were placed in her hands.

Deep in thought, her back to the shower door, she didn't hear the intruder until the door opened, admitting a sweep of cool air into her saunalike cocoon. Dane, naked and smiling, stepped into the shower.

She moved back into the corner, crossing her arms over her breasts and looking stern. She found it difficult to do while wearing nothing but shampoo.

"I'll be finished in a few minutes," she said.

"I'm glad I'm not too late," he replied.

She continued to frown. "You're going to get your wound wet."

He pointed to the plastic wrap wound around his bicep. "Saran Wrap."

He stepped under the shower head, having to raise it from where she'd positioned it. He pulled her to him to save her from a blast of water in the face.

Holding her loosely against him with a hand splayed across the middle of her back, he made a rumbling sound in his throat as the water spilled over him. "God, that feels good."

"I'm happy for you," she said, having to inject the edge of sarcasm into her voice. "I get the water just the right temperature and you reap the benefits of it. How long do you think the hot water will hold out?"

She didn't feel sarcastic at all. She didn't even feel angry. Dane's body was large and warm and seemed to steal all the room and the air in the confining little stall. It made her feel soft and malleable and alarmingly unresolved.

It would not work, she told herself firmly. *Whatever other compensations might be involved in marrying Dane, it would not . . .*

"For ages," he replied. "It's an eighty-gallon tank. Want me to finish your shampoo?"

"No, thank you, I'll leave you to your..."

Before she could reach for the door, he'd reached his long fingers into the cloud of suds in her hair and began to scrub. The sensation of his fingertips against her scalp rose goose bumps all over her and she stood transfixed by the ripple of feeling.

His first pass through was very thorough, almost rough, as he scrubbed from her nape to over her ears, to just above her forehead. She had to put her hands on his waist to steady herself and felt warm, wet muscle.

He did a second pass through her hair, this one gentler, longer strokes drawing the shampoo to the ends of the strands, then mounding it all up to do it again. She began to lose her focus. She tried desperately to reach for the anger she'd felt earlier, the complete conviction that he'd deliberately deceived her and that nothing could excuse that. She couldn't find either.

She felt vaguely disoriented, as though the world were turning with the round movements of his hands.

He turned her so that she stood under the water, adjusting it to rain down on her. He worked his fingers through it as the spray rinsed the suds away, tipping her head back to let the water smooth the hair out of her face.

"A second shampoo?" he asked, shoving the shower head up so that she could respond.

She shook her head, her voice a frail croak as she replied, "No. I'd already done one."

"All right," he said, reaching to the shower caddy for the shampoo. He handed it to her. "My turn."

Instinctively she took it, but the disparity in their heights would make the job an uncomfortable experience for her without a ladder.

"You'll have to get on your knees for this to work," she said.

She knew she was in trouble when he grinned. "I've a better idea," he said, and lifted her against him, placing her legs astride his waist. "There. Comfortable?"

She had no air with which to speak. It left her the moment she felt his bristled chin against her breast, the wiry hair on his chest against her stomach, the muscled warmth of his flat stomach against the gate of her womanhood.

He gave her one little bounce to hold her closer, his hands crossing each other to cup her bottom. It heightened her awareness at every point of her body in contact with his. One of his hands tapped her lightly as he reminded, "Shampoo, Polly."

She tried to wriggle free, but worried about his arm. "You'll hurt yourself," she gasped.

"Then don't struggle," he advised softly.

She squeezed a quarter-size spot of shampoo onto the top of his head because he'd told her to, and her mind didn't seem to be functioning without specific instructions. She was lost to common sense and reasonableness. Her body was so alive with feeling that every other function was lost.

Pressing his advantage, Dane planted a kiss on the tight tip of a breast.

"Da-ane," she whispered in tortured protest. "I can't do this if you..."

"Sorry." He raised his head, looking suddenly very proper, despite the white suds crowning his dark hair.

"Go ahead." When she looked doubtful, he repeated, "Go ahead."

Paula began to scrub, and one of Dane's hands began to wander. Paula resolutely ignored it through the first shampoo, then reached overhead and placed the spout of the shower directly over him, giving it a turn for maximum force.

He moved out from under it, still holding her, coughing and choking. He looked up at her, hair and amusement in his eyes. "That wasn't nice," he said.

She raised an eyebrow. "And I suppose what you were doing was?"

"Wasn't it?" he asked softly, doing it again and longer so that she could judge.

She closed her eyes on a helpless little moan, hitching her body up and succeeding only in placing a breast within easy reach of his lips.

He kissed and nipped and kissed again until the eyes she opened to him were dilated and distant—until she focused on him, and a smile that said a million things to him, which she probably didn't even understand herself, formed on her lips.

He stroked the roundness of her hip. "One more shampoo ought to do it," he said, burrowing his nose between her breasts. "Hurry."

As though controlling her movements from the snare of a trance, Paula shampooed while Dane explored inside her with the deep stroke of a fingertip that soothed one moment and taunted the next; soothed and taunted until she dropped the shampoo and grabbed a handful of his hair, tugging it back under the shower. As the water beat down on both of them, he brought her to spinning, ringing climax, bracing a foot forward as she tipped her head and shoulders back. A little whimper came from her throat. It was music to his ears.

Paula was still in a mindless whirl when Dane shifted her slightly and entered her. She sighed with the pleasurable wonder of being filled with him, bound to him, locked with him forever. Because now she knew she was. It didn't matter what she wanted, what she feared, or what decision she ultimately made, she would always be his and he would always be hers—together or apart, they were one.

The world spun out of control a second time as he groaned her name against her breastbone. His shudders rippled into her and her body tightened on his as though he belonged to her, as though the moment could go on forever.

CHAPTER THIRTEEN

THEY ATE ROAST BEEF sandwiches at ten o'clock in the breakfast nook. Dane wore gray sweats, and Paula a navy-blue sweatshirt that fell to her knees. Dane had refused to give her the bottoms.

"Knees like yours shouldn't be hidden," he'd said.

"I was thinking more of protecting my bare backside on the wooden bench," she'd said reasonably.

He'd wrapped his arms around her and nuzzled her neck and suggested, "You can sit on me." Then he'd reached under her shirt, distracted both of them from their purpose, and dinner had been delayed yet another hour.

Now she sat in his lap, an arm comfortably hooked around his neck while she ate tender roast beef on sourdough bread. The table was littered with jars of Dijon mustard, stout horseradish, and dill pickles Dane had added to his.

Paula frowned at his concoction. "Are you going to be able to sleep?"

He chewed and swallowed, his eyes bright with amusement, his thick wiry hair full and curly from her shampoo. He looked disarmingly young. Curiously she felt both flattered by and afraid of the look in his eyes.

"I don't intend to sleep," he teased. "Do you?"

She laughed softly. "Even the pride of the Marines has to regroup sometime." Then she added, looking into his eyes, "I'm going to be here a few days, you know. You might want to pace yourself."

He put his sandwich down and tightened his grip on her, his eyes darkening. "Thank you, Paula," he said.

"It isn't a promise," she clarified quickly. "I . . . I really don't think this is going to work, but the truth is..." She hesitated, almost afraid to say it aloud, to give him more ammunition to make her stay with him than he already had.

"What is the truth?" he whispered.

She finally admitted with a helpless little sigh, "That I can't bear the thought of leaving you."

Dane, who seldom remembered to pray, thought fervently, *Thank you!* He cupped the side of Paula's face, pulled it down to him and kissed her long and deeply.

"And I have to be in L.A. after the holiday weekend to close my deal," she said.

He nodded. "I'll drive you."

"Wrapping it up might take a couple of days."

"Then what? You still want to take the cruise?"

She had to think about that and finally leaned her cheek against his hair, planting a kiss in the thick, wiry mass. "No. When all this first happened, all I wanted was to be left alone." She sighed deeply against him. "You've changed all that, I just don't know if I'm strong enough to do..." she waved a hand at the very domestic kitchen ". . . to do this again."

"Nobody's rushing you," he said. "You can have another hour to think about it."

She tugged playfully at his hair and he complained loudly. She stiffened suddenly at a stealthy sound from the living room.

"Dane!" she whispered, clutching at the shoulder of his sweatshirt, the sense of physical safety of the past fourteen hours wiped away in that subtle little sound. Had they missed one of Hailey's men? Had Hailey himself somehow gotten free?

"Relax," Dane said quietly. "It's just the midnight marauder."

"Who?"

"A creature who lives by night," he explained in a dramatic undertone, "responds to the opening of the refrigerator door and can only be appeased by getting half of whatever you're eating."

A little figure wearing a frilly flannel nightgown and clutching a naked doll appeared in the kitchen doorway several feet from the nook. Paige's eyes squinted against the light, zeroing in on the pair sitting cozily in the booth. Paula tried to move off of Dane's lap, but he held her in place.

She watched Paige come to Dane's extended arm, kneel up on the bench with the help of his strong tug and smile sweetly into his eyes. Her eyes were bright with love and happiness.

"I thought it was a dream that you camed home," she said.

"No, I'm right here." He hugged her tightly, then kissed her noisily and blew air into her neck until she laughed hysterically.

Paula found herself laughing, unable to resist the infectious giggle.

Finally calming, Paige looked at Paula, apparently not at all upset at finding her in her father's lap. She announced importantly, "Polly starts with a *P.* Like Paige."

"That's right. But my name is really Paula." She enunciated the name clearly.

Paige shook her head. "Daddy said it was Polly." And apparently, that was that. "Chandler starts with a ..." She grimaced and turned to Dane. "What is it?"

"A *C*." He made a half circle of his thumb and index finger. "That one."

"Oh, yeah. That's tricky," she explained to Paula, "'cause it's not the right sound. *Ch* doesn't sound like *C*. What does your last name start with?"

"Mine starts with a *C*, too," Paula replied. "For Cornell."

"Wow!" Paige smiled at Dane, obviously delighted with that knowledge. "Her letters are just like mine."

When he agreed that they were, she got down to business. "What are you eating?" she asked gravely.

He cast a quick, grinning glance at Paula. "Roast beef sandwich. Want a bite?"

She made an ugly face. "Does it have the yucky stuff on it?"

"Horseradish. Yes. You can have a bite of Paula's."

Paula held her sandwich up to the little bow mouth and felt a stab of pain and a curious longing as Paige clamped down on the bread and meat and withdrew a mouthful. How many times had she fed Natalie from her plate just like that? Paige leaned against Dane and chewed mightily.

When she was finished, she told Dane, "She likes to eat things my way, too."

Dane nodded. "Amazing, isn't it?"

"Yeah. Can I have another bite?"

Paula relinquished her sandwich to Dane's daughter and watched and listened with that same feeling of painful pleasure as Paige alternately talked and ate nonstop for half an hour.

She had a strong vocabulary for a four-year-old, Paula noted, a charm she used on her father to great advantage, an inherent sweetness and a wicked little sense of humor.

"Are you sleeping over?" Paige asked Paula, her eyes beginning to close.

Paula glanced worriedly at Dane.

"Yes," he replied. "And speaking of sleeping, it's late and we should all be doing that."

Paula eased off of his lap, and Dane held Paige over his head as he slid out of the booth. Paula began to gather up plates and cups.

"Don't worry about that," Dane said, settling his daughter against his shoulder. She watched Paula over it. "I'll take care of it in the morning."

"I don't mind." Paula carried the stack to the counter and opened the dishwasher. "I'll clean up while you put Paige back to bed."

"I want you to come," Paige said. Even in her sleepy state, the request had the sound of a royal edict. She looked at her father and said, "Tell her she has to come."

Dane turned to Paula, biting back a grin. "You have to come," he said gravely.

Accepting defeat, Paula put everything into the sink, flipped the light off and followed Dane and his daughter up the stairs. Over Dane's shoulder, Paige watched Paula with heavy-lidded blue eyes.

"Daddy can tuck in one side," Paige instructed as Dane placed her in the middle of a single bed covered with a patterned bedspread that matched the drapes, "and Polly can do the other one."

One on each side of the bed, Dane and Paula tucked Paige's blankets.

Paige closed her eyes tightly, her little brow furrowed in the glow of a night-light. "Now you have to kiss me," she said, "and say good-night."

Paula was almost shaking with the effort to be stronger than the pull of her memories. The only thing that helped, she realized, was that the beautiful little martinet waiting for her kiss would be hurt if she ran from the room.

Dane leaned over his daughter and kissed her cheek. "Good night, Poo," he said softly. "I love you."

He straightened and Paula made herself lean down to the child. Her cheek against the goose-down softness of baby skin was almost her undoing. She planted a kiss there and whispered, "Good night, Paige," her voice thick with tears.

"Good night, Polly," Paige replied with a sleepy smile. She opened her eyes and looked into Paula's with that stunningly astute gravity. "Are you gonna cry?" she asked.

"Ah...no," Paula said, quickly swallowing emotion. "I'm sleepy and...my eyes hurt."

She leaned up on an elbow and proposed in concern. "Daddy can tuck you in, too, and sit by your bed. Then you won't feel like crying anymore."

Paula kept her eyes averted from Dane, afraid she'd lose her fingernail grip on control if she did. "That's a good idea," she said.

"Are you gonna stay for breakfast?" Paige asked, leaning back against her pillows.

Paula braced herself. Conversation with this child was fraught with pitfalls. "Yes, I am."

Dane had no idea what was coming next. He moved closer, ready to gently but firmly put a stop to more questions, when Paige hooked an arm around Paula's neck and pulled her closer, whispering something into her ear. Paige giggled, then turned over and snuggled into her pillow.

Paula straightened with a frown of confusion, her face showing signs of strain from the encounter. "Good night, sweetie," she said.

He held the door open for her to pass through. He was beginning to doubt the wisdom of his plan. In his love for Paula, it had seemed to him a relatively simple matter to immerse her in his family for a few days, let her see what special children he had and help her realize she could and should be a mother again.

But he'd failed to realize how close in age Paige was to the daughter Paula had lost, and how the daily contact might remind her of her loss, rather than introduce her to a new future. Had he been wrong?

When she turned to him in the hallway, her eyes large and dark and filled with emotions he couldn't separate and isolate, he still couldn't be sure.

"I'm supposed to ask you," she said, her tension momentarily suspended by a look of confusion, "to make Newberry's pancakes for breakfast. Does that make sense?"

Dane nodded, smiling. "To Paige, it does. She means blueberry pancakes. She's a product of modern consumerism. She knew the name of the dime store before she heard the word blueberry and she still gets them confused." The tension in her took over again, and he put a gentle hand to the back of her head, massaging. He hated himself for causing her pain, however inadvertently. "Would you like that for breakfast? It isn't French toast and champagne, but that'll come, I promise."

Her face crumpled and she took a step forward, wrapping her arms around his middle and leaning her weight against him. He walked her slowly toward his room at the end of the hall.

"I'm sorry," he said softly, sitting her on the edge of the bed. "I hadn't anticipated her putting you through the tucking-in ritual. That was hard, wasn't it?"

"Only because she's so bright and beautiful," Paula wept. "I kept wondering if Natalie would have been like that."

Dane laughed softly, tugging the sweatshirt from her and pulling the blankets back. "Undoubtedly she'd have been more like you and less like me—elegant and cool, rather than brash and bossy."

Dane shed his clothes and crawled in beside her, pulling her close and rubbing warmth and comfort into her back and shoulders. "I suppose this is something like cleaning a wound before stitching it up. It hurts like hell, but it won't heal otherwise."

"I hope I'm strong enough to do this."

"You felled Hailey with your knobby little knee. You can do this."

They lay quietly for a few moments, then Paula remembered something Paige had said. "Have you slept by Paige's bed when she cried?" she asked into the quiet darkness.

"When I first came home from Saudi, she didn't want to sleep and she didn't want me to sleep," Dane replied, his voice hard-edged. "Joyce had taken off while the kids were asleep. She called Sandy and told her she'd just left and that the kids were alone. When they woke up they were with their aunt and uncle and I was halfway across the world."

Paula's eyes filled and spilled over as she imagined Paige's plight.

"Sandy said Paige was remarkably calm, and that she kept telling her that I would be home soon. When I finally did come home, she was afraid she'd fall asleep and wake up and I'd be gone forever, too. I'd rock her to sleep for hours, but the instant I put her down, she'd wake up, screaming for me. I had to sleep sitting up in the chair by her bed so she could hold my hand or my pant leg while she slept."

Paula sniffed. "How did she let you go to take me to the woods?"

"I explained to her," he said, his voice taking on a smile, "that a beautiful lady was in trouble and I had to help her. And I was beginning to see that if I left for a few days and came back, she'd finally realize that even though I might have to leave her for a few days at a time, I'd come back, that I loved her too much to ever leave her forever."

She sighed, the last of the tension leaving her with a little shudder. She kissed his chin. "Whatever happens, I love you, Dane."

He kissed her forehead and squeezed her to him. "I love you, Polly."

He didn't want to give their relationship the leeway of a "whatever happens." He wanted her desperately and forever. He could no longer contemplate life without her. But he kept that to himself. She felt enough pressure from too many sides already.

She sighed contentedly against him, and he leaned his cheek against the top of her head, closing his eyes.

"Dane?" she asked.

"Yeah?"

"You said my hair looked like a camouflage helmet," she said, her tone faintly sulky.

He laughed softly and kissed her again. "I was desperate to make you stay. I knew suggesting your appearance wasn't perfect would keep you from leaving."

"Hmph!" she said lazily, not sounding convinced. "Just now you said my knees were knobby."

"I meant delicate."

"Knobby does not mean delicate. It implies..."

In an instant he knelt astride her, pinning her hands over her head with one hand, his eyes bright and wicked. "I'm about to express very clearly," he said, "how I feel about your hair, your knees and everything above, below and in between. Are you awake enough to pay attention?"

"Well..." she said with exaggerated, grinning reluctance. "Just to make sure I get it straight..."

Either the children had bubonic plague, Paula decided the following morning as she walked into the kitchen, knotting a dark blue terry robe that was huge on her, or Dane had made blueberry pancakes for breakfast.

The purple lower halves of their faces appeared to be a textbook symptom of the first possibility, but their glaring good health as they ran from the table to watch cartoons pointed to the pancakes.

Dane frowned at the robe as she went into his free arm for a kiss. The other hand turned a beautifully browned circle of batter filled with blueberries.

"What happened to the blue sweatshirt?" he asked.

"It isn't decent. Mmm." She looked approvingly over his shoulder.

"Your stuff's already in the dryer," he said, reaching into the oven with a hot pad to pull out a plate stacked with pancakes. He flipped the last one onto it and carried it to the table.

She followed him, smiling indulgently. "For a tough guy," she said, "you're really very domestic."

He kissed her on his way to the refrigerator. "I have everything," he said with exaggerated modesty as he pulled a carton of orange juice from the refrigerator door. "I keep telling you that."

She nodded, sliding into the booth. "I know, but hearing you tell me that and seeing it for myself are two different things."

He smiled as he put the juice on the table and slid in opposite her. "Good. Want to go ring shopping today?"

She gave him a scolding look.

"Okay. Second choice is Disneyland."

"What?"

"Paige asked if we could go to Disneyland," he said, pouring two cups of coffee. "Sounded like a good idea to me. They could use a little excitement in their lives, and God knows you and I need a little lightening up."

"You're recovering from a bullet wound," Paula reminded him.

He shrugged. "I feel fine." His bright eyes and good color seemed to substantiate that claim. Last night hadn't disproved it, either.

Paula frowned at him. "Then why am I here? I'm supposed to be helping you deal with life one-handed."

"You're here," he said, leaning toward her, "because you can't bear the thought of leaving me, and I can't bear the thought of letting you go."

That was true and she knew it. She tried to pretend otherwise. "A multimillion-dollar deal had been suspended, awaiting my convenience, and I'm going to Disneyland?"

The kitchen door burst open and Paige ran in, clad only in pink panties with teddy bears all over them. She had a ruffly white sundress in one hand, and a neon pink shorts set in the other. She came to Paula, asking gravely, "What should I wear?"

Her eyes sparkled with excitement as she awaited an answer. Looking into their bright blue, Paula had difficulty putting the million-dollar deal over Paige's happiness.

"The shorts," Paula said. "The dress is very pretty, but the shorts will be comfortable. Do you have a hat?"

"Yeah. A baseball one."

Paula looked across the table at Dane. "We should put sunscreen on them before we go."

He nodded seriously, smiling to himself. *Gotcha!* he thought. *You're thinking like a mother.*

Sam appeared, also with two choices of what to wear, but without the convention of underwear. He went to Dane and held up a pair of pajamas and a Batman pillowcase.

Dane scooped him onto his lap, wrapping the pillowcase around him. "I don't think you've quite got the idea, Sammy. We'll work on it right after breakfast."

Paige climbed onto her knees on the bench beside Paula. "Will you help me with my hair?" she asked. She smiled across the table at Dane. "Daddy's not very good."

"That's 'cause you're too fussy," Dane said, defending himself while wrestling Sam for the butter knife. "And you lose all your barrettes."

Paula nodded, smiling thoughtfully. "That's a universal problem. I used to buy them in packages of twenty-four."

Sam began to squeal at being deprived of the knife, but Dane expertly stuffed the source of noise with a bite of pancake. "That settles it," Dane said. "Her hair is your responsibility until..." Their eyes met as he hesitated. Neither wanted to consider what he left unsaid.

Paige wrapped both arms around Paula's one and smiled winningly up at her. "Could you hurry?" she asked, indicating her pancakes. "So we can go."

"'IT'S A SMALL WORLD after all, it's a small world after all...'"

Singing at the tops of their lungs as they trudged home up the slate walk after dark, Dane carried Paige and Paula carried Sam, who was fast asleep despite the discordant three-part harmony.

As Dane dug into a pocket for his keys, Paige put a hand over her mouth and giggled. "Your ears are crooked, Daddy," she said, pointing to the rounded mouse-ears hat he wore.

"Your ears are perfect," he said, kissing her cheek.

Paige looked over his shoulder at Paula and smiled sweetly. "Your ears are perfect, too," she said.

Paula curtsied in the shadows as Dane fiddled with the lock one-handed. "Thank you."

Paige stiffened suddenly, her eyes going large with dismay. "My wand!" she said, pushing against Dane's shoulder. "Daddy, I left my..."

"I've got it." Paula produced it from the tote bag slung over her shoulder that had carried extra diapers, cloth wipes, sweaters, animal crackers and the dozens of other things that always traveled with children.

Paige relaxed against Dane's shoulder, touching Paula on the head with the sparkly star at the end of her wand. "Thank you, Polly," she said.

"My pleasure."

Dane opened the door and put the child on her feet. As Paige ran into the house, Dane turned to take Sam from Paula. His eyes were gentle with love. "Thanks," he said.

Paula shrugged a shoulder. "Hey. She can't work magic without it."

"I mean for today. For everything."

She reached up to adjust his hat, her eyes reflecting the love in his. "It truly was my pleasure."

"Hi." Kurt appeared from somewhere inside the house. He looked from Dane's ears to Paula's ears and raised an eyebrow. "Do people grow those when they spend too much time together, or what? I noticed the kids have them, too."

"We've been to Disneyland," Paula said unnecessarily.

"Daddy, Polly, look what Uncle Kurt brought!" Paige ran between the adults, a ball of orange fur wriggling mightily in her arms.

"Peaches!" Paula cried, dropping to her knees to take the cat from Paige. "Oh, Peaches! You're all right. You made it!"

Kurt folded his arms and eyed Dane with dry amusement. "You send me back to scour the wilderness for a cat that led me halfway up a tree then jumped on my head—" he indicated two fresh, livid scratches across his right cheek "—and you went to Disneyland?"

"Dane, look!" Paula raised the cat up for Dane's inspection. Dane reached out to stroke Peaches's head and heard a loud purr issue forth.

"All *right.*" Dane smiled at Kurt. "Yeah," he said, "Thanks."

Paula put the cat on the carpet, then reached up to hug Kurt and kiss his cheek. "Thank you, thank you!" she said emphatically. "I was so worried about him! We didn't see him after the shooting started and we didn't know if he'd been stuck in the cabin or..."

"Look what else Uncle Kurt brought," Paige said, drawing two adults forward, one by each hand.

Paula turned away from Kurt to find herself face-to-face with her father. She shrieked and threw her arms around him, shocked and delighted to see his strong, smiling face. An arm still hooked around him, she reached for her mother, who stood at his side.

"Paula," Barbara Emmett said softly, the word filled with strong emotion and a sort of...welcoming sound Paula was afraid to believe meant what it suggested. Was everything all right between them again?

Paula drew away and looked into her eyes. Her mother's eyes looked into hers a moment, filled with the love that was always there but with a kind of friendship now that had been missing for some time. Then her gaze slid up to the ears perched on Paula's head.

"Funky has never been your style," she said, "but I like it. An earring maybe—" she reached a thumb and forefinger up to loop the side of one round black ear "—right there...and it becomes a fashion statement."

"I thought Paula might feel less inclined to run off," Kurt explained quietly to Dane, "if she could see that her parents were all right."

Dane looked at him, thinking he might have asked him first, or Paula. But he thought he understood what motivated him—what probably always motivated him. It occurred to him that it was possible the outcome of a gesture was never quite as important as the intention that inspired it.

"Thank you," he said. He indicated Paula's beaming face, and her parents' broad smiles. "I'd say you made the right move."

Barbara Emmett suddenly disengaged herself from her daughter and came to put a hand on Dane's free shoulder and reach up on tiptoe to kiss his cheek. The expression in her eyes was complex, but the gratitude was easy to read. "Thank you," she said. "I can't tell you what her father and I owe you."

"In the end, Paula saved herself," Dane said.

Barbara smiled up into his eyes. "I don't believe that's true," she said. "Not at all. Who is this?" She put a hand to Sam's back.

"Sam," Dane replied, resisting when she tried to take the child from him. "He's full of pop, cotton candy, ice cream, caramel corn..."

Barbara insisted. Sam opened one eye halfway, looked suspiciously at the woman looking at him, then apparently decided she didn't pose a sufficient threat to make a fuss. She put him against her shoulder and he went back to sleep.

"I've made coffee," Barbara said, heading back toward the sofas where Paul and Paige were getting acquainted. "I hope you don't mind that we made ourselves at home. When you weren't here when we arrived, the choice was driving all the way back to Kurt's, waiting in the car or coming in. Kurt insisted you wouldn't object."

"Of course not."

"I'm going to be on my way," Kurt said, backing toward the door.

Dane followed him. "Don't you need a cup of coffee first?"

"No, thanks. I just want to get back to Sandy and Nancy."

Dane held out a hand. "Thanks for finding Peaches. And thanks for bringing the Emmetts over."

Kurt looked into his eyes, reading. Dane knew what was there and couldn't change it yet. He was grateful, he was no longer angry, but the rift wasn't completely healed. He was trying, but he needed more time.

Kurt, who seemed to be able to give everyone and everything the time it needed, nodded. "Sure." He pulled the door open. "Oh. Almost forgot. It's Labor Day weekend. Sandy wants to know if you guys want to come over Friday night and stay through. We'll barbecue on the beach, take the boat out if the weather's good." Kurt glanced toward the laughing conversation on the sofa. "Paula will still be here, won't she?"

Dane jammed his hands into his pockets and raised both shoulders in a shrug. "You got me. I hope so, but I can't say. Tell Sandy the kids will love it. We'll come. Hopefully, Paula will, too. Hold up a minute. There's something I almost forgot."

Dane went to Paula's tote and pulled out a large paper sack. He handed it to Kurt. Kurt opened it and looked inside, then up at Dane, grinning. "Three sets of mouse ears?"

"Paige insisted."

Kurt laughed. "Thank her for me. Good night."

"Good night."

Dane went to the sofa that faced Paul, Paula and Paige. Barbara sat in the rocker, humming quietly to a sleeping Sam.

"I suppose Mom doubled her winnings from Kurt," Paula was saying, "when you stayed the extra day in Vegas."

Paul frowned at her. "We didn't stay an extra day. Buck flew us home right after we got word they'd picked up Hailey and that you and Dane were all right."

Paula turned to Dane, her gaze narrowing. He tried to look innocent. "You told me..." she began to accuse quietly.

"I lied," he admitted with no apparent sign of remorse. "If I hadn't, you'd have run home to your parents instead of staying with us as you'd promised."

"That wasn't fair," she insisted.

"Sure it was. Would you rather have missed today?" he asked, his eyes pinning her. And silently they added, *Or last night?*

Bringing into focus only one of the hundreds of memories they'd made the night before melted her indignation and formed a distracted little smile.

"Why don't I put the kids to bed," he said, pushing to his feet, "while you get the coffee your mother made. Sandy usually keeps the cookie jar full."

Paige hugged Paula noisily, then scrambled up into Dane's arm. He winced, shifted her to the other side.

"Does your owie hurt, Daddy?" Paige asked, gently rubbing his shoulder.

"Kurt told us you'd been wounded," Paul said with a frown, getting to his feet. He held his hands out invitingly. "Maybe Paige will let me carry her up."

Paige considered him a moment. "What's your name?" she asked.

"Paul," he replied. "I'm Paula's daddy."

"That starts with a *P*," she said. "Like Paige and Paula." She stretched her arms out to him and confided as he took her onto his hip, "Only 'cept we call her Polly."

"Well, so do I," Paul said, stepping back to let Dane, with Sam over his shoulder, precede them.

Paula and Barbara watched the men head up the stairs, Paige chattering happily as they went.

Barbara put an arm around Paula as they went into the kitchen. "Polly, eh?" she asked.

CHAPTER FOURTEEN

"IT'S JUST A NICKNAME," Paula said, busying herself with taking down cups and finding a plate for cookies. She was conscious of her mother's watchful gaze and carefully avoided it.

"The children are beautiful," Barbara said.

"Aren't they?" Paula checked the cookie jar and found it filled with oatmeal-raisin cookies. She began to arrange them on the plate.

"I didn't know he had children."

"Neither did I."

"Is that why you would have run home to us when he brought you back here?"

Paula looked up, her expression quelling. Barbara looked boldly back into her eyes. "I admire him for making you stay."

"He lied to me," Paula said. The placement pattern of the cookies became more intricate the longer she tried to avoid her mother's eyes.

"He loves you." Barbara leaned against the counter at which Paula worked.

"He just hasn't dropped the bodyguard job yet."

"When he looks at you, one gets the impression you've graduated from a job to his life's work."

"Mom, please," Paula said quietly, reaching for the coffeepot. "This is hard enough as it is."

"What's hard about it?" Barbara persisted. "It looks to me as though you've had a second chance dropped right in your lap."

Paula put a hand to her forehead. "I didn't do very well the first time."

"That's nonsense." Barbara slid aside as Paula reached into the cupboard behind her for sugar bowl and creamer. "You're just playing with him, then?"

Paula gave her mother an annoyed glance. "Of course not."

"Then why are you here?"

"Because my home no longer exists," Paula reminded her, "and he told me you and Daddy stayed in Vegas."

"Darling, I know you," Barbara said with a wry smile. "If you didn't want to be here, you wouldn't be. It's all right to love him, you know. It's all right to love his children and to—" she hesitated, drawing a breath before going on "—to hold Natalie in your heart, but let the reality of her slip into the past where she now belongs. Kurt told us a little about Dane's first wife. These children need a loving mother. He deserves a loving wife."

"Every child needs a loving mother," Paula said, glancing at Barbara significantly as she put everything on a tray. "A mother who understands and tolerates her child's failings. And who'll mind her own business."

"Mothers aren't produced by cookie cutter," Barbara said, following Paula as she headed for the living room with the tray. "We all have our own particular bag of gifts, hang-ups, strengths and failings. But our job is to be there anyway, not to run away when the job becomes difficult—or the child."

SAM HAD BEEN TRANSFERRED from his father's shoulder to his crib without waking. As Dane and Paul left Paige's room, the night-light gleamed on the mouse ears worn by the teddy bear on her toy chest.

"Beautiful children," Paul said as he and Dane walked down the corridor.

"Thank you," Dane replied.

Paul pulled him to a stop at a deacon's bench halfway to the stairs. "I'd like to talk for a minute."

Dane nodded, waiting for the older man to sit before taking his place beside him. He wondered with a private smile if Paul Emmett had ever been in the military. He had a way of posing questions as statements and leaving little doubt about the answers he expected.

"You're almost ten years younger than my daughter," Paul said without preamble, keeping his voice down. Quiet feminine conversation could be heard downstairs.

Dane smiled openly now. Paul Emmett was his kind of man; no preparatory small talk, no careful approach to the issue.

"I'm older than I look," Dane replied. "And it never mattered to me. I think it's stopped mattering to her."

Paul frowned, and Dane knew he was hurting for his daughter. "You know about Natalie?"

"Yes."

"She was a good mother. The best."

"I never doubted that for a minute."

"You know about Bill?"

"Only that he's a lawyer in Taos."

Paul looked him full in the face. "He thought he loved Paula. But he didn't understand what she needed. She drove him away and he went. She needed him to fight her—she needed him to make her understand it wasn't her fault.''

Dane returned his steady gaze. "I haven't been able to make her understand that, either. But she's coming around a little. A couple of days ago she wouldn't even have considered being in the same room with a four-year-old girl, but today she had one or the other of my kids in her arms or in her lap most of the time.''

Paul nodded, a small smile forming. "I saw the difference in her when you walked in the door. She's in love with you.'' The smile disappeared and was replaced by a frown. "I couldn't stand to see her hurt again.''

"I love Paula, Mr. Emmett,'' Dane said gravely. "Believe me when I tell you I'd die before I ever hurt her deliberately.''

Paul considered him a moment, then put a hand to his shoulder. "Thank you for the lengths you went to to keep her safe from Hailey. There are no words to tell you how grateful Barbara and I are.''

"I don't need them,'' Dane said. "It wasn't long before her life became more important to me than my own.''

Paul offered his hand as they stood. "Then, good luck with her. She's a stubborn woman.''

Dane shook his hand, smiling. "Gets that from her mother, no doubt.''

Paul narrowed his gaze on Dane, looking at him with new interest. "You ever consider acting?''

Dane blinked, then laughed. "No. I've got my eye on a hardware store in Oregon.''

Paul frowned. "Oregon? You mean you're going to take her away from us?''

"I'm going to try,'' Dane admitted without apology.

Paul continued to frown, then finally smiled reluctantly. "You don't have the least doubt you can make her happy, do you?"

Dane looked at him as they started down the stairs. "No, not if she'll let me."

Paul put an arm around his shoulders and laughed. "My money's on you, son," he said.

Paula watched Dane and her father come down the stairs, sharing a companionable laugh. Instinctively she knew her father had cross-examined him and been pleased with the results. *God,* she thought worriedly. *Three against one.*

"YOU SHOULD HAVE let them go to a motel," Paula said into the darkness, hands behind her head on the pillow as she stared at the ceiling.

"That wouldn't have been very hospitable." Dane lay on his side of the bed, biding his time. She was angry with him because he'd invited her parents to stay the night despite her pleading glances to the contrary, and they'd accepted.

"Daddy has arthritis."

"The sofa bed is very comfortable. You're just upset because they like me."

She turned onto her side and propped up on one elbow. "I'm upset because you keep pushing me into things over which I have no control."

"If you'll recall," he said patiently, "Kurt brought your parents here without my knowledge. And if you want control, take it. Tell your parents to go home. Leave in the morning for your deal with Ferrante and take the damned cruise. If you want to settle for half a life, do it."

"I'm just trying to be sensible," she whispered harshly.

"Sensible," he repeated doubtfully. "You'll have to explain that one to me."

She sighed. "The timing's wrong, Dane. You haven't even reached your prime, and I'm..."

"Beginning to decay," he said wryly, "I know."

"Your sarcasm isn't helping."

"I'm sorry. Do go on."

"We're both too vulnerable now to make far-reaching decisions," she said stiffly, fiddling with the blanket binding.

"In the military," he said, "you wait too long to make a decision and, one way or another, it's made for you."

"This isn't war," she said.

He shook his head in the darkness. The hell it wasn't.

"When you're in love," he said, trying another tack, "you're always vulnerable. Do you then just put decisions off indefinitely?"

Paula punched her pillow and lay on her stomach, turning her head away from him. "Go to sleep. You're obviously not willing to listen to reason."

"You mean I'm not willing to agree with you, to let you make a negative decision for both of us."

She propped up on both elbows leaning over him to whisper angrily, "And who's been making the decisions for both of us for the past week?"

He reached up to clear the hair from her face. "That was because your life was in danger," he said, "not because I was trying to protect myself from you."

"Maybe I'm trying to protect you from yourself," she said.

He twined his hand in her hair and in a swift movement she never suspected, he reversed their positions, pulling her down to the pillow and leaning over her. "I'll look after myself, thank you very much. I'm looking for a wife and a lover in this relationship, not a big sister."

A tear glistened on her cheek in the darkness, startling him. He freed her hair, afraid he'd inadvertently hurt her.

"I'm afraid," she whispered, wrapping her arms around his neck and pulling him down to her, "it's...it's too perfect."

"Paula," he scolded tenderly. "Stop punishing yourself. You deserve to be happy." He lay beside her and pulled her into his shoulder, stroking her hair back, feeling the tears on his hand. He held her close, kissing the top of her head. "If it's any comfort to you, I'm far from perfect. My kids are far from perfect. I'm sure we'll drive you crazy more often than not, but we need you and we love you."

"When you've been needed and loved, and then you aren't," she said, tipping her head back to look into his face, "being offered those things again *is* perfect."

"Then why are you thinking twice?"

Because she didn't want to fail him and his children. Leaning into him and all the love he offered, Paula prayed she had what it took to take a second chance. "You're sure?" she asked.

His heart lurched. She felt it.

"I'm positive," he said.

She smiled up at him. "Then, will you marry me?"

He answered her with a kiss that erased all her doubts and insecurities, and made her wonder why she'd ever hesitated in the first place.

A CHANDLER SECURITIES CAR came for Paul and Barbara two days later.

Dane insisted they were welcome to stay longer, but Paul was just as insistent that he had several projects to take care of at home before the studio called him back to work at the end of the following week.

"We'll be expecting you to stay with us," Paul said, hugging Paula, "when you come back to L.A. to tie things up with Ferrante."

"Thanks, Dad." Paula hugged her mother, then leaned down to wave as they climbed into the back of the car. "I'll probably be coming early next week. If you get the deck finished, I'll help you stain it."

Barbara leaned out to blow Dane and the children a kiss. "Seems as though we're always leaving her in your care. I can't believe one day soon we'll be doing it permanently."

They'd taken the news of Paula's decision with more excitement than surprise. Paula felt sure her mother had known she'd give in before she had. Her father just seemed relieved.

"If your hardware store deal falls through," Paul said, "remember I can get you a job on Phantom Lake. Just say the word."

Dane laughed and pulled Paige and Sam back as the driver closed the back door and Paul opened the window.

"Thanks, but I don't think all that angst is for me. Take care."

They waved as the car pulled away from the curb, then turned at the corner and disappeared from view. Paula hooked her arm in Dane's and drew a deep breath, her mood a strange mixture of excitement and terror.

Dane kissed the side of her neck and the terror receded.

"Did I remember to tell you you're supposed to make a potato salad and bake a cake for the barbecue?" he asked, turning her to lead her lazily back up the walk, the children running ahead of them.

Her arm looped around his waist, she looked up at him in puzzlement. "You forgot to tell me about the barbecue. What barbecue?"

"Kurt and Sandy have invited us for the weekend."

"Where?"

"They live just beyond Santa Monica in a quiet little cove."

She stopped him in the middle of the flagstone walk. "Does this mean the two of you are friends again?"

"I'm trying," he replied.

"Good." She took his face in her hands and made him look into her eyes. "If you want me to forget, then you have to, too. Forgive, and forget. The world's too full of guilt and grudges. If we're going to do this, then let's clean everything up. No little dark pockets anywhere. Just love. Lots of love."

He pulled her to him in the bright afternoon sunshine, feeling the heat of it on her back, in her hair, on his face. He almost couldn't believe she had happened to him: that the life that had looked so bleak just a year ago was now so promising.

"I love you more than I could ever tell you," he said softly.

She drew back to smile into his eyes. "Then find another way to show me."

He leaned forward to kiss her, finding it difficult to resist the impulse to make love to her right there in the nasturtiums. "We've got two nosy little kids now probably sitting in front of the television."

"I can wait until they go to bed," she said, nibbling his bottom lip. "Anticipation only heightens the final experience. Didn't you know that?"

As they walked arm in arm into the house, he tried to believe it. But he suspected he'd be dead of anticipation by dinner.

"MY GOD." Paula brought the stroller containing Sam and a sack of groceries to an abrupt halt on the concrete walk that ran around the house to the beach side. "The girls have decapitated their fathers."

Sandy shaded her eyes to look toward the bright blankets on the beach where they'd all spent most of the afternoon until the sudden realization that they were out of microwave popcorn sent Paula and Sandy to the store. Dane's body was completely covered in sand, only his head visible.

With a determination that would have been worrisome had they not been giggling so hard, Nancy and Paige swept and patted sand onto Kurt's shoulders, the only part of his body that remained uncovered.

After two days in the company of Dane's little niece, Paula had learned she was curious about everything, and virtually fearless—a singularly terrifying combination. And Paige adored her, following eagerly into every adventure Nancy conceived. Paula had been watching them like a hawk all weekend.

"That's all right," Sandy said philosophically. "They're insured. We'll just say they were attacked by terrorists."

Paula laughed. "As long as we can collect."

"No problem."

"Daddy! Daddy!" Sam, spotting his father and sister, stood up in the stroller, pointing urgently to Paula as he bounced up and down.

Paula untied the safety belt and put him on his feet. He ran unsteadily toward the little crowd, giggling excitedly.

Dane spotted them and shouted, "Help! Polly!"

Kurt, his Chandler Securities baseball cap on his head, turned in their direction. "Sandy!" he called. "Sandy, help!"

Paula started forward, but Sandy held her back.

"Don't you think they're kind of pathetic?" Paula asked. "The girls have been running them ragged for two days now. They probably couldn't fight their way out of that sand if they wanted to."

"Trust me," Sandy said enigmatically, folding her arms. "I know what I'm doing." Across the sandy beach, she called, "Yes, dear?"

"Sandy!" Kurt said, exasperated. "Get over here!"

"But, darling, I have dinner to prepare."

"You can do that later!" When she didn't respond, he added, "Dane will help you."

Dane's surprised voice as he turned to Kurt carried to Paula on the late-afternoon breeze. "*I'll* help her? What's the matter with you?"

"All right, *I'll* help you," Kurt shouted. "Sandy?"

Sandy smirked at Paula. "Now we're getting somewhere." To Kurt, she shouted, "Just how will you help me?"

"I'll make the drinks!" Kurt replied desperately as the girls patted sand around his throat.

Sandy looked bored. "Big deal. We have Bloody Mary mix."

"I'll barbecue the steaks!"

"Dane always does that."

He choked as sand flew around his face. "I'll toss the salad."

Sandy grabbed Paula's arm and turned her and the stroller toward the house.

"Wait!" Kurt shouted. "We'll clean up!"

Again, Dane turned to him. *"We?"*

Sandy changed directions, leading Paula toward the men and the children. "Am I good at this, or what?" she asked on a low giggle.

Paula patted her hand. "You're an inspiration."

DANE WATCHED the women coming toward them and felt emotion rise to lodge in his throat. He had never imagined he could be this happy. He'd actually begun to believe that the loving, devoted wives other men had, the close families that enjoyed being together, were something fate had chosen to deny him. Now he was being handed everything—absolutely everything. He was almost afraid to believe it.

"All right, girls," Sandy said, walking around Dane's mounded feet to examine Kurt's incapacity with detached interest. "That's enough. Time to get washed up for dinner."

Nancy pointed to the ocean. "We were in the water most of the time."

"That water isn't clean," Sandy reasoned.

Nancy frowned up at her. "We eat the fish that come out of it."

Sandy hesitated only a moment. "But we cook them first."

Nancy looked at her hands. "I don't look dirty."

"No, but you do look like you're going to go to bed right after dinner if you don't do as I say."

Nancy, sitting on her father's mounded chest, turned to him for support. "Do you think I look dirty?"

"Germs are invisible," Kurt said. "Go wash your hands."

Dane coughed as Sam and Paige poured sand into his hair and giggled as it streamed onto his face. "And take your cousins with you," he suggested.

"We didn't get to go out in the boat yet," Nancy stated grumpily.

Kurt groaned dramatically.

"Daddy promised tomorrow if the weather's nice," Sandy said, pulling her off Kurt's chest and pushing her toward the house. "Go on now. I'll be right behind you."

As the children ran in the direction of the house, Kurt rose out of the sand, arms curled and threatening as he growled at Sandy. "The Teenage Mutant Ninja Sand Crab is going to get you. Wa-ha-ha-ha-ha!" he threatened in a deep voice.

She looked up at him, arms folded over her protruding stomach, as he loomed over her. She grinned.

"I happen to have a thing for mutant sand crabs. Not teenagers, though. I like the ones that know their way around..." She waggled her eyebrows. "If you know what I mean?"

He dropped the threatening pose and put an arm around her. "Oh, I do, I do," he said, drawing her toward the house. "You should watch that, though," he said, patting her tummy. "I'll bet that's just the kind of attitude that got you in the trouble you're in."

"Guys? Guys!" Dane called as his brother and sister-in-law walked across the sand, oblivious to his call. "Hey, Kurt! I happen to be stuck here!"

"Poor thing," Paula said, sinking to her knees beside him. She reached out to brush sand from his face. "Maybe there's something I could do for you."

The look in her eyes alerted him. "You could get me out of here," he said, fairly certain that was not her intention.

She sat back on her heels. "I could," she said. "But the girls worked so hard to bury you, it's kind of a shame to just obliterate their hard work."

"No, it's not," he said. "Tomorrow they can do you. Or they could do Sandy. Now there's a challenge."

Paula shook her head scoldingly. "That'll cost you, Chandler." She began to brush at the sand in the vicinity of his waist. "If I tell her you said that, she'll make your life..."

"What's your price?" Dane asked, his entire body suddenly awake to the playful look in her eyes.

She widened them in bland innocence. "Price? Why, what a tawdry suggestion." She now worked on the sand at his waist with both hands. He could feel her fingertips through the sliding grains. He had to concentrate on control. "I wasn't thinking in terms of material things, I was more in mind of acquiring certain... liberties...."

Liberties. He liked the sound of that, but still—it wasn't very clear. "What... liberties, precisely?"

She braced an arm on the other side of his waist, sidling right up beside him so that he felt her hip against the side of his.

"I happen to know," she said, baring a patch of skin just above his hipbone on his left side with a last swipe of her hand. "That you're very ticklish..." She blew on the spot, presumably to clear away the last few grains of sand.

"Polly," he warned.

"Right about..."

"Poll."

"Here, I think." She scraped her fingernails with agonizing gentleness just above the line of his trunks.

"Or maybe it's just a little lower?" The tips of her fingers dipped into the waistband.

"If anyone comes along," he said, his voice sounding strained, "you can explain what's going on."

She looked up to check just that possibility. Their little cove was very private, but beach strollers did happen by now and then. He took advantage of her distraction to roll them both over, showering her with the sand that had covered him.

She lay pinned, one eye closed against the sand in her face, the other accusing. "You were stuck, huh?"

He swept a hand up the wide leg of her shorts, into the tap leg of her panties.

"Dane!" she shrieked, then quickly lowered her voice, remembering that though she hadn't seen anyone, this would be the moment fate would send some hapless sunbather on a stroll. "We could be seen!"

A slight inclination of his hand found what he was after. She groaned, trying to sit up. His other hand on her shoulder kept her firmly pinned.

"We could have been seen just an instant ago when you were toying with me."

His other hand moved and her cry became a little higher, a little more desperate. "What... what's your price?" she whispered.

"An early night," he said. "No card playing until 3:00 a.m. with Sandy."

"But she has trouble sleeping," Paula explained.

His hand moved again and she shuddered, capitulating. "Okay, okay. I'll plead a headache at nine o'clock."

"Nine-fifteen," he said, releasing her. "We don't want to be too obvious." With a firm yank, he pulled her to her feet. She slammed into his arms, into his lips with all the desire he lived with on a daily basis, growing stronger every day.

"I'm going to kill you," she said, even while she held his face and dipped her tongue into his mouth.

He couldn't wait.

CHAPTER FIFTEEN

PAULA AWOKE clinging to the side of the bed. It was still dark, and something pushed against her back and hips, threatening to dump her on the carpet.

"Dane!" she whispered. "You're hogging the bed!"

"Guess again," he said. He sounded far away.

Paula reached behind her cautiously and found a pair of matchstick legs. No, three of them. Three? There was a snuffle, a stir, the mattress heaved and suddenly there were four small legs within reach of her hand. She felt the definite imprint of a foot against her spinal column.

"I can't move," she said. "I have four feet in my back."

"I know," came Dane's quiet reply. "I've got the heads in my chest. We've had a thunderstorm and we got company. Just a minute."

She felt movement behind her, little baby sounds, then Dane's caution in an undertone, "You can turn around if you don't fling anything."

She turned cautiously, to find Sam and Paige between them, their blond heads bright in the darkness. Dane reached along the pillow to stroke her hair. "If you're very uncomfortable I can move them. They probably won't even wake up."

"No, it's all right." She laced her fingers with Dane's, kissed his knuckles and sighed contentedly. Sam turned into his father's chest, snoring gently.

Thunder clapped and Paige whimpered. Paula stroked her hair, shushing her. She leaned into her and went back to sleep.

DANE AWOKE to an empty bed. He sat up guiltily, thinking that Paula had done all the early-morning chores this weekend. She'd gotten up with the kids, seen that Sam was dry, helped Sandy get breakfast.

She'd insisted she hadn't minded, that she had to adjust to his household routines, and so he'd let her. It hadn't been so much that he'd enjoyed the break, although that had been true. But he found such pleasure in watching her with his children, doing the little things Joyce had done in the beginning and then lost interest in when she'd lost interest in him.

Paula seemed to enjoy them so much, and the children soaked up her affection greedily and returned it eagerly.

It was looking as though he was really going to pull this off.

He pulled clothes on and went down to breakfast. Rain pounded against the kitchen windows where Sandy and Paula sat at the table over coffee. Kurt waved a good-morning from the telephone at the corner of the counter.

At the other end of the long room, his children watched cartoons, while Nancy stared disconsolately out at the rain.

"Daddy said we can't take the boat out if it's raining," she grumbled at Dane. "How come?"

"Because you get all wet," he said, smiling at her as he poured coffee. "It isn't any fun."

"You get all wet when you swim," she reasoned.

Dane went to kiss his children good-morning, and to hug the grumpy Nancy. "We'll just have to find another way to have fun today."

Nancy looked at him doubtfully and continued to stare out the window.

"Don't try to placate her," Sandy said, pushing a plate of doughnuts toward him as he joined her and Paula at the table. "Her highness is in a royal snit. Here, we saved you a cinnamon twist."

He frowned at the plate. "I don't like cinnamon twists."

"I know." She smiled, trying to hand him something with pink frosting and nuts. He shook his head. "You like apple fritters and maple bars. Unfortunately so do Polly and I. There just weren't enough to go around. You're not going to go into a royal snit, too, are you?"

Dane shook his head and reached for a plain doughnut, looking from Sandy's to Paula's grin with an air of supreme disappointment. "Don't give it another thought. I'll just eat this dry old thing."

Kurt hung up the phone and came to the table to sit across from him, his eyes clouded and distracted.

"Morning," Dane said.

Kurt focused on him with obvious difficulty. "Good morning." Then he seemed to slip back into his thoughts.

"Something wrong?"

Kurt focused on him again, then leaned back in his chair. "That was my attorney. He wants to know what I want him to do about Harriman."

"What are you going to do about him?"

"It wasn't his fault," Paula said, topping off Kurt's coffee. "Hailey had threatened his daughter."

Dane turned to her with a frown. "He almost got you killed, Polly."

"But I'm still here," she insisted, "and I can understand his reluctance to cross those creeps."

"When anyone joins my company," Kurt said, "he signs an agreement that if he's ever threatened or bribed, he's to report it immediately. It's the only way I can offer the best protection possible."

Paula shrugged. "He was in an understandable panic. I think you should give him another chance."

Dane, who had a vivid memory of Hailey with a fistful of the front of Paula's shirt and a .357 Magnum pointed at her temple, took a sip of coffee and chose not to comment.

Kurt ran a hand over his face and said heavily, "I should have the book thrown at me for having allowed that to happen."

Paula and Sandy looked at him in surprise. Dane frowned at him. "You didn't *allow* it to happen. Someone you trusted reacted in a way you couldn't have anticipated."

"I'm suppose to prepare for the unforeseen," Kurt insisted. "That's my job."

"That's ridiculous," Dane said. "You set up the whole operation so that it should have been foolproof. But life is full of things that don't go according to plan. You're not to blame here. Harriman is."

"I hired him." Kurt's eyes darkened and filled with fear, and Dane saw at last what was at the bottom of his self-imposed guilt. "I almost got you killed."

Dane shook his head. "Harriman almost got us killed. Anyway, a miss is as good as a mile."

"I made a mistake."

Dane slapped a hand on the table. The crockery jumped and Sandy and Paula blinked. "I don't think that's true in this case," he said, "but if it were, you've got lots of company. In fact, it runs in the family. I married Joyce. You can be excused a personnel error."

It took a moment for everyone to realize what he'd admitted. He looked into Kurt's surprised expression and finally realized it himself—and felt the cleansing effect of owning up to stupidity and moving on.

"You can even be excused," he went on, looking into his eyes, finding all the old ties there that had pulled him through most of the crises in his life, and anchored him in good times and bad, "doubtful judgment in making my decisions for me."

Kurt swallowed, then glanced at Sandy, as though needing corroboration that he understood what he'd heard. "Could you make that clearer?" he finally asked.

"Sure." Dane leaned an elbow on the back of his chair and said, straight-faced, "You're an interfering, meddlesome pain in the..." Dane hesitated, remembering the children.

"Yes," Kurt said. "Go on."

"But you probably define the word 'brother,' and in deference to all you've put up with from me, and all you mean to me..." He hesitated, his throat tightening. He reached to the doughnut plate. "I present you with this pink thing as a symbol of peace and harmony."

Kurt looked at it doubtfully. "I'm...touched."

"Yes, I know," Dane retorted, pouring himself more coffee. "That accounts for a lot."

Kurt broke the doughnut in half, handing a piece to Dane.

Dane smiled. "No, thanks."

"It's like a peace pipe," Paula said, elbowing him. "You both have to smoke it. Or, in this case, eat it."

"But it's pink."

"Contrary to what most men think," Sandy said, leaning sideways to plant a kiss on Kurt's cheek, "pink doesn't kill. I had one of those. The frosting is buttercream flavored."

Dane turned to her. "You ate the fritters, the maple bars *and* a pink doughnut?"

She patted her round tummy. "I have an excuse."

"An excuse that's going to stay with you," he warned, "long after the baby's born."

He bit the half doughnut in half, chewed, grimaced, drank coffee and frowned at his brother, who still held his entire half. "Your turn."

"I was going to wait a few minutes to see if you survive."

"Nice guy. Eat it!"

"I WAS BEGINNING to think things would never be like they were again," Sandy said, stirring a bubbling pot of spaghetti sauce.

Paula tore lettuce into a large stainless-steel bowl and turned to smile happily. "Did you ever see such a fuss over a doughnut?"

"They were able to hide their feelings behind the dumb doughnut," Sandy said, tasting. Satisfied, she put the spoon aside and pulled a loaf of French bread down from the top of the refrigerator. "And I doubt seriously that it took two of them to run to town for a bottle of Chianti. I think they just need to talk. When I married Kurt, I'd never seen brothers as close as they were. They were all each other knew of family." She reached into the drawer for a long knife and wielded it threateningly. "Joyce was poison. Before we got married, Kurt told me how much he mistrusted his brother's wife. I suppose you know Kurt was going with her when Dane came home on leave?"

Paula nodded.

"Kurt had just been laid off from a little suburban police force because of budget cuts, and Dane had just gotten a promotion and a raise in pay. She dropped Kurt, and Dane fell like a ton of bricks. Once he married her, all she did was complain and spend money and flirt. Actually, 'flirt' is an insipid word for what she did toward the end."

Paula glanced to the sofa near the television where Sam was asleep under a red plaid blanket. Upstairs, the girls' giggles and shouts could be heard from Nancy's room.

Knowing the men had gone off, content in each other's company, that the children were safe and happy while rain fell outdoors, and that Sandy was sharing family confidences with her made her feel like a Chandler. The domestic harmony was everything she'd ever wanted.

"You gave Dane a life again," Sandy said.

Paula pulled tomatoes, green onions and radishes out of a plastic bag. "Before Dane," she admitted, able to feel within herself how long ago that was, "I didn't care if I lived or died."

Sandy looked up from slicing the bread, her eyes grave. "Kurt told me about your little girl. I'm sorry."

Paula sighed. "Thank you. I... She's sometimes still so alive to me. Paige and Sam have given me a place to put all the love I still wake up with every day."

Sandy grinned as she went to the refrigerator for butter. "If you have any left over, I'll be glad to send you Nancy for a few days."

Paula laughed. "Now there's a child to challenge your parenting skills."

"It's the Chandler genes," Sandy said, waddling back to the bread. "They're all smart and stubborn and like things their own way. I presume you've noticed that."

"Oh, yes."

"And you're going to marry him, anyway."

Paula smiled thoughtfully. "The killer is, that the things he wants to have his way are always things he wants for me."

Sandy nodded. "That's what makes them irresistible. It's hard to fight a man who always has your best interests at heart."

Paula frowned at her in concern. "It doesn't worry you that I'm older?"

Sandy looked up and down Paula's slender body in jeans and sweater and sighed defeatedly. "It worries me that you're perfect."

She stopped in the process of unwrapping a butter cube and looked up at the ceiling, frowning. "It also worries me that it's suddenly so quiet."

Paula stopped chopping green onions to listen. There was not a sound upstairs—not a footstep, or a bump, or a giggle.

"I'll go check," she volunteered, sure the girls had finally just slipped into some quiet endeavor after a long day of trying to remain occupied inside.

She cleared the top of the stairs and walked into the bedroom the children shared, stopping several steps inside when she found it empty. A board game and its playing pieces littered the floor, and dolls and stuffed animals covered the bed.

She checked Kurt and Sandy's bedroom across the hall then the room she shared with Dane. No little girls.

Forcing herself to remain calm, she ran downstairs. They had to be hiding. Paige loved to do that. Then she would jump out at her, yelling, "Surprise."

Sandy met her in the middle of the living room, wiping her hands on the white apron that dangled from her neck because she could no longer tie it around her ample girth. Seeing no children trailing her, she went to the window. "Where on earth could they have gone? It's raining cats and dogs, and it's time for cartoons... Oh, my God!"

Paula, checking the front porch where they sometimes made a fort of the card table set up in one corner, heard the distress in Sandy's voice and went cold. She ran inside as Sandy ran out the back door, shouting, "Nancy!"

Paula followed her and felt her heart stop at the sight of Nancy and Paige untying the little boat from the dock. The wind threw Sandy's call back in her face, and she started down the stairs to the sand, holding the railing as she tried to hurry.

Paula ran past her, shouting, "Paige, come back here! Nancy!" They won't be able to work the knot, she told herself. They're just tiny, little girls and that's thick, heavy rope. Then she watched in horror as the thick stuff slipped right off the piling as the girls pushed and pulled together.

The boat drifted away almost immediately. Hand in hand the girls jumped for it and fell short.

In a kind of disbelieving daze, Paula heard Sandy's scream from somewhere behind her as she trudged, heavy and awkward, across the sand. Then she heard her own disbelieving cry of fear and anguish. *This can't be happening again,* she thought as she ran into the water. *Not again. Please, not again.*

Already drenched from the rain, she barely noticed the water as she ran waist deep in it, then stretched out to swim. In a kind of horror that seemed to exist apart from the body in which she methodically reached and pulled and kicked, reached and pulled and kicked, she saw two little heads bobbing at a distance from her that she didn't seem able to close.

Little voices screamed, little hands flailed the air, heads bobbed up and disappeared.

She heard herself praying. "Oh, God, oh, God!" she said over and over, her ability to think now so thin she decided He understood what she wanted and she didn't have to be specific. "I'm coming!" she shouted at the girls. "Kick your feet and keep your chin out of the water!"

She reached and pulled and kicked, the distance still seeming no smaller than it had been before. She reached longer, pulled harder, kicked with all the waning energy she had, all the time praying, "Oh, God. Oh, God. Oh, God."

She reached Paige first, gathering her into her arms, trying to stop her hysterical sobs long enough to give her brief instructions.

"We have to get Nancy," she said, holding her away as the child tried to clutch at her. "You're going to swim on my back and hold my neck, okay?"

"No," she wept, trying to put her arms around her. "Hold me!"

"After," Paula promised, keeping an eye on Nancy who went under several yards away. Firmly she swung Paige behind her, pulled her little arms around her neck and kicked off. Paige held tight, screaming in her ear.

She had Nancy in seconds, feeling a relief so great she was afraid for a minute she might faint and sink all three of them. Then she became aware of the combined effects of near panic and a body covered in heavy denim and cotton knit in water over her head.

A screaming little girl in each arm, she kicked to keep them afloat and tried desperately to devise a plan to get them all back to shore with a body that didn't feel as though it could even make it on its own.

"EVEN IF YOUR OFFER on the hardware store is accepted," Kurt said, shifting the grocery bag he carried as he and Dane turned onto the beach walk, "you could still work for me from time to time on special cases."

"Maybe," Dane said, switching the six-pack of beer to his other hand. "I'll talk to Paula about it. What you ought to do is move Chandler Securities headquarters to Oregon where the air is clean and there are still trees."

"Actually we've talked about—" Kurt stopped in his tracks, frowning at the sight of his pregnant wife standing on the shoreline and screaming at the water. "What the hell is going on?"

Dane narrowed his gaze and spotted the drifting boat and the odd little clump in the water. "Oh, God," he said, dropping the six-pack. "It's Paula and the kids." He started running. Kurt followed with a whispered epithet.

Dane stopped long enough to pull off his shoes. Sandy was now in the water up to her knees, and Kurt ordered her back to the sand as he kicked off his espadrilles.

Dane ran into the water until it reached his chest. He leapt forward into a strong crawl stroke, fighting the fear that tried to inch away his competence and his sanity. Kurt swam beside him with the same grim concentration.

They were only yards away, but Paula had her back to them and couldn't see them coming. He shouted, but she couldn't hear him over the screams of the girls. Unable to swim with a child in each arm, she seemed to be trying to kick toward the boat, but it was drifting away, out of reach.

Beyond them, a wave bulged and grew, and she turned away from it. He heard her shout at the girls to hold on tight and take a big breath.

PAULA TURNED HER BACK on the wave and waited with a prayer for it to crash over them and push them closer to shore. She would worry about the backwash later. Maybe she'd get close enough in to throw one of the girls toward Sandy.

Then she saw how far they were from shore, that they'd even left the dock far behind. It was a stupid idea. They'd never make it. She was going to die with a little girl in each arm, and Dane...

The water hit them with shoving, rolling force. She held desperately to Paige and Nancy as the wave spun them over and over. Her lungs burned as she struggled to right herself. The girls clutched at her, their legs instinctively wrapping around her, preventing her from guiding herself out of the water.

"Oh, God," she prayed. "Oh, God. Please!"

Then strong hands grabbed her and she rose out of the water, the girls still attached to her, as if she were some less-than-exotic Venus.

She sputtered and choked while the girls were taken from her, their screams renewed now that they could breathe. She finally cleared her eyes sufficiently to see Dane supporting her, Paige in his other arm. Kurt held Nancy. Had Dane not been holding her, she thought she might have fainted from relief and drowned after all.

She smiled at him, letting her forehead fall for a moment against his shoulder. "Hi," she said between gasps for air.

Kurt looked over his shoulder at the drifting boat. "Hold on to Nancy," he said, passing her to Dane. "And we can all have an easy ride back to the dock."

He kicked off and swam to the boat, hauled himself into it, yanked on the cord until the motor growled, then expertly turned it and chugged back to his waiting passengers.

Dane passed the children up, then Paula, then she and Kurt pulled him in. The brief trip to the pier was silent, except for the sound of the motor.

On the pier, Sandy greeted them with blankets and towels. Nancy screamed anew in her mother's arms, her fear, Paula guessed, having more to do with the look on her father's face than her experience in the water.

Paige simply clung to Dane in white-faced silence.

"Where's Sam?" Dane asked suddenly.

"Fast asleep on the sofa," Sandy replied, on her knees, rubbing at Nancy with a towel. "I checked him when I ran in for the blankets and towels."

"What in the hell happened?" Kurt demanded.

"Let's talk about it inside," Sandy replied. "We need to get the kids and Polly in a hot shower."

In moments, Sandy had taken both little girls into the bath off the master bedroom, and Paula was under the comforting warmth of the shower's spray. The water washed away the adrenaline-pumping tension of the past half hour, but it couldn't touch the fear that had taken hold deep inside and wouldn't let her go. She had almost let it happen again.

Dane hadn't said a word to her. But she'd seen the anger in his eyes and she didn't blame him for it. She'd been chatting with Sandy and enjoying her new status in his family, when she should have been watching his children. Consequently, Paige and Nancy had almost drowned.

The eagerness for life she'd developed in the past few days slid away from her like the clothes she'd shed to get into the shower. With the realization that she couldn't have life with Dane, everything else lost importance. The beautiful future that had stretched out before her shining with potential crumpled in on itself and disappeared.

Paula allowed herself a moment to mourn it, then turned off the taps, knowing the men awaited their turns to shower and that Sandy would need help with the children.

She drew in a ragged breath when she saw Dane waiting beyond the shower door, holding a large, fluffy bath towel. He wore that same grave expression.

DANE THOUGHT he'd never seen anything as beautiful as Paula, wet from the shower, her eyes wide and uncertain, her slender body perfect and *safe*. God, he wouldn't relive the last half hour for anything. He'd rate that as more frightening than any close call he'd ever had in the military, and that included times when he'd been shelled and shot at.

He draped the towel on Paula and pulled her to him, closing the ends of it and his arms around her. "Thank you," he whispered into her neck. "Thank you."

"Are the girls okay?" she asked in a voice made rough by the water she'd swallowed.

"Paige is all right. I chewed her out, but I think the whole thing scared her so much she'll probably be an angel—for a few days, anyway. Nancy might not have gotten off so easily. Kurt and Sandy were shouting at each other in their bedroom over how to handle it." Aware suddenly of how quietly she stood in his arms, he pulled her away from him and looked into her eyes. "Are you okay?"

She nodded, but her eyes didn't agree.

He took the towel from her and handed her a short yellow robe he'd found in her suitcase. "What is it?"

She looked at him in surprise, as though she were expecting him to grasp something he'd apparently missed. He took a corner of the towel and began to buff at the crown of her head. "What?" he asked again.

"I let your daughter almost drown," she said in a calm, stiff voice. "I almost . . . did it again."

For a moment, he couldn't believe his ears. Then he looked into her eyes and saw what lay behind the uncertainty. He'd thought at first it was residual fear from the close call, but now he saw that it was a return of the old guilt.

"What?" he asked flatly. His own emotions, barely held in check to keep her and his daughter calm, to keep his brother from exploding, to prevent himself from flying off the handle began to roil inside him. He had a grim feeling he knew what was coming.

"I should have been watching." She took the towel and hung it over the rack. Her hands were shaking.

"You thought she was in Nancy's room. They crept out."

"I was talking to Sandy. I should have..."

"Nancy was the instigator," he said, trying desperately not to raise his voice. "But you don't consider Sandy a bad mother, do you? They pulled their little caper on her, too, remember? And anyway, you're forgetting the most important point. You saved both of them."

She gave him a disbelieving look. "Because you and Kurt came along. If you'd been five minutes longer at the store..."

"Stop it!" he shouted, forgetting he'd promised himself he would remain calm. "I know what you're working up to and I'm getting tired of fighting you on it. Go ahead. Say it! Say it, so we can get at the real issue here."

She squared her shoulders, trying to look firm. Instead, wet and sad, she looked vulnerable and frail. "I'm going home tomorrow."

He leaned a hip against the bathroom counter and folded his arms. "You don't have a home, remember?" he said heartlessly. "It's gone. Burned to the ground. Your past and everything in it is gone. Your reality is here—with me."

"I meant my parents' home."

"Ah," he said. "Where it's safe. Where you don't have to confront the rest of your life."

Anger colored her cheeks. "Where I can tie up my deal with Ferrante, deal with the insurance people and..."

"Plan your cruise?" he suggested coolly.

She closed the lapels of the robe around her and drew a breath. "I can't be a mother to your children," she said, her eyes imploring him to understand. He had to force himself to remain unmoved. "I thought I could, I wanted to, but—" tears pooled in her eyes and she turned away from him, shaking her head "—but I can't tell you what it felt like to hold her trembling body in my arms and Nancy's and feel like I couldn't get her back to you, like I was going to lose her for you..."

Dane spun her around, holding her firmly by the shoulders. "Paula, I know I'm beginning to sound like a broken record, but what happened to Natalie was an accident. What happened today was an accident. Two headstrong little girls took it upon themselves to sneak out and have an adventure. It wasn't your fault."

"Dane," she said, tears spilling over, "this ended happily, thank God. But I've lived long enough to know that it doesn't always. You haven't."

He straightened with an expression of exasperation, took two long strides that brought him to the end of the tiny room, then turned around. "I've lived long enough," he said loudly, "to know that a mother can be nothing more than a face on the other side of a glass partition in prison, or a dead-drunk body on the living room floor. I've lived long enough to know a mother can just walk away and never look back."

He saw her bring the shutter down between them. She didn't want to understand. She understood her pain and her fears, and she didn't feel strong enough to go beyond them. The black chasm of acceptance opened at his feet. He knew he couldn't force her.

"All right," he said. "I'll take you back tomorrow, but you have to explain to Paige."

"Dane." She caught his arm as he would have opened the door. He turned to look down at her. "Tell me you understand," she pleaded.

He shook his head. "That would be a lie."

"Then tell me you forgive me."

He thought of all they'd done together in the past ten days, all he'd taught her, learned from her, enjoyed with her—and he thought of the nights in her arms, tangled in her scent and her hair and her complexity and knew it wasn't in his hands.

He put a hand to her face, and shook his head. "Forgive yourself, Paula. You can't live again, even without me, until you do."

CHAPTER SIXTEEN

PAIGE'S APPROACH to logic was a lot like her father's, Paula decided after she'd explained to her that though they'd all be driving home together, she, Paula, would then go on to her parents' house.

They sat together in the back seat of Dane's Scout. In the front, Sam slept in his car seat and Dane listened to a Phil Collins tape.

"You mean, you're not marrying Daddy?" Paige asked.

Paula nodded, trying to look serious but not crestfallen so that the child would take her cue from her behavior. The ploy didn't work. Large tears began to fall.

"Because I was bad," Paige guessed.

"No," Paula said quickly, taking her hand. "You did something you shouldn't have done, but that's not why I have to leave."

"Why?"

Why. Because I have a lot of work to do. Because you and your brother are beautiful and I almost lost you and I'm consumed with worry and guilt and . . .

"Because I have to take a trip," Paula said, skirting a truth she could never explain in favor of a palatable fib. "And I'll be gone a long, long time."

"Why can't we come?"

"You're going to preschool next week, remember? And Daddy has to go back to work."

Paige turned big blue eyes on her. "I don't want to go to school. I want you."

Breath stalled and lodged in a painful lump in Paula's throat. "I have to take my trip," she insisted gently. "But I'll send you something pretty. What would you like?"

Paige could not be bought. "Nothing. I want you to stay. Daddy!"

Paula watched Dane turn the volume down. She knew he'd put the tape player on to give her privacy, but that he'd probably been attuned to every word. "Yes, baby?"

"Make Paula stay," Paige said plaintively. "I want her to stay."

"She has to go, Paige."

"But I don't want her to."

"I know. But you can't always have what you want. Remember yesterday? You wanted to ride in the boat, even though it wasn't the right kind of day for it and you aren't old enough to do it by yourself. You tried to do it anyway, and look what happened."

"I almost drownded," she said solemnly. "And Nancy, too. Only Polly saved us."

"That's right."

"What if I do that again," Paige reasoned, "and Polly isn't here?"

Dane caught her eye in the rearview mirror. "I told you what would happen if you did anything like that again."

Paige frowned and folded her arms, apparently unwilling to consider what he'd told her.

"Well, then, we'll never have another mom," she pouted.

"Of course you will," Paula made herself say cheerfully. "Daddy will find the perfect mom."

Some beautiful, blond, buxom young woman in Oregon, she thought with a pang of jealousy so strong it was almost physical pain. *Someone a few years younger than he, with youthful instincts and reflexes, who could care for and protect his children. Someone who loved to camp and fish and walk for miles . . .*

In deference to his daughter's dreams and Paula's brave attempts to explain her departure, Dane didn't bother to correct her. He'd lost his heart, probably even his soul, to a redhead almost ten years his senior who was as different from him as it was possible to be.

"Daddy?" Paige's worried voice penetrated his thoughts. "Polly's crying."

BOTH CHILDREN were asleep by the time Dane pulled into the Emmetts's driveway. Paula studied Paige for one long moment, then kissed her fingertips and put them to the top of Sam's head. Then she slipped out of the car, closing the door carefully.

Dane walked beside her to the fountain filled with colorful koi as her parents ran out to greet her. He didn't touch her. She looked as though one wrong word and she might shatter, and he certainly felt as though he might.

"Hi, you two!" Paul Emmett called cheerfully as he took Paula into his arms. "Come on in. I'll make daiquiris and we can—"

Barbara stopped him with a hand on his arm, looking from her daughter to Dane with a sharpness that reminded Dane of a five-star general. She knew.

"Hi, Mom," Paula said, giving her a quick hug. "Dane can't stay. He's got the kids in the car."

"Of course."

"Not even for a minute?" Paul, less astute than Barbara, tried to insist. "I want to show him the deck, and the spot under the oaks where your mother thought we'd have the minist—"

"He's a busy man, Paul," Barbara interrupted. "And he's probably seen lots of decks. We'll bring your things in and pour the daiquiris, Paula. Come in when you're ready." She took a step forward and took Dane into her arms. He thought he saw sympathy in her eyes. "Thank you for all you've done for Paula. We're very grateful."

"It was my pleasure, Mrs. Emmett."

Paul frowned from Paula to Dane. "I don't understand."

Barbara gave him a smile that told him not to ask any questions. "I'll explain later, darling."

Dane offered his hand, wondering if, despite his national celebrity, he wasn't always just a little behind his wife and daughter.

Paul took it, still frowning. "I owe you," he said. "If there's anything I can ever do for you in any way, I expect you to call."

"Thank you. I will."

Barbara tugged him up the walk, and Dane and Paula stood alone in the court with nothing but the sound of the bubbling fountain and the lazy buzz of a bee in the roses.

It seemed best not to touch her. It was contrary to everything he wanted, every need that screamed for one last touch of her lips, one last moment in her arms. But her eyes were full and her mouth was trembling and his throat was so tight he doubted he'd ever swallow again.

"Thanks for everything," she said, her voice barely a whisper. She cleared her throat and said more firmly, "I hope your offer is accepted on the hardware store."

He tried to smile but his mouth refused to cooperate. "Me, too. And I hope your deal with Ferrante goes smoothly. And, all teasing aside, I hope you enjoy the cruise."

Something twisted in Paula's middle. "I'll send you something from some exotic port."

The look in his eyes reminded her sharply of Paige's when she'd made the same offer to the little girl earlier and been rejected.

There was nothing left to say, except goodbye. Again, his lips refused to do his brain's bidding. He spread his hands, trying to tell her wordlessly what he couldn't bring himself to say. He turned and started for the car.

He heard the sob and turned back in time to catch her as she flew into his arms. He felt her fingernails against his shoulders and her tears against his cheek.

"I'll always love you," she wept.

He held her close, accepting the gift of these last few seconds greedily. "I'll always love you," he said. Then, because he couldn't bear the thought of her feeling the depth of pain he felt, he pulled her away and made himself smile. "I'll never bait a hook again without thinking of you making such a fuss over it. And you'll probably never put on one of your lacy nightgowns again without longing for my T-shirt."

She smiled with such sadness his heart broke. "Love the kids for me. And Peaches."

"Right." With all the self-control he could muster, he dropped his hands from her and went to the car. He blew her a kiss at the door, then climbed inside, turned the key and drove away without looking back.

Dane took the children to McDonald's for dinner, bathed a sleepy-eyed Sam and put him to bed, then let Paige watch television with him until she lolled heavily in his arms.

"I miss Polly," she said sleepily, curled up against his chest. "How come all our mommies go away?"

Because your daddy's cursed, he thought, but aloud, he tried to sound as though it were just another bump in the upheaval that had been his children's lives.

"People have to go where they'll be happy. Even mommies."

She sighed, obviously considering that. "We're going to go to Ogeron," she said.

"Oregon," he corrected, saying it slowly. The message had been waiting on his answering machine when they'd returned from the Emmetts's. He felt nothing. His dream come true seemed to mean nothing. But he'd called the realtor and told him he'd be sending a check the following day. He had to go on for the children's sakes. He would take them where the air was clean, the land still green and beautiful and where he could know that just across the mountains he'd spent five days of his life with a woman who had changed him forever.

"We're going to have lots of space for you to play in," Dane said as he stood her on her bed and pulled a nightgown over her head. "We'll have a dog and a horse..."

"And we're gonna bring Peaches," she said, her voice muffled as she tried to fight her way out of the neckline.

"And we're gonna bring Peaches," he assured her, unfastening the button at the back that was causing the trouble. Her tumbled hair and pink-cheeked face emerged with a little smile. "Maybe Peaches will have kittens."

"Peaches is a boy," he said, tugging the bunched-up nightgown down her slender body. Then he noticed the bright red scratches just above her waist.

"What happened?" he asked, carrying her into the bathroom and reaching for the antiseptic cream.

"Polly did it," she said, holding the gown for him while he sat her on the counter and dotted the medicine. "Nancy has one, too, on the other side. Aunt Sandy put stuff on it when we were in the bathtub."

Of course. He saw the pattern of fingernails. He remembered Paula clutching the girls as the wave broke over her, and how she still held both of them when he pulled her out of the rolling water.

He sent up a silent prayer that one day the guilt she carried over Natalie would ease and she would see that she hadn't risked his daughter's and his niece's lives, she'd saved them.

He put a bandage over the livid scratches and placed Paige in the middle of her bed, pulling the blankets up.

"Maybe Polly will want to come and visit Peaches," she said hopefully, snuggling into her pillow. "Maybe I could send her a cross-stitch picture when she comes back from her trip."

"That would be nice," he said, afraid one more word about Paula would send him over the edge. He reached to the bedside table for the storybook he read from every night. "What'll we read tonight?"

"Something about dogs and horses."

He took it as a good sign that Paige was thinking about their future. He'd have to do that, too. Someday. When his thoughts weren't haunted by a beautiful redhead.

"WHAT ARE YOU GOING to do now?" Barbara placed a lacquered tray with a cut-crystal pitcher of iced tea and three tall glasses on a little round table set up under an umbrella on the back lawn. Several yards away Paul Emmett hammered a railing onto the nearly finished deck.

Paula studied the cruise brochures spread out around her. The previous day she'd stood in her father's arms in what had once been Natalie's bedroom in the burned-out shell of her home and cried her heart out. She'd found no evidence of Benny. Everything was gone.

"It's over now, Polly," her father had said. "Now, it's really over."

Tears spent, she'd let him lead her away and felt the door close on her past. Natalie still lived in her heart, but she felt as though all the years with Bill in that house had been lived by someone else.

It was time to look ahead.

"I was thinking I'd sail to Europe," Paula replied, "then you and Daddy can join me for a couple of weeks at the end of filming. After that, I'll play it by ear. What do you think?"

Barbara smiled and poured tea. "I think it sounds wonderful. Gives me an excuse to go clothes shopping."

Paula leaned back in her paddle-backed chair and looked at her mother suspiciously. "What's the matter with you? You've been agreeable for days."

Barbara turned innocent brown eyes on her daughter. "Is that a complaint? You're always telling me to leave you alone, that you know what you're doing with your life. If you want to take a cruise when there's a perfectly wonderful man with two beautiful children madly in love with you and eager to start his life over with you, then I think you should take a cruise. Certainly at forty, you know your own mind.''

"I'm only thirty-nine."

"Yes. For a few more weeks."

"Mom, I *do* know what I'm doing," Paula insisted defensively. Trying to rid herself of a feeling of restless anxiety, she'd tried to lure her mother into an argument for days, but she wouldn't bite. "I almost lost his daughter for him."

"Sandy said you saved her, *and* Sandy and Kurt's little girl."

"After I lost track of what she was doing."

Barbara put a lemon wedge on the rim of a glass and passed it to Paula. "Remember when I lost you in Bullock's when you were six? You could have been kidnapped, fallen into a freight elevator or sold to some grandmother from Santa Barbara who mistook you for a doll. But, you weren't. I found you unharmed. I was lucky. Paula..." She turned to her, her eyes dark with love and frustration. "You lost Natalie, but you saved Paige and Nancy. If you insist on assuming the blame for Natalie, doesn't that at least make you even?"

"I don't think the scales are balanced that way, Mother."

"Darling, I know you tried so hard to have Natalie, that finally having produced that beautiful baby, you might have gotten to think you were somehow divine. But you're not. You're human like the rest of us. You're susceptible to the agonies and blessings that make up the human condition, just like the rest of us. Natalie didn't die because your divinity somehow slipped, she died because that's life. Paige and Nancy didn't almost drown because you weren't watching, but because little children can't be second-guessed. They act on impulse.

But they're alive today because you swam out to get them.''

"If Dane and Kurt hadn't..."

"If you hadn't been there, they'd have drowned because there'd have been no one to keep them afloat until Dane and Kurt did come along. Think about that."

She tried and couldn't. She couldn't think about anything. She'd banked several million dollars and set herself up in comfort, even luxury, for the rest of her life. But the effort involved seemed futile, because there seemed to be no "rest of her life." The cruise that had once seemed so appealing, now seemed to be a waste of time.

The only place she wanted to be right now was in a cabin that no longer existed, in a woods she'd never be able to erase from her mind.

She turned to her mother, asking desultorily, "How do you know all that? I didn't tell you."

"Sandy told me," Barbara said, waving at Paul and holding up the icy pitcher of tea in an attempt to lure him to join them.

"When?" Paula demanded.

"She's called several times in the week you've been home."

Paula gasped indignantly. "Why didn't you tell me?"

Barbara shrugged, sipping her tea. "Because she didn't ask to talk to you. She called me."

"Why?"

"First, just to see how you were. Then to tell me Dane's offer on the hardware store was accepted. Then to tell me he's packing up the kids and leaving next week."

Paula swore she could feel the life flowing out of her. Dane and the children were leaving. Moving a thousand miles away. Not that she'd have been able to see them anyway, but there'd been a certain . . . comfort in knowing they were just half an hour's drive away.

She tried to calm herself. She'd made the decision to live without them; this was only her decision being carried out to its logical conclusion—separation. Final, permanent separation.

It was better for the children. It was better for her. She wouldn't be a bundle of nerves every moment, afraid to let them out of her sight for fear they'd endanger themselves. She could be at peace.

Peace. Was this state of restless agitation peace? she wondered. Was this relentless sense of loss, this dire loneliness, this endless longing for the sound of Paige's little voice, for the touch of Sam's baby skin, for a night in Dane's arms—peace?

Paul joined them, wiping his brow on a handkerchief while pulling back a chair. "Well, you little capitalist," he said, winking at Paula. "Have you decided where you're going with part of your earnings?"

"She's cruising to Europe," Barbara said, pouring his tea. "And we're going to fly out and join her at the end of filming. What do you think?"

Paul took a long pull on his glass then leaned back in his chair, eyeing Barbara with a knowing look. "That you're going to use this as an excuse to buy a new wardrobe."

Barbara grimaced. "How did you know that?"

"I've been married to you for forty-one years. You're a brilliant and beautiful woman, but you're very predictable. Your solution to any problem involves buying clothes. It's okay," he added, when she tried to look indignant, "I find it charming. If the two of you do this shopping tomorrow and stay out of my hair, I'll have the deck done, and Paula can help me stain it before she embarks on this cruise.''

Barbara patted Paula's hand. ''Excellent idea. You up for this, Paula?''

Paula smiled thinly. ''Of course.'' Buying clothes was the last thing she wanted to do, but there didn't seem to be a first thing she wanted to do, so it would be easy enough to go along.

''HOW'S THE PACKING coming?'' Kurt asked.

Dane cradled the phone on his shoulder while he boxed the contents of a kitchen cupboard. ''I'm down to pots and pans. I'll be ready for the movers day after tomorrow. Look, would you mind if I picked up Nancy to spend the next two days with us?''

There was silence for a moment. ''You want Calamity Nancy around while you're packing?''

Dane tucked a hot pad between two rattling pans. ''Paige is kind of blue. I thought having Nancy around might help.''

''Why don't you just bring her here?''

''I suggested that to her, but she said she'd rather stay with me. I think she's feeling clingy because the packing's making her nervous.''

Kurt sighed. ''That's understandable.'' He was quiet a moment, then he asked, ''How are *you* doing? You going to be all right?''

''Sure.''

''Dane . . .''

''Well, what do you want me to say? It hurts like hell? I can't sleep without her? I don't even care about going to Oregon anymore?''

''There,'' Kurt said gently. ''Was that so hard?''

Dane sighed and sank into a kitchen chair. "I don't ever remember feeling this desperate."

"Why don't you call her?" Kurt suggested.

"No," Dane replied, pushing the box away and reaching for the now-tepid coffee he'd poured earlier. "She's doing what she thinks is right for her. I'm sure she isn't finding it easy, either."

"Then maybe she'd welcome a chance to reconsider."

"She has to do it without prompting from me, or it wouldn't be her own decision."

"What about prompting from me?"

"I'd see that you spend the rest of your life with your legs where your arms were."

Kurt made a scornful sound. "You really think you could do that?"

"Without a doubt. I'm four years younger, remember? And I'm not a happy man. For your own safety, stay out of it."

"Okay, okay. I've got a meeting in L.A. tomorrow. I'll bring Nancy in after breakfast. That all right?"

"Sure. Thanks, Kurt."

There was quiet conversation on Kurt's end of the line. "You're welcome," he said finally. "Sandy says she's sending over that sausage-and-kraut casserole you like so much, and burger and noodles for the kids, so don't bother cooking."

"Ask her if she wants to run away to Oregon with me."

PAULA LEANED against the polished slate on the side of the house, balancing a tottering stack of boxes from Bloomingdale's. Barbara hooked a hatbox over her arm, added two bags to the stack then dug into her small Paloma Picasso purse for her keys.

"How can you lose anything in a bag that small?" Paula asked, shifting her grip on the weighty burden. "Why don't you just ring for Daddy?"

"Because he'd like that," Barbara replied. "Didn't you hear him say yesterday that I was predictable? I always have to ring for him or Louise to come to the door. I'm so glad you bought those jeans."

Paula leaned her head back against the slate, accepting that she would have to stand there like Atlas with the burden of the world on her shoulders—or at least the contents of a large part of the second floor of Bloomingdale's—until her mother was ready to admit she'd forgotten her house keys.

"I'm not sure jeans are the right thing for a cruise," Paula said. "I shouldn't have listened to you."

Barbara leaned around the boxes to look her in the face. "How could you fit into a size-six anything and not buy it? Aha!" She held a key up in triumph and opened the door. "Paul! We're home!"

"Good." Her father's voice came to Paula's ear as she headed blindly for the living room. "Maybe you can tell me what to do about these?"

Paula's knees bumped the sofa as her mother's voice said softly and with great concern, "Oh, dear."

"What?" Paula dropped everything on the pale blue cushions and turned, expecting to confront a pair of slacks he'd torn working on the deck, or stains he'd put in the carpet when he'd come inside. She hadn't expected to find Paige and Nancy Chandler looking worriedly up at her.

She went with her first instinct, and dropped to her knees, gathering both of them to her in delighted surprise. She hugged and kissed Paige, then Nancy, then Paige again. "Where's Daddy?" she asked, getting to her feet and looking around. "Where's Sam?"

"At home," Paige replied, twisting her little hands together. "We comed by ourselves."

Paula gasped and dropped to her knees again, looking from one to the other. "By yourselves? How?"

Nancy shrugged. "In a taxi."

Paula looked up at her father in disbelief.

"It's true," he confirmed. "I paid him forty-seven bucks. He says he picked them up in Glendale. They said they were lost. Paige gave him this piece of paper...." He passed her a torn square of brown packing paper with her return address on it. She remembered that it had wrapped a box she'd sent to Paige containing a small cross-stitched bag she could take to preschool. "And told him her mother lived at that address."

"Paige!" Paula breathed, so happy to see her she had difficulty mustering a proper scolding. "Does Daddy know where you are?"

Nancy shook her head, her wide adventurer's eyes gleaming with excitement. "We sneaked out when the telephone rang. There's always a taxi where the hotel is right up the street from Uncle Dane's house."

Paula tried not to think about the two little girls crossing the highway with its four lanes of traffic.

Paige shook her head, her eyes wide. "I missed you. Daddy's sad all the time and Sammy won't eat." She wrapped her arms around her as her face crumpled. "And we're going away!"

Nancy leaned an arm on Paula's shoulder as she wept with Paige. "Daddy says if you knew what was good for

you," she confided, "you'd go to Oregon with Uncle
Dane."

Paula looked at her father. "Have you called Dane?"

He shook his head. "They got here just before you
did. Your mother and I will give them milk and cookies while you make the call."

Paul lifted Paige into his arms and kissed her damp
cheek. "Stop crying," he said gently. "Polly's going to
make everything all right." He took Nancy's hand and
led them toward the kitchen.

Barbara turned to follow him, murmuring over her
shoulder, "Don't make a liar out of your father."

"WHERE THE HELL could they be?" Kurt demanded for
the hundredth time in the past fifteen minutes.

"I don't know!" Dane shouted at him, tired of answering the question. "I've driven around the neigh-
borhood for an hour, I've checked all the neighbors, the
park..."

"Well, think!" Kurt shouted back.

"Kurt, calm down," Sandy ordered gently.

"Calm down? He calls us and tells us he's lost his kid
and our kid and you want me to calm down?!"

"That's enough!" Sandy stepped between them,
looking like a hilly little valley between two erupting
volcanoes.

Kurt, pale with fear, turned his accusations on her.
"You're not tough enough with her. Nancy's turning
into a disobedient, reckless little..."

"Listen to you!" she said, shouting to be heard over
him. "The two of you spend your lives being adventur-
ers, and you expect to sire children who sit in front of
the television! If our children are turning into anything, they're being true to their genes. Now calm

down, stop putting the blame on somebody else, and think!" She turned to Dane. "Have you called Paula?"

The possibility that Paige had gone to her had occurred to him, then he'd dismissed it. "Sandy, Paula's living with her parents, thirty miles away. Paige wouldn't even know how to find her."

The telephone rang and the three stared at each other for a moment. Then they ran in a stream toward the kitchen.

"Hello?!" Dane said sharply.

"Dane, it's Paula." Her voice did a million things to him. It gave him pleasure, caused him pain, lit his heart and punched him in the gut. It also built a fragile hope in him that Sandy had been right. "Paige and Nancy are here," she said quickly. "They're fine. I know you must be frantic, but don't worry. Tell Sandy and Kurt not to worry."

He closed his eyes and dropped the receiver to his chest for an instant as relief made it impossible for him to function.

"What?" Kurt and Sandy demanded simultaneously.

"They're fine," he said on a ragged breath. "Paula's got them." He held the receiver up.

"Thanks, Paula," he said. "We've been wild."

"I knew you would be. I'll bring them back."

"I'll come for them."

"No, I'll bring them. Mom and Dad are giving them cookies. See you in about an hour?"

"Great. Paula?"

"Yes?"

He knew what he wanted to say, but didn't dare.

She knew what she wanted to hear, and worried when it wasn't said.

"Drive carefully," he said. "The freeway's like Le Mans at this hour."

"Right."

Sandy, who'd remained calm and practical and lucid enough to tell them off, dissolved into hysterical sobs. Kurt led her to the sofa and Dane made coffee.

PAULA DROVE without conscious thought, the girls belted into the front seat beside her. She'd been getting around greater Los Angeles on the freeway since she'd been a teenager and the bumper-to-bumper traffic going at racetrack speeds had never frightened her.

Her mind was occupied with what *did* frighten her. She was putting Natalie away. She could feel it happening. For two years, she'd hardly had a thought that hadn't involved her daughter. But for days, her entire being had been consumed with memories of and worries about Dane and his children. And at this moment, every thought in her head was for them, to reunite them, to...join them.

That was the concept that truly scared her. Joining. Linking her life again to the lives of others and taking her chances that they would remain safe and whole and together. She'd learned in the darkest, sharpest way that life made no such promises.

But she'd also learned that—for her, at least—the safety solitude provided was not a comfortable option. One cross-stitch, however perfectly made, would never form a pattern unless it attached itself to others.

And she knew now, the pattern she wanted to make— had to make, because Dane was sad, Sam wouldn't eat and Paige missed her.

And the deepest, darkest fear of all was that it was too late. Dane was packed and ready to go. He'd had time away from her to remember that she was almost ten years older than he was, inclined to like things her own way, and couldn't bait a hook or cook over a camp stove or do all the dozens of other things with which he wanted to fill his life.

He'd had time to wonder if everything between them had just been the result of two lonely lives overlapping in a beautiful wilderness.

CHAPTER SEVENTEEN

DANE AND KURT were running down the path to the sidewalk, Sandy waddling behind, as Paula pulled up to the curb. She reached over to unbuckle the girls' seat belts as Dane opened the door and reached in for them. He passed Nancy to Kurt, then pulled Paige out. He held her up, gave her a little shake, crushed her to him, then looked at her sternly.

"Paige Margaret Chandler," he said. "I'm going to blister your bottom!"

Paige nodded as though that were an outcome of her adventure she'd already considered. "But I brought Polly back," she said, her hopeful blue eyes suggesting that rated a commutation of her sentence if not a reprieve.

Dane turned to Paula, trying not to notice how magnificent her loose hair looked in the day's dying light, or how the breeze toyed with the amber-patterned silk of her long skirt and blouse. "I'm sorry," he said. "She just doesn't understand."

Paula looked into his eyes, searching for something to quiet that darkest of her fears. She saw it as his eyes went hungrily over her face, feature by feature, stopping at her mouth to remember as she remembered.

She nodded, holding her hands out to Paige. "I know," she said. "That's because it doesn't make sense. But the girls and I have straightened things out." She looked firmly from one child to the other. "Don't you have something to say?"

Paige looked at her father with glowing blue eyes. "Polly said I'm suppozta tell you I'm sorry," she said. She fidgeted a little, her expression taking on a somewhat dramatic pleading quality. "And she said you wouldn't spank me if I promised never to do that again."

Dane looked from his daughter to Paula, unsure whether or not to succumb to their manipulation.

"She said if we run off like that again," Nancy, who'd been offered the same deal, explained from her father's arms, obviously feeling the deal needed a little sweetening on the parental side, "she'll spank us herself. So we hafta be good."

Dane glanced down at Paula, trying desperately to keep himself together until he was sure what that implied.

"I suppose the deal depends," he said, "on whether or not you're around to carry through."

"That's reasonable," she said, flipping the ring of keys she held in one hand. She went to the trunk of the car, opened it and extracted a suitcase.

"She's sleeping over," Paige said.

Sandy cleared her throat and took Paige from Dane, setting her on her feet. "We'll wait inside."

Paula, smiling, gave Sandy a quick hug and handed her case to Kurt.

Dane thought the case looked very small. He looked into Paula's eyes. "Is that an overnight bag?"

She giggled and wrapped her arms around his neck. "I don't have many clothes, remember. Mom's going to exchange my cruise clothes and send more jeans and flannel shirts. That's what they wear in Oregon, isn't it?''

She looked radiant. He could find no evidence of the pain that had haunted her when he'd left her at her parents' the week before. He didn't want to question his good fortune, but it was all too good to be true. He was afraid to trust it.

Paula kissed his cheek and, wrapping her arm around his waist, started slowly up the walk. "When Paige and Nancy showed up at my parents' door," she said, "I realized if two wily little girls could get away from a trained bodyguard, then I guess I can accept that they got away from me." She stopped, turning to face him, her eyes brimming with happiness and a trace of grief that would always live with her, but was finally being folded away with the past. "Paige and Sam need me. You need me and I need you. God, I need you." She wrapped her arms around his waist and looked up into his eyes. "The timing's right, isn't it? It doesn't matter that I'm . . ."

He enveloped her in his arms and smothered her concern with a deep, lingering kiss. "All that matters," he said finally, his voice thick with emotion, "is that you're home."

Paula closed her eyes and leaned against him, letting herself absorb the welcome to which she'd been so afraid she was no longer entitled.

She drew back to tell him a little reluctantly. "We should talk money," she said.

He frowned. "Why?"

"Because I banked five million dollars on Monday."

"Holy sh—" Long conditioning to the presence of children stopped the word before it came out. "Five? Really?"

"Really," she said. "You're not going to be weird about it, are you?"

"No," he said with a laugh. "It's yours. Buy whatever you want with it. But we'll run the house on what I..."

She resisted as he tried to lead her toward the house. "That's being weird," she said firmly. "You said you dreamed of renovating the store."

"No."

"Why not?"

"Because I'm not taking chances with your money. Businesses fail all the time." He kissed her cheek and tugged her along. "In fact, if you had a good business head, you'd insist on a prenuptial agr—"

He lost the last syllable of the word as his backside hit the lawn, followed quickly by his back and shoulders. Paula straddled him, holding his shirtfront in both hands. "Take that back!" she ordered.

"Paula," he laughed breathlessly, "I just..."

"I'm taking my share of everything you have to give me," she said, leaning over him until they were nose to nose, "and you're taking what I have to give. Do you understand me?"

He grinned wickedly. "Are you going to give it to me right here on the lawn."

She scolded with a glare. "Don't be crass, I'm talking money."

He put his arms around her and turned them so that she lay on the grass and he knelt astride her.

He studied her as though she were some delicious morsel he contemplated. "We'll do any damn thing you want with the money. And I was teasing you about the prenup. I'm not ever letting you out of my sight, much less out of my life."

She sighed under him, her eyes and her smile warming him to the center of his being.

"That's better," she said.

"Where'd you learn the fancy throw?" he asked.

"You," she replied. "I saw you use it in the restaurant parking lot that night." Her eyes grew dark and turbulent, mirroring a love that ran spiritually deep but smoldered with physical excitement. "I've learned so much from you. I hope I can give you a fraction of what you've given me."

She pulled up to touch his lips with a reverence that humbled him. He stood and pulled her to her feet, enveloping her in his arms. "You gave me everything when you came back to me," he said. "I'll make you happy. I promise."

She laughed softly. "I know that. I'm already so happy I could burst."

"See? I'm not one to say I told you so, but..."

"What?" she challenged with a frown.

He shrugged, as though it should be obvious. "The timing was perfect."

EPILOGUE

"Now, you be good for Grandma and Grandpa."
Paula held Sam in her arms and looked into his bright,
mischievous eyes. At three years old he was a little devil
with the face of a cherub. "No spitting your vegetables
at Sissy, okay? Promise?"

"Yes, Mommy." He nodded vehemently, but Paula
wasn't fooled. He agreed to every request with great diplomacy, then happily went in search of trouble.

Paula handed him to her father. "Watch him. He
loves heights and sharp things."

Paul Emmett rolled his eyes. "You don't remember,
of course, but you were prone to the occasional mis-
adventure yourself at his age. I'm experienced. Just relax. Your mother and I are perfectly capable of keeping
your children safe for two weeks."

Paula wrapped her arms around two of her three favorite men. "Thanks, Dad. I know you are."

"Although, why you want to leave this little para-
dise," Barbara said, indicating the old Victorian house
set in the middle of an enormous green lawn sur-
rounded by fruit trees just a block away from Heron
River Hardware, "to vacation somewhere else is beyond me."

"I told you," Paula said softly, "it's a surprise for
Dane. Now you know how to reach us?"

Barbara patted the pocket of her slim khaki pants. "Got all the numbers right here. Chill out, will you?"

Paula rolled her eyes, biting back a smile. "Chill out? Where have you been hanging out?"

Barbara pinched her cheek. "I'll always be younger than you, Paula. Now, if you can pry Paige away from her father, we can start for home."

Paula gave her mother a fervent hug. "I really appreciate the two of you coming all this way to take the kids while we're gone. I'll be able to relax, knowing they're in good hands."

Barbara squeezed her. "We're excited about it. Your father has quite an itinerary planned. We're going to hit all the hot spots. Disneyland, Knott's Berry Farm, Sea World, and then, of course, he's going to take them on a private tour of the studio." She pointed across the lawn to where Dane stood with Paige in his arms, apparently in the midst of a serious discussion. Paige's arms were folded and she did not look pleased. "But your daughter needs a little coaxing."

Paula walked across the lawn toward Dane and the little girl who now lived in her heart right beside Natalie. When Paige saw Paula, she turned the pout on her. "You said you would never leave me," she reminded with an air of high drama. Paula often wondered if she, too, would be working before the cameras one day.

The trip had been planned for weeks and Paige had been excited at the prospect of visiting Disneyland again and spending time with her grandparents. But now that it was time to go, she was worried about leaving her secure little world.

"We're not leaving you," Paula said, patting her back. "Daddy and I are taking a little vacation and you're going to visit Minnie Mouse. Then we're going to come and get you and we'll all drive back home together."

"I want to go with you," she insisted.

"Where we're going," Paula said, "there are no morning cartoons, no *Sesame Street,* no television at all."

Paige frowned. "Then why do you want to go there?"

"Because . . . we're going to do other things." Paula carefully avoided Dane's eyes. "Now, are you ready to go with Grandma and Grandpa?"

Paige looked at the car in which Sam was being comfortably buckled, then back at Paula and Dane. Her little lip quivered. "I'm going to miss you."

Paula reached up to hug her, her eyes filling. She felt Dane's arm come around her. "We're going to miss you, too, sweetie, but we'll all have lots of fun and have lots to talk about when we come home. Okay?"

Paul joined them, large and deep-voiced and cheerful, and pried Paige from her parents. "Let's go," he said, "the Minnie Mouse Express is leaving. Do you have your ticket?"

"My ticket?"

"A kiss," Paul said, pointing to his cheek with his free hand. "Right there."

Paige giggled and paid.

In a moment the car was heading down the road toward the highway, horn honking and hands waving. A startling silence descended on Dane and Paula. She stared worriedly after the car.

Their car already packed, Dane began to tug her toward it. "Come on. I don't know how far we have to go on this mystery ride, but if you're driving, I don't want you driving after dark."

Paula allowed herself to be pulled along, still frowning at the road. "Do you think they'll be all right?"

"I know they'll be all right," Dane said firmly. "You haven't let those kids out of your sight for a whole year. They need a little time away from you, and I need a little time *with* you. Now, come on. You're sure you don't want me to drive?"

Paula turned to him, forcing herself to stop worrying about the children and concentrate on her husband. This trip had been her idea after all, to let him know in some small way how happy he'd made her, how much she loved him and his children and his family— how very much alive she felt.

"No," she said, taking his arm and tugging him to the passenger side of the car. She opened the door, gestured him inside then stopped him when he would have climbed in. He looked at her in perplexity.

She put a hand on her hip. "Have you got your ticket?" she teased.

Dane suspected that a man could die of being so happy. He loved the contentment he saw in her eyes these days, the excitement and the satisfaction and the occasional flare of temper that only meant life was real and very wonderful.

He slipped his hand under her hair and leaned down to kiss her slowly, lengthily. She responded fervently, then pushed him into his seat and ran around the car to get in behind the wheel.

HE'D SUSPECTED their destination for the past hour, but when she nudged the car into the thicket late in the afternoon near the very familiar trail, it became very clear. She was taking him back to the cabin where they'd come to know each other and made love for the first time. Only the cabin no longer existed.

As she turned off the engine, he stretched an arm along the seat behind her. "I appreciate the gesture, my love," he said, "but it's October. I hope you brought your longies for sleeping under the stars."

She pushed an empty pack at him. "Take whatever you need out of your suitcase," she said, "and put it into the pack."

She tied her jacket around her waist and shrugged into her pack. He grinned at her as he did the same. "Shades of the first time we did this. That aerobics class has made you cocky, hasn't it? You think you'll make it up the hill this time?"

She made it three-quarters of the way, and he happily supported her the last quarter, teasing her mercilessly and stealing what little breath she had left with long kisses. Until they reached the clearing and he almost dropped her.

"What the hell?" he demanded on a startled gasp.

At the other end of the meadow where the old cabin had stood, was a large, two-story log house with a broad stone fireplace and a wraparound porch. He closed his eyes and opened them again, half expecting it to disappear.

"Happy anniversary," Paula said, delighted by the disbelieving smile forming on his lips. She tugged him across the clearing. "Come on."

"Wait a minute." He pulled her to a stop, his expression suddenly stern. "How did you do this? We had an agreement about your—"

"I know," she said interrupting him. "We live on your money, but I'm free to buy whatever I want with mine."

His head tilted as he scowled. She looked back at him intrepidly. "It's a silly rule, but I've lived by it. I wanted to buy this for you—for us and the children and Kurt and Sandy and their girls. Kurt and Sandy are joining us next week, incidentally. So do we want to waste our precious week alone standing here arguing, or do we want to go inside and drink the champagne that's chilling, and eat the cold capons and see if the old canopied bed I bought is as comfortable as it looks?"

Dane toured the house in a kind of daze. It was decorated in comfortable country style with light wood and floral-patterned fabrics. There were dried flowers everywhere. Water still had to be pumped, but a generator provided electricity so that the large new kitchen boasted a range and a refrigerator. But there was no television.

He stood in the middle of the room, remembering the primitive old cabin, and looked awed and just a little worried.

Paula wrapped her arms around his waist and explained urgently, "Oh, Dane. I didn't do this because there's anything lacking in what you've given me. It's *because* of all you've given me this year that I wanted to give you just a little back." Her eyes dark with emotion, she smiled up at him. "I feel like I was born on this spot, Dane. You brought me back to life here. It's a special place. Now we can come here with the kids, and Kurt and Sandy and their kids can come. It'll be good for all of us."

He crushed her to him as love and dreams flowed between them. "Polly!" he said heavily. "As though you haven't given me everything any man could ask for. God! I can't tell you how I feel about you. It's like all the things I've always wanted are all wrapped up in you—and things I didn't know about, things I never suspected."

She expelled a sigh of relief. "Then you're not angry?"

He kissed her lightly. "Of course not."

"Then, what do you want to do first?"

He lifted her in his arms. "Silly question," he said and headed for the stairs and the canopied bed.

HARLEQUIN SUPERROMANCE®

A PLACE IN HER HEART...

Somewhere deep in the heart of every grown woman is the little girl she used to be....

In September, October and November 1992, the world of childhood and the world of love collide in six very special romance titles. Follow these six special heroines as they discover the sometimes heart-wrenching, always heartwarming joy of being a Big Sister.

Written by six of your favorite Superromance authors, these compelling and emotionally satisfying romantic stories will earn a place in your heart!

JAYNE ANN KRENTZ

A two-part epic tale from one of today's most popular romance novelists!

Dreams
Parts One & Two

The warrior died at her feet, his blood running out of the cave entrance and mingling with the waterfall. With his last breath he cursed the woman— told her that her spirit would remain chained in the cave forever until a child was created and born there....

So goes the ancient legend of the Chained Lady and the curse that bound her throughout the ages—until destiny brought Diana Prentice and Colby Savager together under the influence of forces beyond their understanding. Suddenly they were both haunted by dreams that linked past and present, while their waking hours were filled with danger. Only when Colby, Diana's modern-day warrior, learned to love, could those dark forces be vanquished. Only then could Diana set the Chained Lady free....

Take 4 bestselling love stories FREE
Plus get a FREE surprise gift!

WELCOME TO

The quintessential small town, where everyone knows everybody else!

Finally, books that capture the pleasure of tuning in to your favorite TV show!

GREAT READING...GREAT SAVINGS...AND A FABULOUS FREE GIFT!

Each book set in Tyler is a self-contained love story; together, the twelve novels stitch the fabric of the community. The covers honor the old American tradition of quilting; each cover depicts a patch of the large Tyler quilt.

With Tyler you can receive a fabulous gift, ABSOLUTELY FREE, by collecting proofs-of-purchase found in each Tyler book. And use our special Tyler coupons to save on your next TYLER book purchase.

Join your friends at Tyler for the seventh book, ARROWPOINT by Suzanne Ellison, available in September.

Rumors fly about the death at the old lodge! What happens when Renata Meyer finds an ancient Indian sitting cross-legged on her lawn?

If you missed *Whirlwind* (March), *Bright Hopes* (April), *Wisconsin Wedding* (May), *Monkey Wrench* (June), *Blazing Star* (July) or *Sunshine* (August) and would like to order them, send your name, address, zip or postal code, along with a check or money order for $3.99 for each book ordered (please do not send cash), plus 75¢ postage and handling ($1.00 in Canada), payable to Harlequin Reader Service, to:

In the U.S.

3010 Walden Avenue
P.O. Box 1325
Buffalo, NY 14269-1325

In Canada

P.O. Box 609
Fort Erie, Ontario
L2A 5X3

Please specify book title(s) with your order.
Canadian residents add applicable federal and provincial taxes.

TYLER-7

Harlequin Superromance ®

Come to where the West is still wild in a summer trilogy by Margot Dalton

Sunflower (#502—June 1992)
Robin Baldwin becomes the half owner of a prize
rodeo horse. But to take possession, she has to travel
the rodeo circuit with cowboy Matt Adams, living
with him in *very* close quarters!

Tumbleweed (#508—July 1992)
Until she met Scott Freeman, Lyle Callander was about
as likely to settle in one spot as tumbleweed in a
windstorm. But who *is* Scott? He's more than the
simple photographer he claims to be . . . much more.

Juniper (#511—August 1992)
Devil-may-care Buck Buchanan can ride a bucking
bronco or a Brahma bull. But can he win Claire
Tremaine, a woman who sets his heart on fire but
keeps her own as cold as ice?

**"I just finished reading *Under Prairie Skies* by
Margo Dalton and had to hide my tears from my
children. I loved it!"** —A reader